I0562722

A Portion of the Journal

Thomas Raikes

Contents

A PORTION OF
THE JOURNAL

BY

Thomas Raikes

PREFACE.

The Author of this Journal was the eldest son of Mr. Thomas Raikes, a rich and respected merchant in the city of London, who was descended from an ancient family in Yorkshire, and himself a personal friend of Mr. Pitt and of Mr. Wilberforce. His son was educated at Eton, where he became a fair classical scholar. In his nineteenth year he was sent abroad with a private tutor. In the course of his travels he visited most of the German courts, and made himself extensively acquainted with modern languages. On his return to England, he became a partner in his father's house; but having little inclination for mercantile affairs, and a marked preference for social and literary pursuits, he very soon established himself in the west end of the town, became a member of the fashionable clubs, and mixed largely in what is, by a somewhat questionable courtesy, denominated the ***best*** society. He married Miss Sophia Bayly, a daughter of Nathaniel Bayly, Esq., the proprietor of large estates in the West Indies. The entries in this Journal will show in what sort of society Mr. Raikes's life was passed, and the intimacies he formed. In the year 1832 (the year in which this Journal commences), embarrassments of the house with which he was connected compelled him to break up his establishment in London, and to settle in Paris, where he remained till 1846. He then returned to England; but by this time most of his early Mends and associates were either dead, or dispersed in various directions; and not long after his own health began to decline. He passed some months in Ireland with his friend Lord Glengall, and then went to Bath, to be near a still older friend, the late Lord Alvanley, who was confined there by illness; after which he took up his abode at Brighton, where he died on the 3rd of July, 1848, in the 70th year of his age. Mr. Raikes visited St. Petersburg in the year 1831, and a few years afterwards he published the result of his observations on Russia in the shape of "Letters from St. Petersburg." In the course of his residence at Paris he likewise published a work entitled "Paris since 1830."

JOURNAL,

&c.

1832.

London, Friday, 6th January.—I had to-day a curious conversation with Matuscewitz [Note *: Count Matuscewitz, who had been employed in the chancellerie at St. Petersburgh, was sent to London in 1830 to act as joint plenipotentiary with Prince Lieven at the Conference. He took root in this country, where he resided many years, speaking the language perfectly, and adopting all the habits and tastes of an Englishman. He left England on being appointed Russian minister at Naples.]; he was just returned from the Conference [Note †: The Conference was opened in London in November, 1830, when the plenipotentiaries of Austria, Russia, Prussia, France, and England met for the purpose of settling by negotiation the affairs of Belgium and Holland. They succeeded in effecting the separation of the two kingdoms, and in averting the war with which Europe was threatened at that time.], which had sat very late, and I could see that things were not going on smoothly, which indeed he allowed very frankly. "Still," said he, "there is a way by which everything now might be arranged finally, and the peace of Europe rendered certain; though one individual seems anxious to do everything which would prevent it, and embroil the question more and more." I at first thought he meant Talleyrand, with whom I knew he had had some difference of opinion on the Conference. "No," said he, "I mean the King of Holland, who is obstinate, and perverse beyond conception, and if anything will produce war, it will be his headstrong conduct." I was rather surprised at this observation, because there seems a general feeling abroad that Russia is secretly abetting Holland not to accede to the treaty, as it could hardly be supposed that so small a state would set all the Five Powers at defiance without some underhand assurance of aid from a powerful quarter. I then remarked that, whatever might occur, one circumstance alone was sufficient, in my opinion, to prevent a war in Europe; that was, the want of money: such an event would produce bankruptcy to the different governments, and, moreover, would tend to throw England, ruled as she now is, into the arms of France. His answer was, "I pretend not to say that there will be war; but if a real cause arises for it, no dread of bankruptcy or pecuniary motives will stop it; and then, should your surmise be true, England will see how little she has to gain by clinging to France in her present state." These words are rather mysterious; but still I cannot help thinking that the Russians are trying what they can do by this semblance of menace. Lord Allen, with whom I dined tête-à-tête, grognon chez lui, comme ailleurs.

Tuesday, 10*th.*—The accounts from Paris alarming, and everything looks woeful.

Wednesday, 11*th.*—French funds fell 5 per cent.

Thursday, 12*th.*—The panic subsiding, a soothing protocol appeared from the Conference. The ***feigned*** delay of Russia to ratify the treaty seems to have had a good effect for Holland, and I think that some modifications will be made in her favour, as to the navigation of the canals and the settlement of Luxembourg; then a formal ratification may probably take place, at least ***pro tempore;*** for which purpose a delay of fifteen days longer is agreed to.

Notwithstanding his permission from the King to create peers, Lord Grey seems evidently unwilling to proceed to this unconstitutional extremity; the feeling to-day is that a compromise may take place between the Government and the Tories, in order to obviate this expedient; that a modification may still be made of the bill in the Commons, to which Lords Harrowby, Wharncliffe, Bristol, Haddington, and it is said the bishops, are not averse.

Saturday, 14*th.*—Périer's [Note *: Casimir Périer, who six months previously had succeeded M. Lafitte as president of the council in the ministry of King Louis-Philippe.] brother and another Frenchman, M. Glasson, arrived last night from Paris, with a ***most private*** dispatch to Talleyrand, to insist at the Conference that the two fortresses of Marienbourg and Philippeville shall not be in the number of those to be demolished. Périer threatens at once to resign if this is not conceded. The ratification was nearly accomplished, and now another stumbling-block to peace is come out. I had this information from a very particular quarter; and as Matuscewitz is at Melton, I immediately wrote to inform him of it.

Sunday, 15 *th.*—Baron Neumann [Note *: Baron Neumann married Lady Augusta Somerset, daughter of the late Duke of Beaufort, and died in 1850, not long after his appointment as Austrian ambassador at Florence.], the Austrian secretary, called on me this morning. He allowed that the news of yesterday was quite true, and said, "What is very odd is, that M. Dethillier, Talleyrand's secretary, crossed them on the road, being sent to Paris with the assurance that the Conference was decided not to yield on *this very point.* We can no longer listen to these threats of Périer's resigning; no sooner is one point granted than a fresh demand is made; ça ne finira jamais. *Besides, things are altered, and his resignation does not seem now to depend* entirely *on himself." He added, that the Prussian ratification came last night. I afterwards met Benckhausen, the Russian consul, in the street, always anxious for news. He thought war would ultimately take place, and said, that even more time would be required by Russia after the expiration of the fifteen days just allowed.* Nous verrons. *The opposition in the French Chambers becoming stronger, the civil list of the Citizen-King reduced to twelve millions in money, with various other deductions of the royal property. A* bon mot *of Talleyrand's at the Conference the other day is cited. He has been much vexed at France not being permitted to have a voice in the fortress question; and being since taxed with creating unnecessary difficulties at the Conference, he replied,* "Oh! donnezmoi le traité, je le signerai."

Monday, 16 *th.*—Received a letter from Greffulhe, who says, "It appears that poor Talleyrand is at his wit's end for some *mezzo termine* to extricate all parties from their present awkward scrape."

Tuesday, 7 *th.*—The Parliament re-assembled. No announcement of peers. The Ministry appears much embarrassed how to act. One of them said, the other day,

"The Tories must concede, as we cannot retract; the people would not let us." This speaks volumes as to the dilemma in which they have got, not only themselves, but the country. Greville told me this morning that Lady Charlotte had lately received a letter from Prince d'Aremberg [Note *: Prince Auguste, second son of the Due d'Aremberg, was born at Brussels in 1753. His maternal grandfather, the Count de la Marck, of an illustrious German house, who possessed a regiment of infantry in the French service, which had been raised by his grandfather, and brought into France in the reign of Louis XIV., engaged the young prince to enter the French service; and at his death, in 1773, he bequeathed to him his regiment, with the title of La Marck. Soon afterwards the court of Spain conferred on him the grandeeship which his grandfather had possessed. From this time a brilliant career was opened to him at the court of France, where he was admitted into the intimate society of the Dauphiness, afterwards Queen Marie Antoinette. In 1789 he married Madlle. de Cernay, who brought him a considerable property. In the preceding year he had formed the acquaintance of Mirabeau, which soon ripened into an intimacy that only ceased with the death of the latter. His curious correspondence, which was published in 1851, shows the important part which the Count de la Marck played in the secret negotiation between Mirabeau and the court, which was still proceeding when the sudden death of Mirabeau, in April, 1791, extinguished the last hopes of succour and safety to the royal cause. In October, 1791, the count quitted Paris, and his property was confiscated. He soon after took employment under the Austrian government; and, after passing some time in Italy and Switzerland, he established himself at Vienna in 1798, and remained there till 1814, when (having resumed the name of d'Aremberg and recovered part of his property) he returned to Brussels, where he continued to reside till his death, in September, 1833.] at Brussels, which says that none of the old Flemish nobility had appeared at Leopold's court. One of them had even gone so far as to give a ball on the birthday of the Queen of Holland.

Wednesday, 18*th.*—Received a letter from Lord Hertford at Rome, with an account of the Lyons insurrection, which he had witnessed on his journey.

Thursday, 19*th.*—Talleyrand's **bons mots** always fly about. His friend Montrond has been subject of late to epileptic fits, one of which attacked him lately after dinner at Talleyrand's. While he lay on the floor in convulsions, scratching the carpet with his hands, his benign host remarked with a sneer, "C'est qu'il me paraît, qu'il veut absolument deseendre." No news from the Continent.

Friday, 20*th.*—Dined with Irby, and went with him to see Lord Francis Leveson's tragedy of "Catherine of Cleves" at Covent Garden. Sat in the box with Lady Francis and the two Grevilles. It is a translation of M. Dumas' "Henri III.," the story interesting, and Miss Kemble acted better than in any other character. The House of Commons went into committee on the Reform Bill; and their first division not so favourable to ministers. They had only a majority of fifty.

Saturday, 21*st.*—No political news. The Tories at White's in spirits, and begin to talk of throwing out the bill; *spes vana!* The cholera-morbus seems subsiding in the country. The attempt at making a commercial treaty with France, which George Villiers [Note *: Now Earl of Clarendon.] has been sent over to negotiate with that government, does not seem likely to succeed.

Monday, 23*rd.*—Received a letter from Greffulhe, who seems to think that Périer will remain in office, in spite of the fortress question. He says, "The king was observed to be extremely violent in his manner with Baron Werther, the Prussian minister, at the Tuileries the other night, but no very great importance is attached to his majesty's words or manner; royalty, in fact, is at a dreadful and increasing discount. That is the great, the alarming evil, for which none but violent remedies, I fear, can be a cure. The funds keep up pretty well, though all our sores are sadly laid bare by the discussion of the budget."

Wednesday, 25*th.*—Had some conversation this morning with Lord Wharncliffe at White's, which proves that there is no chance of any compromise now between his party and the Government. His language was most decided, that they were sacrificing everything to party spirit, and love of place; he could allow the propriety, as matters now stand, of some reform; but the present Ministry seemed placing themselves at the head of the people, to urge them on to fresh innovations.

Thursday, 26*th.*—Mr. Herries' motion to bring the Government to account for paying the dividend on the Russian loan, after the separation of Belgium from Holland, contrary to the intentions of the treaty, was lost in the Commons only by the small majority of twenty; and the ministers are, as may be supposed, very sore on the subject. Ellice, Lord Grey's secretary to the Treasury, said, that if they had been beat, they would have resigned the next day. But this the opposition does not want, till after the Reform question is settled, and then it seems hardly possible they can remain. Poor Mr. Greenwood [Note *: A partner in the firm of Messrs. Cox and Greenwood, the well-known army agents.] died at the Pavilion at Brighton, in his eighty-fifth year. He was taken ill when playing at whist, after dinner, with the King and Queen; was removed by Sir H. Taylor and Lord Erroll into an adjoining room; and expired, without any apparent suffering, in less than a quarter of an hour. He was a great friend of the late Duke of York, in whose society at Oatlands I used formerly to see much of him. A more amiable, kind-hearted man never lived. His loss will long be regretted, particularly by the army, to whose members he was a most liberal agent.

Saturday, 28*th.*—Matuscewitz to-day did not seem to think political matters looking well; from whence I infer that the Russian ratification will not come on the 31st, on which day he goes out of town. The division on Thursday night in the Commons has impressed the foreign ministers here, that the Government will not stand long.

Monday, 30*th.*—Sir H. Parnell dismissed from his post of secretary-at-war, because he did not vote on the Russian loan question in the Commons on Thursday night. It appears clear that the foreign ratifications will not arrive to-morrow.

Tuesday, 31*st.*—Sure enough no ratifications came from the Three Powers. England and France ratified last night, tête-à-tête, ***to the great exultation of Talleyrand, who has now got Palmerston in his*** wily embrace; the other powers do not refuse, but the P. P.'s [Note *: Sic in MS.; probably ***the Prussian Plenipotentiaries.***] await orders. Dedel [Note †: M. Dedel, who had for many years represented the King of Holland at the court of St. James's, died in 1848.] arrived last night from the Hague, with a further **strong protest.** Sir J. Cam Hobhouse appointed to succeed Parnell as secretary-at-war. A bold and inconsiderate measure in the Government to hazard a fresh Westminster election in these times.

Wednesday, 1*st. February.*—The papers mention the murder of Archdeacon Whittye within a short distance of his own house, six miles from Tipperary, for enforcing payment of his tithes.

From Count Matuscewitz
"Melton, near Grantham, Jan. 31.

"Dear R.

"I have received here your very interesting letter of the 29th, and hasten to return you my sincere thanks. I am looking forward with great anxiety to the King's speech. Meantime I fancy no war will arise out of the Belgian question, or out of the storm which threatens the superannuated empire of Constantinople. In both cases some compromise, even temporary, will and must [*be*] devised and agreed upon, as all leading powers in Europe are determined to maintain peace. In this pacific policy Russia fully participates. You may depend upon it, therefore, however circumstances may appear menacing, my opinion is, that general war will be avoided. With the recent example of St. Domingo before one's eyes, it is difficult not to consider the immediate emancipation of the negroes as pregnant with danger and bloodshed, and very little calculated to allay the angry feelings or terminate the serious discussions which have arisen in the West Indies between the respective administrations and legislatures. However, I sincerely wish I may be deceived in these forebodings. I am going tomorrow for two days to Willoughby's. After which, I shall return to Melton if it thaws, or go to town if it continues to freeze.

"Yours truly,

"M."

Thursday, 2nd.—At dinner at my brother's, H. R., the conversation turned chiefly on M——y's failure, who seems to have been very unpopular, and not to have excited much sympathy. I hear that the late coronation only cost 37,000*l.* The Queen was so anxious that no expense should be incurred on her account, that she would not permit either the purchase or hire of a crown from Rundell's for her; but ordered that it should be composed of her own jewels, and made up at her own expense. At the prior coronation of George IV. Rundell's charge for the loan of jewels only, was 16,000*l.,* as interest on their value.

Saturday, 4th.—The Nottingham rioters were executed on Tuesday last, as those at Bristol were the preceding week. The cholera has got to Edinburgh, but its violence seems abating up to this time; there have been in all 3489 cases and 1091 deaths.

It is asserted that the Austrian troops have again entered the Italian States, in order to assist the Papal troops in putting down the insurrections; and the French Government not only makes no remonstrance, but affects to approve it, such is the time-serving policy of M. C. Périer.

Sunday, 5th.—The Speaker told me this morning at White's, that Ellice had assured him the night before, that the Government never was so strong as at present. This is *un peu fort.*

Monday, 6th.—Joke of Holmes in the House of Commons. When Mr. Morrison, the member for Leicester, who, being a haberdasher, had made himself conspicuous by a speech on the foreign glove question, came up to him, and asked him if he could get him a *pair* for the evening: "Of what," said Holmes, "gloves or stockings?"

Wednesday, 8th.—Went from Lord Worcester's, where I had dined with Allen, to the Olympic. It appears that Lord Grey appears determined to enforce the Tithe question in Ireland, which will alienate the Irish members. It is too late now, the mischief is done.

Saturday, 11*th.*—Glengall arrived from Ireland. He says that Lord Anglesey has made a fearful mistake in his view of pacifying Ireland; he called in Dr. Doyle, Lord Cloncurry, Blake, and some other Catholics, whom he attempted by kindness and attentions to bring round to the Government. He thus displeased and alienated the Protestants, who were his real friends, without attaching the other party; he is therefore unpopular with all. Arms must be used to enforce the tithe system, and then the rising will become general.

Wednesday, 15*th.*—Lords Althorp and Stanley, for the ministers, recanted in the Commons Earl Grey's high language in the Lords about enforcing the payment of tithes in Ireland, and O'Connell publicly boasts that he has beat the Government. Matuscewitz agrees with me about the pitiful policy of Périer, who is sending 5000 French to assist Austria in quelling the insurrections in the Papal States. He crouches to the Holy Alliance, but can never gain their confidence, while he sacrifices the principles of the Revolution and must become odious in France. The only consistent powers are Russia, Austria, Prussia, and Holland, who make head against the revolutionary system without flinching; while England and France, who profess to advocate it, are daily shuffling and shifting about like ***girouettes.*** A letter from Lord Hertford at Naples tells me an American minister is come there as resident for the first time; his real object is to get an island as a pied à terre in the Mediterranean.

Friday, 17*th.*—A letter from Greffulhe says, "The Périer ministry seems to gain strength. A foolish expedition is preparing at Toulon, for the avowed purpose of intermeddling with the Papal States and the Austrian proceedings there; which will, I hope, be prevented by an opportune account of the latter having again retired. It is meant as a sort of os à ronger ***to the opposition, and therefore still more objectionable on that account. But the most striking and serious subject on the*** tapis is Don Pedro's expedition, which the Court of Madrid is determined to counteract and oppose, being therein strongly countenanced and supported by Russia, and perhaps Austria and Prussia. Diplomatic remonstrance from hence has proved quite ineffectual; and in this dilemma our Government are trying, I believe, to discourage Don Pedro, who will now scarcely be induced to desist, especially if backed and pushed on, as reported by your cabinet. This may breed a storm with Spain here, or is quite sure to breed a storm with the opposition, if Périer and Co. wisely determine to remain quiet."

Here, then, is Périer again blowing hot and cold. After all the support and assistance given to Don Pedro at Paris, he now wants to desert him and truckle to Spain, as he already has to the northern powers.

Saturday, 18*th.*—A duel has taken place within these few days under rather peculiar circumstances, the particulars of which were related to-day by Sir Robert Peel at White's.

A Mr. Stapylton, of Richmond in Yorkshire, was staying last year at Florence, where he became acquainted with the family of General Moore, and soon afterwards proposed to his daughter, who declined his addresses. Piqued by this refusal, it appears that he not only traduced her character, but lampooned her in some scurrilous verses, which he caused to be printed and circulated. The general has in consequence called him to account, shot him, and he now lies in great danger. There are some odd and contradictory reports of what passed on the ground; but as the general is in custody, if death ensues they will be investigated in a court of justice. The cholera seems to make no progress.

Sunday, 19*th.*—Strong reports at White's that twelve new peers will be created this week, which I cannot credit. Bad news from Jamaica; a serious insurrection of the slaves, which had been repressed by the troops; but it is said that fifty estates have been destroyed. This alone was wanting to complete the misery of the West India interest.

At dinner at Lord Foley's we had a long discussion on Mr. Baring's intended motion for rendering M.P.s liable to arrest. The reformers do not like liberty when it trenches on their privileges.

Friday, 24*th.*—The news of the cholera being in London has been received abroad. According to the feelings of the different nations towards England, France, who wishes to court us, has ordered a quarantine in her ports of three days; Holland, who feels aggrieved by our conduct at the Conference, one of forty days. The fog so thick in London, that the illuminations for the Queen's birthday were not visible.

Tuesday, 28*th.*—Last night, in the House of Lords, the Duke of W—attacked Lord Grey violently on his whole system, foreign and domestic.

Wednesday, 29*th.*—Last Sunday died an old schoolfellow of mine, Emilius Delme Radcliffe, at his house in Conduit-street. He was sitting with Lord Albemarle and Sloane Stanley, who were paying a morning visit; without any previous affection, he laid back his head in his chair, and expired without even a groan. His disorder was ossification of the heart. He was gentleman of the horse to the late King, who was very partial to him, and had the superintendence of all the royal racing studs. In his youth he was reckoned the best gentleman jockey-rider in England, for which his light weight was singularly adapted. He was a quiet, inoffensive character, and lived formerly much in the sporting society at Carlton House, but of late years had been more secluded from the world. He never changed his style of dress from the lime he left Eton, his single-breasted coat, long breeches, and short, white-topped boots.

Monday, 5*th.*—A melancholy event indeed—my poor friend Henry B. destroyed himself this morning in his room at Limmer's Hotel, Conduit-street. Continued losses at play and other pecuniary embarrassments drove him to despair, and he cut his own throat, after shaving and dressing himself completely, while the breakfast was preparing by his servant. It was an infatuation of long standing; his father had twice paid his debts to a large amount, and they were unfortunately not on speaking terms for some time past. His poor mother was burnt to death not two months ago, and he never saw her in her last moments. This sad event, and the recollection of his intimate friend——, who last year drowned himself in the Serpentine from the same dreadful cause, most probably accelerated this catastrophe.

He left no letter to any one,—merely the following words, scribbled on the back of a kind note which he had received the preceding evening from his friend the Duke of Dorset: "I cannot pray, and am determined to rush unbidden into the presence of my God!" What a sickening thought.

He was an amiable, gentlemanlike man, had many friends, and was one of the commissioners of the customs, which, with his original expectations, might have rendered his situation not only comfortable but affluent. The real object of commiseration now is the father, whose many domestic misfortunes will probably send him to the grave.

Thursday, 8th.—Walking with Matuscewitz, the conversation turned on the late French expedition to Ancona, one more of Périer's blunders; a *faux calcul,* which may recoil on himself, but cannot interest the powers of Europe. 5,000 French could do nothing in Italy against 80,000 Austrians, supposing the worst, but at home it must damage his influence. This useless demonstration will alarm the friends of peace and order, while it is too contemptible to give any satisfaction to the *parti du mouvement.*

Sunday, 11th.—Mr. Stapylton having recovered from his wound, General Moore was released from confinement. A duel has taken place in Paris lately, which has terminated fatally. The party who was killed, Captain Hesse, was my acquaintance. The dispute originated at play. Count Léon, a natural son of Bonaparte, lost to Hesse at écarté a sum of 17,000*l.*; and, some insinuations having been thrown out by the loser as to the dexterity of his adversary, satisfaction was required. They first repaired to a notary's, where security for the debt was given by Count Léon, and then to the field, where Hesse met his death. He was a Saxon by birth, had been in our service, and had been formerly notorious as a protégé of Queen Caroline.

Monday, 12th.—Precious news from Ireland this morning. At the assizes to try the murderers at Knocktophet, the jurors refused to be sworn and the witnesses to give evidence, from fear of their lives. The prisoners, therefore, could not be tried, and the sessions were adjourned. No law can now be said to exist in Ireland.

The plea was that, as they were all sworn to oppose the tithes, they could not co-operate in bringing to justice the murderers of tax-gatherers who had been appointed to levy them.

Tuesday, 20*th.*—Charlton, who dined with me to-day, said, aptly enough, without some reform we should have a rebellion in the country; but, with the present extravagant plan, we shall have a revolution.

Wednesday, 21*st.*—The general fast-day for the cholera. The political unions tried to excite a tumult in the city, but failed. Upon the whole, the day was observed with much decency; the churches were well attended, the shops shut up, and the streets even more quiet than on a Sunday.

Monday, 26*th.*—This day the [Reform] Bill was brought for the second time into the House of Lords from the Commons. Lords Harrowby and Wharncliffe expressed their intention to vote for the second reading, reserving their comments for the committee. They might as well have said nothing. The Duke firm.

Tuesday, 27*th.*—The cholera seems increasing still. Count Orloff arrived this evening from the Hague; but, as the Dutch funds seem declining, it does not augur much for the success of his mission to the King of Holland: after all, it is still a question whether his master the Czar is really in earnest. I see there will be no Russian ratification.

gancies, was this day ordered by Sir H. Halford to be under the superintendence of a keeper. Here is a man with high rank, character, very cultivated talents, and a colossal fortune, courted in society, surrounded with every means of receiving and conferring happiness,—the most enviable position perhaps in life that could be pictured,—and what is the result? One single dispensation annihilates the whole! Oh, *vanitas, vanitatum!* What a corrective to human wishes! What an inducement to patience under all our disappointments! Perfect happiness seems impossible; but a system of compensation appears throughout to kindly and wisely equalise our lots. No prosperity without some alloy; no adversity without some palliation. Our only course is gratitude and submission.

Saturday, 7th.—From the daily reports, cholera seems greatly subsiding; up to last night the grand total of cases here, since the commencement, are 7435, and deaths 2489. It has broke out in Paris with greater violence than here; in three days they have had 1050 cases and 394 deaths.

How consistent are the monarchical powers, how inconsistent the two liberal!

Civilisation still keeps on her march; even barbarous Egypt feels the impulse,—a stage coach and harness has been shipped from hence, to run between Cairo and Alexandria. As old Europe decays and runs to seed, she scatters the means of fertility to new regions destined to succeed to her prosperity. Bonaparte, when first consul, said to Mr. Livingston, at his levee, "Le vieux monde est corrompu, il n'y a plus que le nouveau monde." It was meant as a. compliment to the American minister, but it becomes daily more and more a truism. Livingston, who did not understand French, appeared rather embarrassed what to reply, when Bonaparte, looking round for an interpreter, fixed his eye on Cambacères, whose moral character was sufficiently notorious, and said to him, "Dites-lui en Anglois, que le vieux monde est corrompu; vous en scavez quelque chose, vous." A new Tory club [Note *: The Carlton.] has just been formed, for which Lord Kensington's house, in Carlton Gardens, has been taken. Lord Clanwilliam and others, having asked me to belong to it, though no party man or political character, I have agreed. The object is to have a counterbalancing meeting to Brooke's, which is purely a Whig re-union; White's, which was formerly devoted to the other side, being now of no colour, and frequented indiscriminately by all. The Duke takes a great interest in the new establishment.

Monday, 9th.—Second reading of the bill began in the Lords.

Tuesday, 10th.—I hear, by a letter from Greffulhe, Périer has been near dying from the cholera, which is making frightful progress in Paris. He says, "War seems equally dreaded by, and impracticable for, all parties, a belief strengthened by the wild Ancona prank, which shows that the pacific spirit at Vienna must be *fire-*

proof, to resist such a provocation."

Friday, 13*th.*—Last debate in the Lords, on the second reading of the Reform Bill, which after a stormy debate through the night, on—

Saturday, 14*th,*—at 7 o'clock in the morning, was carried by a majority of nine. The meeting in committee is adjourned till after the Easter recess, and then will come the real contest. Went to Mr. Rennie's wharf, to see the diving-bell, which we have provided for the Société de Commerce, at the Hague. It is to cost 860*l.*

Sunday, 15*th.*—It seems currently reported that no new peers will be created, and that now a serious modification of the bill will take place in the committee, with the consent of both parties. Lord Dudley's malady seems hopeless; he has just been removed into the country under proper care. On the examination of his affairs, it appears, by his banker's account, that very large sums have been drawn since he was in a state of derangement.

Monday, 16*th.*—General Mackenzie writes, that he has quitted Paris, on account of the cholera, which is making dreadful havoc among all classes in that city; where alone, in three weeks, there have been 10,000 cases and near 5,000 deaths.

Tuesday, 17*th.*—The tide of emigration is rolling fast towards our colonies in Canada and Van Diemen's Land; poverty and want of employment are daily driving thither hundreds of useful labourers, with their families, who will aid the great work of bringing a new world into cultivation. The parent hive is full, and sends out its swarms; but when I look at the tracts of land which remain uncultivated in Ireland, and even here, I fear that we must impute this desertion of home rather to the vicious organisation of our system and of our poor laws, than to an overcrowded population in the empire. There is still room enough for all, and useful employment likewise, were there but less avarice and encroachments among the higher and wealthier classes; everything works to the ordained point, and out of evil good may come.

Wednesday, 18*th.*—Accounts from Russia, that by an imperial ukase Poland has been annexed to the Russian empire as a punishment for her rebellion.

Thursday, 19*th.*—Prussia and Austria have last night exchanged their ratifications, with the stipulation that no coercion shall be used towards Holland; which leaves the matter as unsettled as ever. Upon the same terms I conclude that Russia will also adhere, though the orders are not yet come to Prince Lieven. The division in the Lords on the Reform Bill has probably carried this decision, under the idea that the Government here will be more likely to last, and therefore in appearance to be conciliated; but though prudence may dictate this step, there is and can be no real cordialty on the subject.

Good Friday, 20*th.*—The progress of the cholera at Paris still very frightful: the private letters mention that the government reports have been very much understated; that near 12,000 deaths have occurred, and many in the higher ranks. Among them is Prince Castelcicala, the Neapolitan ambassador, aged eighty years, who had long been known for his self-indulgent mode of life: he was a friend of my father's forty years ago in England. Lord Granville, who is come over to vote for the bill, said many people in his society are dead, and there are sick in almost every house in Paris.

I see that there is a colony of emancipated slaves Called Liberia, on the southwest coast of Guinea, extending upwards of 200 miles, where all the arts of civilised life are introduced, and will gradually spread over the whole of Africa.

Sunday, 22*nd.*—Yesterday, died of the cholera, in ten hours, Lady Ann Wyndham, sister to Lord Jersey. Her first husband was Mr. Lambton, by whom she was mother to Lord Durham, and Mrs. H. Cavendish, &c. After his death she married C. Wyndham, brother to Lord Egremont, and was separated from him on the following day by mutual consent. For many years her health had been much impaired, and she had lived in the completest retirement; her broken constitution could make no resistance to this fearful malady, which carried her off instantly; and she was buried this day to prevent the contagion. Mr. Cunliffe Offley, M.P. for Chester, is also dead, after an illness of twenty-four hours, of the same complaint. Hitherto no other cases have occurred in that rank of society, and the disorder, it is hoped, is now disappearing.

Tuesday, 1*st May.*—I have been reading the "Memoirs of Louis XVIII.," just published, and which M. de Talleyrand says, "Ne peuvent être que de lui." There is one circumstance so extraordinary in the book that I must transcribe it. He says that, on returning home at night after the christening of the young Dauphin, son of Louis XVI. and Marie Antoinette, he found on his toilet a letter in a double envelope, addressed "à Monsieur seul." On opening these, he found a sheet of black paper, with the following lines, written in white ink:—

"Console-toi, je viens de tirer l'horoscope du nouveau né; il ne t'enlevera pas la couronne; il cessera de vivre lorsque son père cessera de régner. Un autre que toi, cependant, succédera à Louis XVI.; mais tu ne seras pas moins Roi de France un jour. Félicite-toi d'être sans postérité: l'existence de tes fils seroit menacée de trop grands maux, car ta famille boira jusqu'à la lie ce que la coupe du destin renferme de plus amer. Adieu! tremble pour ta vie si tu cherches à me connoître. Je suis—
     "La Mort."

His first impulse was to take a copy of the letter, that the original might be shown to the police in the morning; but, to his great surprise, soon afterwards the white characters began to fluctuate on the black paper, and then completely disappeared; being evidently traced in some chemical composition which would only last a certain time, as a precaution for the writer. On the following morning the paper presented nothing but a mass of holes and corrosions. He adds, that he never mentioned the circumstance at the time to any one, but during the emigration he told it to his friend the Duc d'Avaray. Unfortunately, *then,* two-thirds of the prophecy must have been fulfilled; and, as he then bore the title of Louis XVIII., it was nearly made out entirely. Yesterday my brother Henry went to settle at Chester, as chancellor of the diocese.

Wednesday, 2nd.—Montrond has come back from Paris. He says the Memoirs are not doubted at Paris by all who knew Louis XVIII.; and not the least proof of their authenticity is that, in wishing to demonstrate his sagacity, he cannot help showing what a rogue he was.

It appears that the Russian ratification is come in, also with restrictions. Holland remains immovable. The ruin of Mr. Watson Taylor declared, and executions put in his houses in town and country. At his outset in life he was a regular, independent man, with about 1500*l.* a year, and happy. At forty-five years of age he inherits above 60,000*l.* a year, through the death of his wife's brother, Sir Simon Taylor; and in twelve years he is completely ruined. The state of West Indian property may have contributed to this catastrophe; but his wasteful expenditure was beyond all conception;—plate, pictures, houses, furniture, and curiosities of all sorts, and at double the price that others would give, without any order or consideration, and merely to engross public notice. Sir Robert Peel said, the other day at dinner, "No man ever bought ridicule at so high a price."

Friday, 4th.—De Ros said, that in society lately the conversation turned on the horrid scenes which a field of battle presented on the following day. Talleyrand, who was present, described that which he had himself seen after the battle of Austerlitz, which field he visited from Vienna in a carriage with Marmont, soon after the victory. He concluded with saying, "Marmont pleuroit à chaudes larmes, quant à moi je vous assure que cela ne me fesoit aucun effet."

Saturday, 5th.—The King yesterday gave a grand dinner to all the East India directors and others any way connected with that government. In the number was the Duke of Wellington; and though the healths of the generals who had commanded on that station were drunk individually, that of the ***conqueror at Assaye was omitted.***

Monday, 7th.—This evening the House of Peers met in committee on the bill; and on the first division the Government were beat by a majority of thirty-five, to their own great astonishment. Lord Grey upon this immediately adjourned the

House till Thursday. He said to Lord Wharncliffe, with evident vexation, on going out of the House, "You may now take the bill, and do what you please with it." They must, it is supposed, now, either make peers, and not less than sixty, or resign.

Tuesday, 8*th.*—Much anxiety and gossiping at all the clubs during the day, but nothing known. Lords Grey and Brougham went down to the King at Windsor, and returned in the evening. A cabinet council was held on their return, which broke up at twelve o'clock; but nothing transpired. One circumstance alone struck me and others forcibly. Sefton was at the opera in the highest spirits possible; he came at half-past one into the supper-room at Crockford's, having most probably driven in the interim to Downing-street, and I never saw such an alteration. His face was the picture of despair and vexation.

Wednesday, 9*th.*—Sefton's face was a true barometer. The King has refused to make the peers, and this morning the ministers have given in their resignations, which have been accepted. Still they attended at the levee, and the King appeared cheerful. Brookes's Club is full of weeping and gnashing of teeth, so little was the party prepared for this sudden catastrophe. No one knows to whom the King will turn for his new advisers, and the aspect of affairs is cloudy enough; but the funds have not fallen much, the three per cents leaving off at eighty-four. Lord Grey in the House to-night announced the retreat of himself and colleagues, which had been graciously accepted by his Majesty. Very little passed, except some severe remarks from Lord Carnarvon on the atrocious coup d'état which had been meditated by Lord Grey against the privileges of that house. In the evening the King sent for Lord Lyndhurst, and some violent resolutions were passed at Brookes's, to be brought forward to-morrow in the Commons. Sefton told me that he knew the fact early this morning, and went instantly to communicate it to Talleyrand, who was thunderstruck at the news, and sent it off by express to Paris. It must make a great alteration in our foreign political relations, and be much to the satisfaction of Holland, Russia, &c.

Thursday, 10*th.*—Various rumours all he morning. At night it was pretty well understood that the Duke would undertake the formation of a ministry, under certain conditions; but Sir R. Peel persists in his refusal to accept office. He says, that he underwent so much obloquy on account of his vote on the Catholic question, that he will not be induced by any motives of place to alter his opinion; which proves that the Duke means to make great concessions as to reform. The present Government loudly proclaim the impossibility of forming a Tory ministry which can last three weeks under the present exciting circumstances, and exult in the certainty of their speedy return to power. Is not this as much as to say, that they have resigned on the first difficulty purposely to create tumult and confusion in the country, that they may then be brought back on the shoulders of the people in triumph? May they be disappointed! Lord Ebrington's motion in the Commons to approve the conduct of Lord Grey and his colleagues was carried by a majority of eighty, which is not surprising.

A curious circumstance occurred to-day in the conference on Greek affairs. Baron de Cetto, the Bavarian minister, has been for some time holding back from signing the treaty for Prince Otho's accession to the throne, with a view to get more money for him guaranteed by the Three Powers; but on Palmerston representing to him that his powers would cease in a few days, and Talleyrand showing that Périer, whose confidence he so entirely possessed, must soon be replaced by others, who might have very different views on the subject, he has suddenly made up his mind to submit to their proposal, which is a loan of 60,000,000 francs, and will sign the treaty to-morrow. This I know from undoubted authority.

Friday, 11 *th.*—A great Tory meeting at Apsley House, when all party schisms were abjured by the ultra party, and a general reconciliation took place, with a determination to pull together for the common cause. A list was then formed by the Duke, which was carried down to Windsor by Lord Lyndhurst immediately. The result is not known to-night; but it is asserted that a strong measure of reform, as being absolutely necessary to the peace of the country, will form the basis of their policy. I have just seen Adolphus Fitz-Clarence, who told me that he had left the King at two o'clock, who was in excellent spirits, and said to him on parting, "I do not know who are my ministers; but I am determined to do that which I feel is right without consulting any one." The expresses from Manchester and Birmingham mention considerable excitement of course, and a disposition not to pay taxes. This feeling will probably be increased when they hear the Tories are coming into power, and I fear much tumult may ensue in many places; but we must hope for the best.

Saturday, 12 *th.*—The King came to town this morning at one o'clock, when he met the Duke at the palace, who, after a short interview, kissed hands as premier. None of the other appointments are known. The King, it appears, is in very good spirits. The first measure to which he has been advised by the Duke, is not to receive the delegates from the political union at Birmingham, as an association not authorised by the law.

Sunday, 13 *th.*—There was a great Tory dinner of forty covers at the new club. The Duke in the chair. Many speeches after dinner, which concurred in admitting the necessity of reform. In the evening there was a most violent meeting of Whigs at Brookes's, where the virulence of the speeches, particularly that of Mr. Stanley [Note *: Now the Earl of Derby.], the Irish secretary, who got upon the table, showed the exasperated feelings of the party. Yesterday, when Lord Foley went to the palace, to give in his resignation as captain of the band of Gentlemen Pensioners, the King said to him, "I am an old man, and I do not think I shall ever live to see you in place again."

Monday, 14 *th.*—Dined at Sir Robert Peel's, where there is a fine gallery of paintings by the old masters, and the best collection of Sir T. Lawrence's portraits,— particularly those of the Duke of Wellington and Canning. We saw a new picture by Haydon, being a back view of Napoleon on the Isle of St. Helena, contemplating the sea: the effect is not pleasing; and, as the painter had never seen the original, can have no absolute value.

The list not being formed, the Duke did not go to the House, as was expected; indeed, there seems to be still much difficulty in effecting this object. Mr. Baring in the Commons declared, that he now saw reform must be carried; a prelude, it is supposed, to taking office. A meeting of Radicals at St. John's Wood, which ended in nothing. Late in the evening the debate took a most stormy turn, and such violent abuse was heaped on the Duke for changing his politics, that, though I firmly believe he is actuated only by worthy motives, to save the country from the grasp of democracy, yet it is to be feared this virulent excitement, on the part of his political opponents, will be greedily caught up by the public in general, who believe that statesmen can never be actuated by any other feeling than the love of place. I say, I fear, that he will not be able to fight against the storm; that the dread of the world's harsh judgment will damp his energies, will not only prevent his persevering in the formation of a new ministry, but will also deter many others from enlisting under his standard, and giving him that assistance which it is certain his own intentions deserve. Nobody doubts his dislike to the bill; all must see that he yields his opinion, and gives his aid to one evil in order to avoid a greater in perspective; but, nevertheless, the ***protest,*** so lately signed by him in the Lords, stares all in the face as an apparent inconsistency.

Tuesday, 15*th.*—This morning, as was anticipated, the Duke signified to the King that, owing to the excitement produced by the present crisis, he could not form an administration. The King wrote to Lord Grey, whose answer was very long, and, it is said, couched in haughty terms, demanding ***carte blanche*** to make peers, which the King still positively refuses to do. We are therefore still without any government. The feeling at night was general, that the Tory Lords would no longer oppose the bill, but walk out without voting, and allow Lord Grey to carry the measure without a fresh creation; by which means they save the peers from being swamped. This is the line they ought to have taken at the commencement; it would have been consistent, and given a weight to the party, which would probably have enabled them to oust the Whigs hereafter, upon the valid grounds of their insufficiency and ignorance. I fear, however, Lord Grey may still insist on making peers, though sure of carrying this bill, to obtain a support on other matters for the future.

Wednesday, 16*th.*—A day of various and conflicting reports. At one time it was conceived that all was settled, that Lord Grey had carried his point with the King; but at night Sefton's face, which is my barometer, augured that no settlement had as yet been accomplished. There was a levee in the morning, and a grand dinner given by the King to the Jockey Club. The cabinet council was still sitting, and no answer to the King's message decided upon.

The changes here have created much sensation in Paris, and will influence the appointment of a new minister there, in the room of Périer, who is dying.

Thursday, 17th.—Another stormy debate in the Lords, where the Duke made his statement. Nothing settled as to the ministry, or any change in the King's decision concerning peers. An express arrived to-night with the news that Casimir Périer died yesterday morning at ten o'clock.

Friday, 18th.—At last this awful question is settled. Lord Grey announced in the House that he had received **assurances** which enabled him to congratulate the country on the success of the bill. He had the means of carrying it unimpaired in all its branches; but he did not say whether by creation of peers or secession of the opposition. Mr. Hume, the member for Middlesex, and most vapouring radical in the House, has shown that courage is not amongst his peculiar virtues. He in the most uncalled-for manner wrote to the constituents of Mr. Horatio Ross, member for the Scotch burgh Arbroath, Aberdeen, &c., that he had deserted his duty to them, and was become lukewarm in the cause of reform: Mr. Ross instantly wrote to him, that he was a malicious liar, and demanded a recantation or satisfaction. The cautious demagogue submitted to the insult, and retracted his expressions, in a letter which Mr. Ross will be well justified in publishing.

Saturday, 19th.—A numerous meeting of Tories assembled at Apsley House to-day, when the Duke proposed that they should not secede jointly as a body, but each individually refrain from voting on the bill, which in most instances will be adopted, and thus the evil of a creation of peers be avoided. There is much alarm in some branches of the cabinet about the future; they begin to feel that they have raised a power which they can never put down, a power that will only go with them as long as they follow its impulse. The political unions have spoken too loudly now ever to be silenced again, and they will eventually overturn not only this government, but any other which may succeed. The Duke of R. has said to Lord W., "You may think yourselves defeated, but ours is the real defeat; we have created the monster, which will turn upon us as well as you. Attwood and O'Connell will turn the scale in the end." It is plainly to be seen that they dread the Irish bill, as the most tremendous struggle of all, and they must take the consequences, come what will. The die is cast; to go back is impossible: the tide of innovation has set in, and who shall say where it will carry us? From this day dates a new era for England. Placards are streaming about the streets with "Glory and honour to the people." And what is the people? what has the people always been? The most capricious, the most cruel, the most ungrateful and selfish class of society; but we must be governed by this same people which fifteen years ago was the worshipper of the Duke, which hailed him as the saviour of Europe, but now pursues his steps with curses deep and loud, and showers on him all the bitterness of malignant invective, nay, more, which pants for his life! I have heard it frequently asserted by the Government party, that, if on this occasion he took office, before a week was out he would be assassinated. This is the real evil: it is not the disfranchising rotten boroughs, and the enfranchising other places, it is the reckless agitation of the whole country, caused by an unprincipled set of men, to keep themselves in place, which we have now to deplore. Périer's brother is appointed minister in France for the present; a man of no abilities, but merely put up to the foreign powers as a symbol that his brother's system will continue to be enforced.

Sunday, 20*th.*—Ross showed me the correspondence between him and Hume, which places the radical member in a most contemptible light. Lords Londonderry and Ellenborough seem still inclined to prolong the warfare in the Lords, but it will not have effect, the bill now must pass.

Tuesday, 22*nd.*—A division took place in the Lords on the metropolitan clause; the opposition only mustered 36 and the Government 91. This majority must show that a new creation of peers cannot be required. Previous to the late dinner which the King gave to the Jockey Club, Lord Sefton, who was indignant at the resignation of his friends the ministers, and most clamorous at what he called the duplicity of the King, in a fit of pique and vexation erased his name from the list of members, and sent an excuse to the dinner as no longer belonging to the Club. The King, who was not then aware of his motive, graciously requested that he would come as his friend. He never went. Circumstances soon took a different turn. Lord Grey resumed office, and Lord Sefton's animosity subsided. The Queen gave a ball on Friday night, where the whole Sefton family made their appearance, and His Majesty, who was then better informed, turned his back openly on his lordship. ***Dans ces entrefaites*** Lord Molyneux had attended a public meeting at Liverpool, where he made a speech, and, actuated by his father's feelings, alluded very bitterly to the conduct of both the King and Queen. He afterwards came to town, and appeared with his family at the ball. On the following day the King commanded Mr. W. Ashley, as vice-chamberlain to the Queen, to write to Lord Molyneux, and request he would not appear at court again. Nothing could be more just. The Duke of Sussex, having presumed to present an insolent address to the King from the Political Union at Birmingham, but which was not received, is also very justly in disgrace. These are only slight instances of Whig insolence and ingratitude. Sefton has been made a peer, and treated with the most marked courtesy and attention by the present King; and who does not know all that he has done for his brother the Duke of Sussex?

Wednesday, 23*rd.*—Still some talk of peers being made; among others Methuen, who says, that he has a promise to be made Lord Corsham. Copley said, at White's, that if he was disappointed, he would be Lord Curse'm. Our fleet is tomorrow to sail for Portugal to see *fair play* between Miguel and Pedro; and, in case the Spaniards should assist the former, to act on the offensive, in consequence of our system of *non-intervention.* All parties now seem to agree that we are in a dreadful state, and even the Government people lower their tone, and hope that the common danger may ultimately unite Whigs and Tories to resist the common enemy. They have done the mischief, and feel too late their incapacity to remedy it.

Thursday, 24*th.*—The other morning Montrond, coming out of Sefton's house, met De Ros, and said to him, "Ce pauvre Sefton, il est si méchant, si bossu aujourd'hui, ça fait pitié." Greffulhe writes from Paris, that the marriage between King Leopold and Mademoiselle d'Orléans, daughter of Louis-Philippe, has been announced, and is to be celebrated immediately; it is a prelude to the Union, and perhaps hereafter the incorporation, of Belgium with France; and precludes all idea of Leopold's future adhesion to the interests and policy of England, in the event of differences between us and our rival, who now gains as great an influence in that quarter as if the Due de Némours had been chosen King of the Belgians.

The bill is now passing rapidly, but in sullenness on the part of the Tories, through the Lords; few vote against it, but the debates are acrimonious, and marked by the most unseemly personalities. The unfortunate and ill-judged line which the party has taken precludes any chance of modifying the clauses. Thus the metropolitan clause was carried against the general feeling of the House; and there seems to be only one object in view, that of finishing the question. Ministers cannot object to forward their own work, and the opposition in their pique, wish to saddle them with all the responsibility of its most odious defects. Their motto seems to be ***"Vous l'avez voulu, donc vous l'aurez"*** Thus patriotism yields to party feeling. In the meantime the country, though apparently tranquil, does not seem satisfied; that general content which was predicted to follow the settlement of this question is not so evident. The adherents of the Tory party are numerous, wealthy, and influential; and the despondency assumed by such a class must naturally have its weight with the public mind, and particularly with the monied interest, always more alive to alarm than others, and naturally suspicious of a Whig or popular ascendency. The stockholder loves the Tory bolstering system, which put the best face on existing circumstances, and strenuously maintained the doctrine of faith with the public creditor. He trembles at the former republican threats of Lord Althorp, with his pruning-knife and his sponge, though perhaps without much reason, as the maxims of a Whig out of place seldom regulate the practice of a Whig in office. The wand of power makes strange alterations in the feelings and policy of all men. Then the unlucky coincidence, that at this moment two such serious questions as the renewal of the Bank and the East Indian Companies' charters should come into discussion, gives fresh cause for apprehension. The committee of the former is already named, and all the secrets of that massive establishment will be laid open to public view; and from what I have ***some reason*** to know, certain sanguine anticipations of the accumulations of that company may be grievously disappointed. Glad would the

Government now be if they could dissolve the political unions, but of this there is little chance; on the contrary, success seems only to have raised their tone, and Lord Grey will find that he has used a dangerous auxiliary, who will only serve under him as long as he will lead them on to further conquest. They have got their reform, what will be their next war cry? The repeal of the corn bill, which will reduce the income from land one-half, will that satisfy them?

No! Then comes, &c. &c.,—annual parliaments, ballot.

Monday, 28*th.*—The King's birthday, and a very full drawing-room. It was re-marked that the Duke and Lord Lyndhurst were received with particular attention, and much more noticed than the ministers. The usual state dinners were given; but the King did not dine with the Duke, as was at first intended.

Tuesday, 29*th.*—Reports that Lord Grey will resign as soon as the bill has passed through the Lords. The Paris letters mention, that no minister is appointed, and that Louis-Philippe imagines he can act as president of the council himself. The two foreigners most known here are,—

Montrond, who must be near sixty-five years old, a protégé *of Talleyrand, and constant guest at histable. He has lived through the different scenes of the French Revolution, always keeping up a certain scale of expense, is received into all the best houses in London, and is witty and entertaining, though his* ton *is rather* tranchant. *He plays high, and generally wins; is full of anecdotes; tells them well; great epicure and connoisseur at the table; enters into all the gaieties and pursuits of the young English dandies, who look up to him and admire his sallies. He was notorious in Paris as a* roué; grand brétailleur; and fought one duel with the elder Greffulhe, which did not end so fatally as some others. He married the Duchesse de Fleury; a beautiful woman with a fortune, which he spent. Old age has now mellowed the more riotous traits in his character; he feels less independent in a foreign country than in his own; and a life of quiet self-indulgence seems now his only ambition. The other is D'Orsay [Note *: Count Alfred d'Orsay, who married the daughter of the Earl of Blessington, died at Paris in 1852.], very good looking, and gifted with great talents, the son of the General Count D'Orsay, whose mother married Mr. Crawford, well known for many years as a rich collector of pictures and articles of vertù at Paris. His sister, a beautiful person, married the Duc de Guiche, son of the Duc de Grammont, and is now, with her husband, following the fortunes of the exiled royal family, at Holyrood House.

Wednesday, 30th.—This day died Sir James Mackintosh, of a lingering disorder, originally caused by a piece of chicken sticking in his throat, when at dinner, which nearly produced strangulation, and affected his health afterwards. He was a man of great learning and abilities, and a staunch Whig, and he will be a great loss to this Government, under which he was President of the Board of Control. His Moral and Political Lectures, many years ago, in Lincoln's-Inn, will be long remembered by those who heard them. The Pitt dinner was attended today, at Merchant Tailors' Hall, by near 500 persons. The Duke in the chair. Though a complete Tory meeting, no discontent was observed in the mob without, and the Duke, on going away, was rather cheered than otherwise. Schedules A. and B. were carried in the Lords with not above five or six peers on the opposition benches.

Thursday, 31st.—Alvanley and Cooke, dining with me, were both very amusing and full of anecdote of former times. The former, who has lived much with Talleyrand in France, both at Paris and at Valen-çaye [Note *: The Château of the Prince Talleyrand, near Blois.], gave us some interesting recollections of the prince's Memoirs, which had been occasionally read to him when he was staying in his house. From these it appears that there were two points on which Talleyrand's counsels had been uniformly, but unsuccessfully, opposed to the views of Napoleon,—the invasion of Spain, and the elevation of his brothers to the sceptre over foreign states. As far as my memory goes, these were the arguments which he adduced. The error of the first was, that, having already unlimited power in that country, having fascinated the King Charles IV., and bribed the Prince of Peace, who governed the weak mind of the Queen, all the resources, military, naval, and financial, of Spain, were entirely at his disposal. Why then attack by a military invasion the ***amour-propre*** of a country, which, though dead to the degradation of its sovereign, would, and must still be alive to the humiliating occupation of a foreign invader? Why draw upon himself the rancour of a priesthood, all powerful in the country, who must be stimulated to oppose his progress by the apprehension of losing, not only their immense property, but also their moral influence over the minds of the people, by the incursion of his armies, and the dissemination of his principles:—a nation, too, degraded, but loyal, attached to its king, its religion, and its peculiar prejudices, no longer perhaps formidable in the field, but united and desperate in a partisan warfare, to which its native thickets, mountains, and fastnesses gave advantages unknown and unexpected in modern warfare.

Upon the second point of opposition, that is, with respect to the enthronement of his brothers, the language of Talleyrand to Napoleon was equally strong and cogent. Alvanley proceeded to say, as far as I can accurately recollect of the conversation, "You have," said he, "created a great empire by your own transcendent talents and master mind; but look at your brothers, and observe how little they are gifted with those qualities; make them princes, constables of the empire, or what you will at home; load them with honours, riches, titles; but place them not on an elevated pinnacle abroad, where their weakness may only tend to undermine the *prestige* of your greatness. Send thither ambassadors, whom you may select for those qualities and merits, which may *more effectually* promote your purposes and objects, than can be done by crowning weak members of your family, and thereby exciting the jealousy and ill-will of your neighbours."

Talleyrand renders every justice to this great and extraordinary man, as a sovereign and a general; his chief mistake was, to have underrated the credit and resources of England; and as he was tormented by the *ver rongeur* of ambition, which offered to him no excitement but military conquest, so the resistance which he met with from this country was the source of constant irritation in his prosperity, and of his final ruin in adversity. The Memoirs of Talleyrand, whenever published, must be a valuable acquisition to the history of Europe and to the study of human nature. No man ever lived so long in such extraordinary times; he is now near eighty years old. [Note *: He was born in 1754, and died in 1838.] He began life in the reign of Louis XV. He was descended from a good family, but very poor. He defrayed the small expenses of his college education out of the produce of an *abbaye,* which he received on going into the church. He at last was made Bishop of Autun. On the breaking out of the Revolution he joined the popular party, abjured his ecclesiastical profession, and was for some time secretary to Chauvelin, the French minister in England. On his return to France the massacres and proscriptions had commenced; the Jacobin party was waging war to the knife against nobles and aristocrats; his doom was sealed, and he was forced to emigrate. His previous conduct had rendered any asylum where he might meet his brother emigrants dangerous to his personal safety, and America presented the only retreat from the rage of all parties, who were now equally incensed against him. Thither he went, with what little money he could collect; and bitter must have been the time he spent there. Straitened circumstances in an infant and but barely civilised republic must have been galling to one then accustomed to all the luxuries and refinements of the late French court. At one time he meditated, and had almost engaged his passage for a speculative establishment at Calcutta, but another lot was already designed for him. The Government in France began to wear rather a more settled aspect under the Directory [Note *: Madame de Staël.]; his friends in Paris interested themselves strongly in his favour, and at length obtained the erasure of his name from the list of emigrants. He quitted America without regret, as may be supposed; and he says himself, that he arrived in France with only fifteen louis in his pocket. Here his various talents and natural *finesse* soon gained him an ascendency with the people then in power, and in a very short time he became Minister for Foreign Affairs of the republic. His account of this period is very singular. Installed in one of the magnificent hotels of the old *noblesse,* which had been appropriated to the uses of the new government, and after being gutted during the excesses of the Revolution, had been partly refurnished by promiscuous gleanings of finery and magnificence from the Garde-Meuble and the other palaces, he found himself lodged like a prince, without a shilling of revenue, surrounded by servants whose wages he knew not how to pay, and who were using the most costly services of old Sèvres china for the commonest purposes of the kitchen and offices, because they really had not the money to purchase utensils of earthenware.

His first step to extricate himself from these difficulties was the treaty with Portugal, then on the ***tapis.*** The negotiation was soon brought to a favourable conclusion; by which it was stipulated that, in return for certain concessions on the part of France, Portugal should pay an indemnity of eight millions. Of this sum Talleyrand allows that he distributed one million to each of the five directors, and appropriated the remaining three to himself. This was the origin of that amazing fortune which he afterwards accumulated; but which, like every other circumstance in human affairs, having reached the zenith of its prosperity, declined nearly as rapidly as it had risen; for he is now supposed to be in moderate circumstances. Many other anecdotes were mentioned, which I have no time to note down, but Alvanley's opinion seems to be, that his diplomatic talents may have been rather overrated, and that his successful career may chiefly be attributed to a fineness of tact, which enabled him to perceive early the current of the times, and float on its surface.

His fortune was very much diminished by the expense of maintaining the Spanish royal family at Valençaye; a penalty inflicted upon him by order of Napoleon.

Friday, 1***st June.***—Report of the committee in the Lords. Two marriages announced. Marquis of Abercorn to Lady Louisa Russell, daughter of the Duke of Bedford, and Captain H. Rous, brother to Lord Stradbroke, to Miss Cuthbert.

Sunday, 3***rd.***—The Government begin to have apprehensions about the state of things in France. I could see by the questions and manner of J. Walpole, who is Palmerston's private secretary, that they are uneasy on some points of their foreign policy. Talleyrand goes in ten days to pass two or three months at Barège, and reports are beginning to circulate, that he will not return, but be succeeded by Flahault.

Monday, 4***th.***—The third reading of the Reform Bill passed in the Lords, with a majority of eighty-four, only twenty of the opposition peers remaining to vote. Thus is the question put at rest, and the bill unamended is become the law of the land. A new era may be dated from this day for England, and who can tell the changes that may ensue? The House of Peers, as a deliberative body, is trampled under foot; it never again can be a check to popular innovation, as the same threat of a fresh creation may be used by a reckless minister to carry any other point in opposition to their opinion and feelings.

Wednesday, 6th.—Baring's motion brought on in the House of Commons, to make the members liable to arrest for debt, as with others.

Thursday, 7th.—The King gave his assent to the Reform Bill by ***commission,*** to the great annoyance of ministers, who wished to induce him to do it in person. An express from Paris arrived this morning with the news of a fresh insurrection, which broke out on the occasion of General Lamarque's funeral on Tuesday last; the mob was still fighting with the military in the streets, and the bloodshed was very great. In the evening came a telegraphic dispatch that order was restored, and Paris tranquil. St. Giles won the Derby stakes at Epsom.

Friday, 8th.—The accounts from Paris still far from encouraging; more fighting in the streets on Wednesday, and, what is more extraordinary, Talleyrand has no dispatches. The commercial expresses speak favourably of the result, but the interest of the writers is to prevent a fall in the funds; and their reports must be received with caution. The general impression is, that if Louis-Philippe retains his crown, he must throw himself into the arms of the côté gauche, ***who will then come in, and form the government, leaving him the empty title. Thus the two countries will go on*** pari passu, and what is called the popular party will be triumphant on both sides of the water. Should this be the case, the jealousy of the continental powers will be again excited, and the crisis of war, so long anticipated, will soon be realised.

Saturday, 9th.—The military force has triumphed in Paris, after much carnage; the rebellion has been put down by the energetic measures of Marshal Soult. An ordinance has been issued in the name of Louis-Philippe, declaring Paris in a state of siege, dissolving the Ecole Polytechnique, and disbanding the artillery of the National Guard. An attempt will be made to establish a military despotism, which all the foreign powers are anxious to promote. Even our liberal Government, which has been for twelve months truckling to the people here, is most desirous to see a different system pursued in France. Lord Granville sets off immediately to resume his post as ambassador at Paris, with the strictest injunctions to impress on the mind of Louis-Philippe the necessity of acting with the greatest firmness at this crisis, and, above all, of preventing the admission of Odillon Barrot and the other liberals into the administration. This advice will be palatable to Louis-Philippe, but his temporising conduct hitherto has proved how little he is formed to act with decision at such a crisis. The origin of this insurrection, though evidently foreseen by the Government, is not exactly ascertained: its object was republicanism, its feeling a disgust at the late administration, and the Carlist party availed itself of the public ferment to foment the confusion, in hopes to have a chance of promoting their own views against the common enemy. The Duchess of Berri is in the south, trying to raise a corresponding flame in that part of France, but without much effect: if she now should be taken, it may go hard with her.

Sunday, 10*th.*—Talleyrand has received his dispatches, which mention that the rebellion was quite subdued, and the courts-martial were occupied in trying the prisoners. Montrond said last night, "Si j'étais Roi de France je ferais la guerre; la nation n'est plus faite pour autre chose." It would certainly unite all parties, and make the king popular: but, in the present state of things, it might prove a dangerous experiment; the flame, once lighted in Europe again, might consume half the globe.

Tuesday, 12*th.*—I do not think that in all my experience I ever remember such a season in London as this has been; so little gaiety, so few dinners, balls, and fêtes. The political dissensions have undermined society, and produced coolnesses between so many of the highest families; and between even near relations, who have taken opposite views of the question. Independent of this feeling, the Tory party,—whose apprehensions for the future are most desponding, who think that a complete revolution is near at hand, and that property must every day become less secure,—are glad to retrench their usual expenses, and are beginning by economy to lay by a *poire pour la soif.* Those who have money at command are buying funds in America [Note *: Lord Hertford, under this impression, lost 300,000*l.* or 400,000*l.* by his investments in American stock, which was repudiated.] or in Denmark, which they think least exposed to political changes. Those who have only income are reduced to retrench; but all seem impressed with the idea that they cannot long depend on their present prosperity; and these very means of precaution may tend to accelerate the crisis, if such there is. The London tradesmen are first affected; the ***petit commerce*** declines, which creates discontent; the orders to the country are diminished, which disappoints the manufacturer; he in return must discard workmen, which augments the number of those already out of employ; and thus the apprehensions on one side create distress on the other, till at length that which was only imaginary creates for itself an alarming reality. The irremediable distress which has this year overtaken all the West India proprietors, many of whom, my intimate friends, have laid down, some a part, some the whole of their establishments; the miserably unprofitable state of trade, which must affect the expenses of all who are engaged in that department; the retrenchments that are gradually making in all the salaries of the public offices; all tend to the same end, to diminish the circulation of capital, to curtail the demand for the comforts and luxuries of life, and consequently to circumscribe the demand for labour and ingenuity. These circumstances are only beginning to be felt; but the progress is sure though slow, and will be a disheartening contrast to the smiling prosperity which the-advocates of reform have so unblushingly predicted as the immediate result of the success of their measure.

Wednesday, 13*th.*—No news. House of Commons met after the Whitsun recess on the Irish Reform Bill.

Friday, 15*th.*—Something appears still to be brewing in France. Montrond tonight evidently wished to converse with me privately; he dealt in dark hints, and talked of the capability of France to make war, of her 500,000 men, of the facility with which she coped with all Europe in the first revolution, of the amalgamation of all parties in such a case, and of the inability of England to interfere, if such an event should happen. He seemed to expect, what I perhaps should dread, that the present Government would never take a line hostile to France. He said that Belgium would name a day when the Dutch must evacuate Antwerp; if that was not complied with, treaties would oblige France and England simultaneously to interfere, and enforce the demand. He evidently wished to sound me as to popular feeling in this country, and how far I thought we should consent to France taking the initiative. From any one else this would have been of small importance; but his intimacy with Talleyrand, his constant access to the embassy, and his early information on all such subjects, which I have previously experienced, made me determined to keep on my guard. I told him that he had very much under-valued the resources of this country, and the spirit of the nation; that, however we might, from pecuniary circumstances, be averse to war, yet in a just and national cause, we had not only the will but the means, beyond any country in Europe, of asserting our dignity; that we combined in ourselves the sinews of every exertion; that, like France, and perhaps more unanimously, all party spirit would be forgotten; and, however he might reckon on the liberal policy of this Government and its wish to conciliate that country, yet if we were forced into a war, and such a war, which would be contrary to their pledges and system, I foresaw no event more likely to accelerate the downfal of Lord Grey and the restoration of the Duke; that, however the latter might have incurred his share of popular odium from the difficulties of reform, yet still there was a very influential party in the country which looked up to *him* and *him alone* as a beacon in the event of a storm; whose confidence he entirely possessed; and if to this feeling should be superadded the necessity of recurring to his acknowledged great military talents at such a crisis, the sense of danger, aided by old recollections, would produce such a general reaction in the public mind, that he would again come forward triumphant, not only as the leader of our armies but of our counsels. I strived to impress upon him the power of this country, and the folly of conceiving that we could look upon any encroachments on the part of France with apathy or indifference, much less openly join or connive at them.

Saturday, 16*th.*—The news from Ireland to-day is unsatisfactory; and Sir Hussey Vivian [Note *: He was raised to the peerage in 1841, and died in 1842.], the commander-in-chief, has been sent back to his post at a minute's warning. The public funds are declining; for which various reasons are alleged. It is stated from Ireland, that, for some days past, many of the country people are seen running over the midland counties, carrying with them pieces of burning turf, a small piece of which they leave at every house, with the following exhortation: "The plague has broken out; take this, and, while it burns, offer up seven paters, three aves, and a credo, in the name of God and the holy St. John, that the plague may be stopped." The person leaving it lays each householder under an obligation to set fire to his piece of turf and run to seven other houses where no holy fire has been left, and leave it to each, under a penalty of falling a victim to the cholera himself. Men, women, and children are seen scouring the country in every direction with this charmed turf: one man had to run thirty miles before he could perform his task. The priests, however, pretend entire ignorance of the matter; and when we recollect the bearing of the fiery cross in Scotland previous to a rising, there is too much reason to fear that the ceremony has more of a political than a sanatory tendency.

Monday, 18*th.*—Anniversary of the battle of Waterloo. The Duke, on returning from the Tower this morning on horseback, was assailed in the streets by a mob of ruffians, who hissed and abused him. Their conduct at last became so violent, that a band of the police were obliged to escort him to his house.

In the evening he gave the annual banquet at Apsley House to all the field officers who were present at the battle, and it was deemed necessary to have a large armed force of regulars, besides a numerous police, in the neighbourhood; but no further riots ensued. To such a pass, then, has popular ferment arrived! I am even glad that the brutes have singled out this very day to exhibit their malicious vengeance; that they may show to all Europe what monsters the Radicals really are. May it be, though I fear too late, a lesson to the desperate Government which has relied on such support! may they learn their own future fate from this disgraceful instance, when the fleeting breath of popularity, which they are now so anxious to court, shall no longer fan their sails! These are indeed signs of the times which he that runs may read.

Tuesday, 19*th.* The first day of Ascot races, which was attended by the King and Queen, &c. As soon as His Majesty presented himself in the stand, a ruffian threw a stone at him, which hit him on the forehead, but, fortunately, did him no serious injury. The scoundrel was taken up and sent to prison. The poor King will now see the value of mob popularity. From France the only news is the arrest of Chateaubriand and the Duc de Fitz-James, as concerned in the late riots on the Carlist side. The military tribunals continue in force, but hitherto the prisoners have been acquitted. This proceeding, arbitrary and inefficient, will only tend to irritate the minds of the people.

Wednesday, 20*th.*—An address moved by the Government in both Houses, to congratulate the King on his escape from the stone thrown at Ascot. It would have been wiser to let the subject be forgotten. It appears to have been the act of a half-cracked Greenwich pensioner, unconnected with any political feeling, and therefore not worthy of such public remark; but they wish now to make a show of loyalty and attachment to the King.

Friday, 22*nd.*—On Sunday last, died, at an advanced age, the Earl of Scarborough, and, on the following day, Count Woronzow, aged eighty-eight, formerly Russian ambassador at this court, and since settled in this country. His daughter married the Earl of Pembroke, and his only son is Count Michael Woronzow, general in the Russian service, who commanded in the last Turkish campaign. Martial law still continued in Paris; but the Ecole Poly-technique is re-established for those students who took no part in the insurrection. Talleyrand left London yesterday for France. He is replaced, during his absence, by M. de Mareuil, who has hitherto been the French minister at the Hague.

Sunday, 24*th.*—At the conclusion of Ascot races, Lord Lichfield, master of the Buckhounds, as usual, gave a dinner on Saturday to the royal party at his house at Fern Hill. When the list of guests was submitted to the King's approval, he particularly commanded that Lord Sefton should not be invited. Lady Lichfield made some attempt to interest the Queen, by saying that, if this had any reference to the conduct of Lord Sefton with the Jockey Club, she believed that it had been much misrepresented.

The Queen coldly replied, that she hoped it was so, and made no further comment.

Monday, 25*th.*—The day before Chateaubriand was arrested in Paris he had attended the funeral of a young lady, and had promised the father to write a few lines on the interment of his daughter. I have just learnt that the deceased was Miss Eliza Frisell, whom and her father I had known both here and in France. She was not more than seventeen, and died of consumption. Chateaubriand has fulfilled his promise when in prison.

"Pour Elisa Frisell, la Fille de mon Ami, enterrÉe devant
MOI, HIER 16 JUIN, AU CIMETIÈRE DE PASSY.

"Il descend ce cercueil, et les roses sans taches
Qu'un père y déposa, tribut de sa douleur,
Terre tu les portes, et maintenant tu caches
Jeune fille et jeune fleur.

"Ah! ne les rends jamais à ce monde profane,
A ce monde de deuil, d'angoisse et de malhenr;
Le vent brise et flétrit, le soleil brûle et fane
Jeune fille et jeune fleur.

"Tu dors, pauvre Elisa, si légère d'années;
Tu ne crains plus du jour le froid et la chaleur;
Elles ont achevé leurs fraîches matinées,
Jeune fille et jeune fleur.

"Mais ton père, Elisa, sur ta cendre s'incline;
Aux rides de son front a monté la pâleur;
Et vieux chêne, le Temps fauche sur sa racine,
Jeune fille et jeune fleur.

"A la Préfecture de Police, ce 17 Juin, 1832."

Tuesday, 26*th.*—The King and Queen and all the royal family were at the Duke of Wellington's fête at Apsley House. Very crowded, but uniforms, stars, and ribbons enlivened the scene, and there were many handsome women. The King looked infirm and tired. The Queen was evidently out of spirits; she had attended a review in Hyde Park in the morning, when the sovereign mob thought proper to greet her with much uncivility and rudeness. Truly enough might the King remark that he feared he had got into bad hands, when he sees that his own wife cannot escape from insult before his face.

Wednesday, 27th.—The King had a levee to receive the addresses from both Houses, at which Lord Durham took leave, being appointed ambassador extraordinary to St. Petersburg. The admirer of the three glorious days in France, and the commiserator of Poland, must be a very unwelcome guest in the Russian capital. Young Paul Lieven, who is *fin* enough, said this evening, "You can never guess how things may turn out. Durham has talent, and may see his position in Russia, and act accordingly."

Thursday, 28th.—The Dutch letters mention that, after a council at the Hague on the subject of the late protocols from the Conference, it was determined by the King not to evacuate Antwerp, as demanded. Matuscewitz says to me, that he is a madman to resist, but that may be a façon de parler; and we shall probably soon know Russia's sentiments on the question. To-day arrived the King of Bavaria's final consent to the Greek treaty, and the acceptance of the crown by Prince Otho, and Saturday is fixed by the Conference for the exchange of the ratifications.

Friday, 29th.—The cholera has broken out again even in London. Sir James Macdonald, who was going out to Corfu as Lord High Commissioner of the Ionian Islands in the room of Sir Frederick Adam, appointed to the government of Madras in place of Lushington, died this morning of that complaint, after an illness of only eighteen hours.

Saturday, 30th.—Lord Palmerston had a meeting of members who generally vote with Government at the Foreign Office; out of seventy-six, forty have declared that they cannot support him on the question of the Dutch Russian loan; and as the Tories are straining every nerve against him, the Government will probably be left in a minority. There will be few opportunities again of voting away the public money, even for the most just and necessary measures. Matuscewitz seems very indignant, and says, that the treaty is binding and must be fulfilled: should the motion be lost, it will not make the reception of Lord Durham at Petersburg more cordial, or his mission more palatable to the Russians. Lord Palmerston, after finding so much opposition to his views at this meeting, then proceeded to say, that he had pledged himself to the payment of this loan *further* than bound by the original treaty, in order to detach Russia from favouring the plan, proposed by Talleyrand at the Conference, of partitioning Belgium between Holland, France, and Prussia, which it was so much the interest of this country to prevent.

Sunday, 1*st July.*—On Saturday the Greek treaty was finally settled, and the ratifications exchanged by the respective ministers.

Monday, 2*nd.*—The Cour de Cassation in Paris has reversed the sentences passed by the courts-martial, and acquitted the prisoners; in consequence of which the ministers held a cabinet council, and annulled the ordonnance, placing Paris en état de siége. This triumph of the liberal party will probably accelerate their return to power, and render Louis-Philippe more unpopular than ever; his imprudence in risking such a step, and being so soon forced to retract, will also render his throne more precarious. The Chambers will soon meet, and if they impeach the ministers, it is no more than they deserve.

Tuesday, 3*rd.*—The cholera very near home; a maid-servant at Lord Clarendon's, who lives only a few doors off in this street, was seized with this complaint at seven o'clock last evening, and died at two o'clock this morning; she was in her coffin at eight o'clock, and buried at ten.

Friday, 6*th.*—Martial law being at an end, Chateaubriand, Fitz-James, and Hyde de Neuville are released.

Sunday, 8*th.*—Matuscewitz says that our cabinet are playing a very rash game. That in the Belgian question they are guided by a false punctilio, which will bring them into very serious difficulty. They are determined, with France, to enforce the protocols against Holland, and no one can foresee the result. There is an opening from the lust Conference of Saturday, which Holland might accede to, but there is little hope of it: on the other hand, what can she do against France and England combined? but this unnatural alliance, in which we are engaged, will convert an ancient ally into a bitter enemy. A collision in that quarter will probably take place; but Prussia, Russia, and Austria will not interfere, except by continued protocols, of which he who is the rédacteur of the Conference has already composed sixty-nine. The former is occupied by putting down in Germany the radical meetings and the press by the most vigorous measures. The other two powers are too far off to send troops. Holland, he says, has not many advocates in Belgium; the Prince of Orange had many friends, but he has lost them by his own conduct. There is no news of Don Pedro's expedition, which is supposed to be dispersed by foul weather on its passage from Terceira; loss of time and want of money will soon separate the mercenaries who compose his little army, whilst Miguel, though also poor, is supported by the priests, and having the advantage of being on the spot, with the resources of an established government around him, will be able to keep the ascendency against his brother. Met at dinner at the Willoughbys' Count Funchal, who is Don Pedro's ambassador here, and who seemed very sanguine for the result of his master's expedition.

Affairs in France remain in the same unsettled state, and no change made in the ministry. Talleyrand has positively refused to take office, which he sees is no very enviable post. He said, "C'est que je ne vaux pas m'attirer un charivari dans la Rue St. Florentin,"—the street in which he lives.

Monday, 9*th.*—Accounts came of Don Pedro's expedition having sailed from Terceira on the 27th ultimo. Went with Lord Hertford and the Strachans to a French play at Covent Garden, where Mademoiselle Mars is now acting; who, though too old for les rôles de jeunes amoureuses, still plays with great effect.

Friday, 13*th.*—At dinner at Lord Hertford's the conversation chiefly turned on the cholera, and though the table was loaded with every luxury, the entrées, the champagne, the ices, and fruits were neglected for plain meats, port, and sherry, the fear of this dreadful malady making all so cautious.

Saturday, 14*th.*—The week is over, and no more news of Don Pedro. Neumann last night seemed ominous about Belgium. The Russian loan question was carried by the Goverment in the Commons, notwithstanding the threats of the Tories.

Monday, 16*th.*—News came of Pedro having landed his army at Oporto. Lord Minto is going to Berlin on a special mission. The cholera seems still to rage in this country. The cook at Arthur's and the porter at Crockford's have both died, after four hours' illness. Lord Sydney is going to marry Lady Emily Paget, daughter of the Marquis of Anglesey by his second marriage; and Lord Howick, son of Earl Grey, is to marry Maria, second daughter of Sir Joseph Copley.

Wednesday, 18*th.*—Lord Nugent is going to the Ionian Islands, in the room of Sir James Macdonald, and Lord Minto on a special mission to Berlin (à la Durham) to try to mollify the King of Prussia, who is moving his troops and looking warlike, though his professed object is only to keep in awe the agitators and the press in the Rhenish provinces.

Thursday, 19*th.*—Sir Thomas Tyrwhit resigns, as usher of the Black Rod; Sir Augustus Clifford appointed in his place. Lord Frederick Fitz-Clarence is made deputy adjutant-general, in the room of Colonel Gardiner. Lord Adolphus Fitz-Clarence is returned from Berlin decorated with the order of the Black Eagle. The cholera still very violent, particularly in the City. Among many other victims within my knowledge was a Mr. Von Rossum, a native of Holland, but established here as an exchange broker. He went to Rothschild yesterday to ask if he would advance money on stock; the old Jew refused him, saying, "In these times I shall not advance money to any one, *by Got;* who knows what may happen? you maybe dead tomorrow." It so happened that the poor man was seized with the cholera that very evening, and the next morning he was dead.

Friday, 20*th.*—The movements of the Carlists in La Vendée seem to have sub-sided, and the Duchesse de Berri has disappeared from the scene of action. There are reports that she has been seen in various places in France, but always disguised. Talleyrand said the other day at Paris: "Je ne sais pas si vous la trouverez en la Ven-dée, ou en Italie, ou en Hollande, mais ce qu'il y a de sur, c'est, que vous la trou-verez **en homme.**"

Saturda, 21*st.*—I called this morning after breakfast on M——. He allows that things are coming to a crisis, that even the answer expected to-morrow night from Holland may decide the question of peace or war; but, happen what may, nothing can exceed the obstinacy and imbecility of our cabinet; they know nei-ther how to conciliate nor how to intimidate. The probability is that, to enforce the protocols, France and England may jointly blockade the Dutch ports, and an embargo be laid on Dutch property in the two countries. What will result from that? The neutral nations will not acknowledge the blockade; Holland will not care for it; and an embargo will be laid on all French and English property in Holland, which must be severely felt by our trade. The great **prestige** of a strict alliance with France, which our cabinet is so anxious to cement, is unnatural and delusive. He says, very justly, that France only clings to it as a protection for the present, and a means of aggrandisement for the future, which she never loses sight of. "I am now," to use his own words, "determined to make no longer any opposition to their mad schemes: they may go to war if they please, and rue the consequences. I can destroy in a week their boasted intimacy with France; I have only to throw out the lure of the partition of Belgium, with the consent of Russia, and what will then happen? France, Holland, and Prussia, will eagerly seize their shares, in spite of England, who will then be left to herself alone, unsatisfied, disappointed, and degraded. Her moral influence in Europe will vanish, and the headstrong cabinet which has re-duced her to this low state will then be overthrown for ever, I have had all the wranglings, all the discussions fall upon me; they look on me as a bugbear, and my advice as insidious; but I have had no other object in view than the general peace. At the same time, do not think that the late interval of suspense has been passed by the Three Powers in idle leisure; they have been increasing their armies, regulating their means, and, whatever people with you may think, they have not only men but money—the whole of the last Russian loan is still in the bank of Petersburg. With regard to Lord Minto's mission to Berlin, it can be of no avail; it shows their wish to interfere and protect the revolutionary meetings in Germany, and will only be met with disgust and neglect. The same would occur to Durham at Petersburg, did I not feel that his talents and agreeable manners would render him eventually popular there; he will have sufficient tact to avoid disagreeable subjects, he will have a pride in counteracting the impression against him that may have preceded his arrival, he will be flattered by the attentions paid to him, and will come back a much greater aristocrat then he went.

"As for the present cabinet, I have never seen people with whom it was so difficult to act; they have no settled plan by which they are guided, no talent to bring any point to an issue. I had rather have to act with a ***Fourbe*** who has talent and consistency to take his own line and adhere to it than to deal with men who hesitate on every question, who try palliatives where firmness is necessary, and obstinacy where conciliation is required. We shall now let them have their own way; but if French troops march into Belgium, they will never retire a second time, and then may be a general war."

I remarked to him, that England was an aristocratic country ruled by a democratic government, while France was a democratic country ruled by a pseudo-aristocratic government. His answer was, "You are quite right, and how can such contradictory elements long maintain themselves?"

Adolphus Fitz-Clarence told us to-day at dinner of his mission to Berlin, and reception; which, if he had been a prince of the blood, could not have been more flattering. On his arrival an aide-de-camp of the king was attached to him, and royal carriages placed at his disposal. He was escorted with every honour to the races at Potsdam; but by his own account was ***bored,*** and left the course before the royal family, for Berlin. The next day he dined at court, and taking his opportunity to glide away from the palace, got into a hackney coach, and went to a ***petit spectacle;*** here he was detected by the aide-decamp, who tapped him on the shoulder, and told him the royal carriage was in waiting to convey him to the opera. The mission itself was a trifle; to present to the King of Prussia the miniature model of a man-of-war, accurately rigged, *secundum artem* at Portsmouth.

Sunday, 22*nd.*—Mrs. Robert Smith was seized with the cholera this morning, and died at eleven o'clock this evening. She was at the opera last night in health and spirits, to-night she is no longer of this world. How short a warning! Even the set at Crockford's was for a *moment* electrified at this sudden catastrophe! She was young, beautiful, daughter of the late Lord Forester, and sister of the present; niece to the Duke of Rutland; sister to Lady Chesterfield and to Mrs. Anson. She was married to Mr. Smith, eldest son of Lord Carington, who is disconsolate for her loss. Where will this scourge end? Each succeeding day increases the list of victims!

Monday, 23*rd.*—This morning died, at Lord Dacre's house in Chesterfield-street, of cholera, Harry Scott, consul at Bordeaux. He was brother to Lady Oxford. Mrs. Orde and he were to have sailed this week with his daughter in Augustus Craven's yacht for Bordeaux. Yarmouth arrived, from Paris. Duncombe was seized with spasmodic cholera yesterday, and was nearly dead; but by timely assistance was saved, and is now recovering.

Tuesday, 24*th.*—Called upon the Duke of Wellington, and had a long conversation with him on politics. He agrees fully with my friend, as to the present state of Europe. He is inclined to keep well with France; but he observed, if she ever takes the initiative as to war, whether in Belgium, in Italy, or in Portugal, it becomes an attack upon us. He does not think that Pedro will succeed. As to the present government, he said, their main object is to take on every point precisely the contrary line to that of the late cabinet. They now wish for war, but of such a nature as would not render it necessary for them to go down to Parliament, and formally announce it to the country and demand supplies; a war that might be carried on with their present maritime peace establishment: and he thinks that, if the Portuguese question was settled, and the fleet in the Tagus at liberty, they would have sufficient means to carry on their views of annoyance on Holland. With respect to the blockade of the Dutch ports, not only would it not be recognised by the neutral powers, but in his opinion the captain of a merchantman (English) might sue the commander of the squadron in the Court of Admiralty for impeding his voyage, provided there existed no absolute declaration of war between the two countries. However England and France might act in unison together, the appearance of a French fleet in the Channel would not be seen with a favourable eye in this country; he rather should expect the march of a French army into Belgium. His opinion on the public funds was very well judged; he did not expect any great decline, unless in the event of a loan being required, when the stockholder would sell, in order to get a better thing, sudden panics being of course excepted. The more I see of this extraordinary man, the more I am struck with his singularly quick apprehension, the facility with which he seizes the real gist of every subject, separates all the dross and extraneous matter from the real argument, and places his finger directly on the point which is fit to be considered. No rash speculations, no verbiage, no circumlocution; but truth and sagacity, emanating from a cool and quickly apprehensive judgment fortified by great experience and conversant with each and every subject, and delivered with a brevity, a frankness, a simplicity of manner, and a confidential kindness, which, without diminishing that profound respect which every man must feel for such a character, still places him at his ease in his society, and almost makes him think he is conversing with an intimate friend.

His whole mind seems engrossed by the love of his country. He said, we have seen great changes; we can only hope for the best; we cannot foresee what will happen, but few people will be sanguine enough to imagine that we shall ever again be as prosperous as we have been. His language breathed no bitterness, neither sunk into despondency; he seemed to me aware of everything that was going on, watching, not without anxiety, the progress of events, and constantly prepared to deliver his sentiments in the House of Peers on all subjects which affected the interests of England. His health appeared much improved, and I trust that, however his present retirement may be a loss to his country, it may be a benefit to himself.

Tuesday, 31*st.*—Yarmouth at dinner at Foley's was very amusing in his attacks on Alvanley and Glengall, who could not make any head at repartee against him.

Thursday, 2*nd August.*—To-day, as I drove down to dine at Greenwich with

Alvanley, Foley, and the Duke of Argyll, we were overtaken near Westminster Bridge by a violent thunder-storm, and went into the House of Lords for shelter. We passed the time in the library, where the librarian showed us various curiosities; among others, the original warrant for the execution of Charles I. signed by Cromwell and the other parliamentary leaders. It was found after the Restoration in the possession of an old lady in Berkshire, and formed the ground of the prosecution against the regicides. It is newly framed and glazed, and preserved in the library of the Lords as a most curious document.

Reports are current to-day that the Belgian question is at length settled. If true, the obstinacy of Holland must have gained its point, at the expense of Belgium. By making some slight concessions the former will have succeeded in securing its principal objects. The next question will be, how the Belgians will bear it!

Saturday, 4*th.*—Matusoewitz said to me this evening, "What are we to think of your ministry, who professed friendship for the Allied Powers; who, whenever a revolutionary movement is made in Europe, affects to sympathise with it, but when the crisis arrives, refrains from giving its assistance; who incurs all the obloquy and suspicion of fostering such principles, but dares not openly avow them?"

My answer was, "We are now governed by men who, whether the principles of the late administration were good or bad, were bound to deviate from them in every respect, and to act in a contrary spirit to the past. They found their claim to power on popular feeling, which alone can carry them through; but, like all other men in power, they feel how untenable such a position is; they are therefore ruled by the press in their language, and they advocate liberal opinions without having the courage to act up to them. There is no certainty in their rule of conduct; they have no fixed principle; they have no other wish than to avoid collision with either party, to live au jour la journée, to keep everything in a state of stagnation and inactivity; they neither wish to heal wounds nor assert rights; they yield first to one side, then to the other, happy if that which is left tranquil to-night may be found tranquil to-morrow, and trusting always to the chapter of accidents, that Providence may steer the ship through the storm, and keep them in their places."

I think Lord Palmerston's speech on Thursday night on Mr. Bulwer's motion about German politics will fully bear me out in this inference. But what is the result of this wavering policy? That we are objects of suspicion to both parties. The Allied Powers see through the veil, distrust our professions, and increase their armaments; the advocates of what are called liberal opinions in Europe, though anxious to catch at every glimmering of protection, at the same time are convinced that in the event of a real struggle, they have no chance of succour from us.

Tuesday, 7 th.—Palmella [Note *: The Duke of Palmella, who afterwards represented the late Queen of Portugal at the Court of St. James's, died in 1850.] arrived yesterday morning at Portsmouth in four days from Oporto. Whatever face he may attempt to put upon it, the affairs of Don Pedro are going on very ill. He is not joined by the natives, and his troops are in want of provisions and money; which latter he will not get easily from this country, as his loan fell immediately on the news to four per cent. discount. The Belgian question seems as interminable as ever. Holland is rather more pacified by the late approximation to her views; but now the Belgians consider themselves as the injured party. Leopold is to be married on the 9th to the French princess, which must throw France into the scale in his favour; and that nation will probably act the same part for Belgium that Russia has hitherto done for Holland.

Lord Durham has arrived at Petersburg, and been received in the most distinguished manner by the emperor. The calembourg à la mode *at Paris is,* Leopold aura le plus bel habit de noces possible, mais sans envers (Anvers).

Wednesday, 8th.—I called on Lord and Lady Heytesbury this morning, who are just arrived from St. Petersburg. He was gone to the levée, but I had a long conversation with her. She does not at all regret the honours of diplomacy, but seems very much appalled at the change in our affairs. The mission of Lord Durham, when first known at Petersburg, created much alarm and disgust; but their feelings were soon allayed, or at least smothered. Nothing could be more flattering than his reception, which was at first private, on his arrival at Cronstadt, where the emperor happened to be reviewing his fleet. He expressed a great wish to inspect the ***Talavera,*** a seventy-four, and came on board ***incognito.*** The crew were just going to dinner, and he insisted on going below deck. He tasted their soup, and then said he was thirsty. Wine was brought, but the Emperor preferred the seamen's grog; and, taking the glass, he drank first the health of the King of England, and then that of the company present, which was of course received with enthusiasm. He captivated the hearts of all ranks by his amiable and condescending manners, which no one has more at command than himself. In the same way will Durham be flatté ***and*** flagorné, when he comes to enter on business! Lady H.'s description of the cholera in Russia was really frightful; but the remedy used there with constant success was twenty drops of laudanum and twenty drops of spirit of ammonia in a wine-glass of peppermint-water; which never failed of success in the first instance.

Thursday, 9*th.*—Matuscewitz said to me, that things were going smoothly for the present; but I see that he has his doubts of the ultimate settlement in Belgium without some struggle between the contending parties. He is satisfied, because all the concessions have been in favour of Holland; and he added ***significantly,*** "I think ***we*** have shown more ***nous,*** after all, than your people."

Sunday, 12*th.*—"Went over to Windsor from Ottershaw, where I was on a visit to Lord and Lady Belfast, to see the Guards encamped in the park. We then went to see the castle, which was magnificently furnished by the late king, and contains the finest collection of curiosities of every description. I was particularly struck with the long picture-gallery, the treasures in which it would have taken several days to examine; and St. George's Hall, where a table of 210 covers was laid for a dinner to be given tomorrow by the King to the officers, who are to be reviewed in the morning, on the occasion of the Queen's birthday. The whole of the late king's gilt plate was displayed.

On our way home we had permission to see the Chinese fishing-temple of Virginia Water, built by George IV., to which he was so fond of retiring in summer. Nothing can be more picturesque than this situation, or more luxurious than the whole scene. These were the enjoyments and indulgences for which alone he separated himself so long from the public gaze, and lived entirely with a little coterie of his own. Leopold was married on the 9th instant to the Princess Louisa, daughter of Louis-Philippe, at Compiègne. It remains to be seen what will arise from this connection.

Wednesday, 15*th.*—The speedy arrangement of the Belgic question, and the certainty of continued peace, is in every one's mouth. The latter, perhaps, may be maintained from the general dread of war in Europe; but the former I can never believe to be practicable. The Emperor of Russia, on leaving the *Talavera,* gave the crew a present of 500*l.* Indeed, when all circumstances are considered, the natural reserve of a Russian sovereign, the disgust shown at Petersburg on the first news of Durham's nomination, the little reason which Nicholas can have to feel satisfied with our Government, or with the feelings that have been expressed in the country about Poland,—it is impossible not to see that he is acting a part, and indeed overcharging it grossly; he oversteps the *modesty of nature,* but he seems to be well informed from hence of the character of those with whom he has to deal. It might be as well for our Government to recollect the expression of Napoleon, about the Emperor Alexander: "Il m'a trompé comme un Grec du bas empire."

Thursday, 16*th.*—This day the King went in state to prorogue the Parliament, which will probably never meet again. He was greeted with some marks of disapprobation by the mob in the streets, and the speech from the throne was of little moment. It allowed that nothing was settled, either in Portugal, Belgium, or Ireland; but it abounded in hopes for the future—a coin in which this Government pays largely. The Reform Bill was mentioned; but so little good has resulted from it, and the nation at large seems now so indifferent to the object, when attained, that little stress was laid upon it.

The Bank Committee has terminated its labours, after ransacking all the secrets and privacies of that establishment, which they have ordered to be printed. They have made no report, but left the question of the charter to be settled by the new Reform Parliament.

Friday, 17*th.*—I asked M. to-day what he thought of the political horizon. His answer was, "I can say nothing; one day it looks peaceable, the next day warlike; it is impossible to tell what may happen." This admission donne à penser.

Saturday, 18*th.*—No news this morning from any quarter; the funds keep up, and the surface of events is calm. Never were the nations of Europe in such a state of armament, never did more jealousy exist between *les deux principes;* and yet the nearer a collision approaches the more it becomes an object of dread to all. Each power feels how little it can depend upon its own subjects, each is aware that the first cannon-shot will set fire to the whole mine, and a general explosion will ensue; thus they are all anxious to temporise, to procrastinate, to protocollise, and, leaving the vital question always unsettled, to defer from day to day, and month to month, that final reckoning which is still inevitable; that struggle of opinions which, only gaining additional force by delay, must eventually be more desolating and tremendous.

Van de Weyer arrived last night from Brussels, and speaks out in a warlike manner. Gobelet, the Belgian minister, says, that he is sure he will do his duty.

Sunday, 19*th.*—The cholera still goes on here, and has extended itself to Ireland; the report of the Board of Health is to-day 764 new cases, and 271 deaths for England alone, and total of cases from the commencement 32,835, and deaths 12,274.

Notwithstanding the unsettled state of affairs in France, there are two points which Louis-Philippe seems anxious to defer as long as possible—the completion of the ministry, and the convocation of the Chambers. While the movement party in Paris is overawed by a garrison of 60,000 men, he thinks public tranquillity is owing to his own firmness and popularity, and that no one is so fit as himself to be president of the council. When the Chambers at length are convened he may probably learn the truth.

Matuscewitz said to me this evening, that he had hopes of a settlement of the

Belgian question; that squabbles would ensue this week in the discussions, but he did not despair of an arrangement. ***Nous verrons.*** I doubt it.

Monday, 20*th.*—Bank stock fell to 185 in consequence of the ill-judged disclosures of their affairs ordered by the Government. This is a fall of 17 percent. in two days.

Tuesday, 21*st.*—Another conference took place to-day. Both parties now are become equally obstinate, and neither will yield; how, then, is a settlement to be made? A duel took place the other day between Count Tolstoi, of the Russian embassy, and a Prince Inchatzkoi, a traveller of the same nation. They each fired once, when the police interfered, and they were separated.

In Ireland they are beginning to combine for the non-payment of rent, having got rid of the tithes.

Sunday, 25*th.*—This evening died Mr. Charles Greville, the father of my friend C. Greville, after a short illness, at his house near Shepperton. He married Lady Charlotte Bentinck, daughter of the late Duke of Portland; to whom he was formerly secretary during his administration. His only daughter is married to Lord Francis Leveson Gower [Note *: Now Earl of Ellesmere.], son of the Marquis of Stafford. Mr. Greville was a very agreeable member of society, and one of the few remnants of the old school.

Tuesday, 28*th.*—G. Villiers said, that he dined on Thursday at Lord Palmerston's; where he met Palmella, who was evidently very much depressed by the state of Pedro's affairs at Oporto; but what appeared to him most extraordinary was, that the ministers of Russia and Prussia, who dined there also, seemed to be on very intimate terms with him.

It is said that the Duke of Reichstadt, who died lately at Vienna of a pulmonic complaint, made the following epitaph for himself previous to his death: "Ci gît le fils de Napoléon, né Roi de Rome, mort Colonel Autrichien."

Saturday, 1*st September.*—I had this morning a visit from M. Koulounoff, a Russian just arrived from Paris, where he has been staying for the last six months, and living much with the Russian embassy there. He told me that Lord Durham had received his answer, and a most decided one; but what his mission was remained a mystery, whether it related to Belgium and Holland, or to Poland; but the *fact* was, *it had failed.* He said, that all the courtesy shown by the emperor at Cronstadt was intended for the British flag *alone;* that to Durham individually the reception was so cool, that it excited general remark, and it was quite evident that both the ambassador himself and the message he conveyed were equally unpalatable. His account of the state of Paris is wretched; no foreign guests left, the hotels, &c., all empty, servants and workmen out of place, great poverty and discontent, constant broils in the cafés and theatres, the king hated and despised, and the mob only kept down by the severest military police. The animosity of Nicholas against France he described as deep-rooted and unceasing. When he heard the account of his ambassador's hotel being attacked last year, he remarked," J'ai reçu un soufflet que je n'oublierai jamais."

Sunday, 2*nd.*—The cholera reports are very much increased; they now amount for England to 44,354 cases, and 16,441 deaths. This does not include the London list; and as many deaths have occurred which are not registered, the amount must be more serious.

The tide of opinion seems daily turning against the present administration, and the press is not backward in exciting this sentiment. "The Times," which was their most earnest advocate during the reform question, has long since been violent in its animadversions on their foreign policy. "The Herald" has often alluded to their want of practical knowledge, and their wavering, inconsistent conduct on all commercial questions; but the "Observer" of to-day throws off the mask entirely, by saying, at the conclusion of its leading article, "We repeat, therefore, that a change must take place; for the country cannot, now that the Reform Bill is passed, brook much longer the utter incapacity of those who are so highly paid for the management of affairs, that to ordinary men of business are neither intricate nor difficult of comprehension. The main step in the ladder on which they climbed to power is crumbling under them. Their *quondam* friends, their thick-and-thin supporters, are now becoming clamorous for their downfal." It appears that the object of Palmella's visit to this country was to obtain from this Government the formal recognition of Donna Maria as Queen of Portugal, in which he has failed.

Monday, 3*rd.*—Louis-Philippe's well-known avarice and parsimony have appeared even on the late marriage of his daughter with Leopold; notwithstanding his immense wealth, he has only given her a million of francs, which would not be thought a very large fortune even for a private lady in England. The Belgians are discontented and disgusted at it.

Thursday, 6*th.*—In politics a dead calm; no movement and yet nothing settled; an armed truce everywhere. War appears more remote than it did a few weeks since; but the prospect of a general peace has not improved nor advanced. This political palsy may be traced to the unsettled internal situation of Germany and France, which makes a *secousse* on either side dangerous. Disarmament is therefore a chimera; but this unnatural state of things must have an end. Louis-Philippe is prosecuting the press for libels on his inconsistent government, and in almost every instance the editors have been acquitted by the jury.

Sir Augustus d'Este, son of the Duke of Sussex, has been dismissed from his post of equerry to the King, and Horace Seymour is appointed in his stead. This nomination of an ultra-Tory to the household must prove to Lord Grey the real bias of the King. D'Este is occupied in preparing a suit-at-law, to prove the validity of his father's marriage with Lady A. Murray, which was celebrated at Rome and in England, in order that he may hereafter claim the Irish title, and eventually, it is said, the crown of Hanover.

Friday, 7*th.*—Met Crampton, formerly attaché to Lord Heytesbury's mission, who is just arrived from St. Petersburg. He says that Durham goes very little into society, and it was supposed there that his mission had no very definite object.

Saturday, 8*th.*—Sir Charles Bagot said to me at White's, that the mission to St.

Petersburg had been really offered to him soon after he returned from the Hague, and previous to Durham's appointment, which he refused for several reasons, which may be easily imagined. My only surprise was that Lord Grey, after displacing him at one court, should have applied to him for temporary assistance at another; but Lord Heytesbury was so urgent to give in his resignation, that he knew not whom to send.

On the 26th ultimo died Colonel Aubrey, aged seventy-six; the deepest gambler and the best whist and picquet player of his day. He had passed through various vicissitudes of wealth and poverty, ***comme de raison.*** He made two fortunes in India, which he successively lost; he then made a third at play from 5*l.* which he borrowed, and at last died in very meagre circumstances.

The elder Dupin, in his late oration before the Academy, alluded to Louis-Philippe in terms of the most extravagant panegyric; and observed that, although the king could address the ambassador of every nation in Europe in his native tongue, he always used French from preference. The following pasquinade appeared the next day in Paris:—

"Il parle Italien, Anglais,
Russe, Saxon, jargon Souabe,
Il écorche aussi le Français,
Mais il ne pense qu'en Arabe."

Standish [Note *: He died in 1840, bequeathing his vast collection of works of art to Louis-Philippe, King of the French.] arrived yesterday from Dieppe, where he had been passing a fortnight. The town is very full of French nobility, almost all Carlists, loud in their abuse of Louis-Philippe; the society gay and agreeable, but living very economically. The Duchesse de Berri had lately a narrow escape of being taken in La Vendée; she was obliged to remain during eight hours in a marsh, nearly immersed in mud and water. Charles X. and his family are all moving away from Holyrood House this week, to take up their residence at Gratz in Styria, by permission of the Emperor of Austria. Cholera register of to-day 48,475 cases,

17,831 deaths, in England.

Monday, 10*th.*—The Duchesse d'Angoulême arrived in town from Holyrood House, on her way to the Continent. She stays here only a few days, but receives at her apartments in the Coburg Hotel, Charles Street, Grosvenor Square, twice a day. In consequence of representations from the French government to our Court, that the exiled family were plotting rebellion and assisting the Carlist party in France, our ministers intimated to them, that they must either give up all correspondence with their old adherents, or quit the British territory; they without hesitation preferred the latter alternative, and so the policy of Louis-Philippe has gained its point *for the present.* The letters from Petersburg mention that Durham has left that capital on his journey home by land. Despatches have been sent from hence to meet him at Berlin.

The evidence given before the Bank Committee in the House of Commons is now published, and the public prints are filled with extracts and daily comments on the disclosures which result from this investigation. Attwood, Cobbett, *et hoc genus omne* of speculative theorists, are propagating, according to their different views, what they call improvements in our monetary system. The first two have met lately in a public forum at Manchester to discuss the merits of their respective doctrines; that of Attwood consisting in the return to an extensive paper circulation; that of Cobbett in what is called an equitable adjustment, or, more properly speaking, a reduction of the national debt. The audience was extremely numerous, and the discussion, which lasted two days, was terminated by a majority of ten to one in favour of Attwood's proposal. So loud an agitation of this question, which compromises so seriously the very essence of the Bank system, has naturally much increased the idle clamour against the renewal of the charter; and although, under a steady and consistent government, we might feel confidence in the wholesome result of their ultimate decisions, yet our prospects, under present circumstances, must be very different. The subjection this administration has shown throughout to what is called the voice of the people, their acknowledged ignorance of all practical commercial questions, their ardour for innovation, and the overthrow of what they term the antiquated system, as no longer coeval or compatible with the present *gi-*

gantic march of intellect,—all this, I say, combined with the fact, that Mr. Attwood has had private interviews and communications with our present Chancellor of the Exchequer, gives too much reason to dread that, when ministers reassemble, the distresses of the country may be attempted to be met in any way rather than with remedies. I am the more inclined to this impression, from reading a letter which arrived yesterday to a high commercial quarter from Manchester, which mentions that a meeting of the political unions will soon take place there, to recommend the adoption of certain measures to the Government, such as the circulation of paper, and the raising of the standard. This letter adds, that the anticipation of such an idea has already begun to produce its effect, by creating great want of confidence in making contracts, and an evident stagnation in trade, which threatens much distress to the manufacturing classes during the next winter.

Wednesday, 12th.—The Belgian question is just as near a settlement as it was twelve months ago. The mandates of the Conference are of no avail. Holland will not abate a particle of its demands. Leopold wishes to yield, but the Belgians will not hear of it. His treasury is empty, and Rothschild will not contract for the loan without binding the Belgians not to go to war. But there will be more temporising, as the stock-jobbing interest must prevail. All the nations of Europe want money, and dread a fall in the funds more than any other calamity. The queen came to town to-day, and visited the Duchesse d'Angoulême. Our funds have reached eighty-five. Pedro remains entrenched in Oporto, and no collision takes place between his troops and those of Miguel.

Saturday, 15th.—This morning the Duchesse d'Angoulâme left London on board the steamer for Hamburg.

Sunday, 16th.—The cholera returns this week from the country are now increased to 53,464 cases, 19,396 deaths; among which is that of my old friend Charles Calvert, M.P. for Southwark, who died at Saxmundham, after an attack of only a few hours.

Monday, 17th.—Charles X. and the rest of his family sail direct from Leith for Hamburg. He is by no means in affluent circumstances, but has brought from France a sum sufficient to maintain him for nine or ten years. The Dauphin and the Duchesse de Berri also had not made that provision for the future which former adversities might have taught them to provide; and even after this second banishment the sales of their private property in France were not only very unproductive, from the disadvantageous circumstances under which they were made, but in many instances have been depreciated by the illiberal meanness and parsimony of Louis-Philippe. D'Orsay tells me, the magnificent *haras* of the Dauphin was ordered to be sold; and the Due de Guiche was sent over to Paris to superintend the arrangements; but, as it was considered an object of national importance to preserve untouched an establishment which contributed so much to the improvement of the breed of horses in France, it was arranged between the Duc de Guiche and M. Thiers, on the part of Louis-Philippe, that he should become the purchaser. Guiche was therefore instructed to make out a valuation of the stock and property, which, as having had the entire management of it, he was alone able to estimate. His calculation amounted to 320,000 francs, including the buildings, which had been erected at a great expense by the Dauphin. It would hardly be supposed, that a man who had so lately been raised to such a state of splendour and affluence, at the cost and upon the ruins of his nearest relations, would have hesitated for a moment at making any pecuniary arrangement (even had it been overcharged, which it was not) that might have slightly contributed to their comfort; but this was not the case with Louis-Philippe, he found the Duc de Guiche's valuation too expensive, and he declined the purchase. The agitation which then pervaded France, and the consequent depreciation of all objects of luxury, afforded little prospect for the sale of this valuable stud; and Guiche at length decided on consigning the horses to Tattersall, for sale in this country. On this decision being known, a fresh negociation was opened by the king, who at length consented to become the purchaser; but here a new quibble was started by his legal advisers. The various buildings had been erected on the property of the Crown, and an old French law was cited, by which all buildings erected by a tenant shall, at the expiration of his term, become the property of the ground landlord; thus expunging the title of the Dauphin to derive any advantage from the money he had invested in that manner. The Dauphin's *haras* was thus bought for the moderate sum of 160,000 francs by the man who had just received a civil list of 12,000,000 per annum from the nation, in addition to his own colossal fortune.

Tuesday, 18*th.*—Lord Howe is reinstated in his place of chamberlain to the Queen, who during the interval had never allowed any other nomination in his room.

Wednesday, 19*th.*—Set out this morning on a visit to Lord Hertford at Sudbourne Hall in Suffolk, and arrived at seven o'clock to dinner.

Sudbourne, Saturday, 22*nd.*—Neumann, who, during the absence of Prince Esterhazy in Austria, acts for him at the Conference, has announced his departure for town tomorrow. He tells me, that the Conference was summoned for Tuesday next, and that affairs in Holland wore an untoward aspect. "It is late in the season for war to commence, but," said he, "we can concede no more, and the time is coming when the Three Powers, who are simply prepared for any alternative, must make a stand. Austria has 70,000 men encamped near Milan, 120,000 men in Italy, and altogether 415,000 of the finest troops she ever possessed, and on whom all dependance may be placed. Prussia has a noble army of 300,000, besides what Russia could bring into the field next spring; the movements in Germany are put down, and let France now pass her frontiers, if she pleases, to join the Belgians. We shall then have 100,000 Dutch to act in unison with us." At the same time all parties must deprecate such extremities at such a moment, when the cholera is raging in Europe; which, if these masses were put in motion, would probably cause a much greater sacrifice of human life than the cannon or the sword.

Sunday, 23*rd.*—The Corsaire French paper says very maliciously, "Fécondée par le coq gaulois, la révolution de juillet couvoit des œufs de la liberté, la doctrine les a brisés, le juste milieu les a brouillés. En y mélant M. Persil, on en a faite une omelette aux herbes fines." It appears that nothing is omitted to excite the hatred of the people against the *juste milieu,* and the King of the Barricades. Accounts received through Paris that Ferdinand VII., King of Spain, died at St Ildefonse of an attack of gout. The cholera list is now 55,711 cases, 20,177 deaths.

Croker has lost his place by the change of government, and his seat in Parliament by the Reform Bill; he has therefore ample personal reasons to be dissatisfied with the present order of things; but no words can describe the desponding, hopeless view which he takes of all public matters, national ruin and bankruptcy with him are inevitable.

Tuesday, 25*th.*—Lady S. had a letter this morning from Sir Walter Scott's son, announcing that his father died on Friday last at Abbotsford. This year has been fatal to many men of science, Goethe, Cuvier, Bentham, Mackintosh, &c.

Wednesday, 26*th.*—Drove over to Kempsey Ash, distant about seven miles, to see a place belonging to the Shepherd family. It is an old house, with a beautiful deer-park and gardens, kept up in the old English taste, with clipped yews, statues, and a fine bowling-green. There are some magnificent trees, particularly the finest cedars, and it has a great air of comfort and respectability. Preparations are making to blockade the Scheldt with a joint French and English fleet, and the letters from London are very warlike. If the Whigs do plunge us into a war, as the allies of regenerated France, against our old ally Holland, we are indeed going back to the times of Charles II., and the consequences to us may be equally disgraceful and deplorable.

Thursday, 27*th*—Much excitement at Madrid on account of the succession to the Crown of Spain. The Queen is left pregnant; which circumstance would require a regency till her *accouchement;* but the party of Don Carlos is backed by the Church, Austria, and Russia, and the Absolutists.

Friday, 28*th.*—Some doubts of the truth of the King of Spain's death. The Conference of yesterday terminated very unsatisfactorily; the French cabinet is afraid to meet the Chambers without announcing the settlement of Belgium, and is trying to induce the Powers to use force. Holland remains firm. Talleyrand was asked his opinion of M.

Barthélemy's poem, called his Justification. He replied, "La corruption engendre les vers."

Saturday, 29th.—French manœuvres will not succeed; no one will believe in war, for the present at least. Pedro seems to be in a bad way, his warmest advocates give up his cause. The king of Spain is not yet dead. A French frigate is arrived at Portsmouth from Cherbourg, to say, that the fleet there is ready to sail, and act under the orders of our Admiral Pulteney Malcolm, in blockading the Scheldt, and already disgust appears to be felt here, at the idea of the junction of the two flags, just as the Duke of Wellington foretold to me on the 24th July.

Tuesday, 2nd October.—Theodore Hook is of the party here. Hook is an author; he has written Sayings and Doings, the farce of Killing no Murder, &c. He is an editor, the chief compiler of John Bull, a wit and a wag.

Thursday, 4th.—The speaker, Mr. Manners Sutton, has been positively refused his peerage by Lord Grey, on the plea that he cannot admit so formidable an opponent into the House of Lords. It must show to the world the miserable shifts to which this government is reduced, that they refuse a claim which, in every other instance, and under every other administration, has been considered undeniable. Mr. Sutton has still further claims; when Mr. Canning came into office he wished to secure his co-operation in the government, and offered him the Home Department, with the power, or rather the responsibility, to nominate the lord lieutenant and chancellor of Ireland; which Mr. Sutton, from his feelings on the Catholic question, declined. George IV. then sent for Mr. Sutton's father, the Archbishop of Canterbury, and, actuated by the same views as Mr. Canning, proposed to raise his grace to the peerage, which would then naturally descend to the son. The Archbishop's reply was couched in the following terms: That he must beg to decline the honour, as his advanced period of life would probably soon transmit it to his heir, and remove him from the House of Commons (which was his present sphere of action by choice) earlier than he wished; whereas, occupying as he did the speaker's chair, he was ultimately sure of receiving this natural promotion when it best suited his own views and prospects. Mr. Sutton has thus a double claim, and the circumstances will probably in time come under the consideration of the King.

*Friday 5*th.—Marshal Soult is made president of the council, and the Duc de Broglie minister for foreign affairs, in the room of Sebastiani.

*Saturday 13*th.—Letters from town mention that Soult's cabinet is composed of *doctrinaires;* and Dupin will not join him. Durham arrived in town on Thursday. His mission is considered a failure. The emperor showed him much *cold civility,* gave him an order, and a malachite table of small value, which he heard he was about to purchase.

Sunday, 14th.—I had a long conversation last night with the Duke of Wellington, who is here, on the renewal of Bank and India charters. He said it was the intention of his government to have granted both, taking from each a tribute of 100*l.* per annum; which would have been fair enough. He considered the late proceedings against the Bank, in exposing all their secrets, as not only unjust, but impolitic.

Three or four of us were sitting round the fire, before we went up to dress for dinner; amongst whom was the Duke, who amused us much with several anecdotes of the late king. He was in a very gay, communicative humour, and having seen so much of George IV., one story brought on another. He said that, among other peculiarities of the king, he had a most extraordinary talent for imitating the manner, gestures, and even voice of other people. So much so, that he could give you the exact idea of any one, however unlike they were to himself. On his journey to Hanover, said the Duke, he stopped at Brussels, and was received there with great attention by the King and Queen of the Netherlands. [Note *: King William L, grandfather of the present king.] A dinner was proposed for the following day at the palace of Laacken, to which he went; and a large party was invited to meet him. His Majesty was placed at table, between the king and queen. "I," said the Duke, "sat a little way from them, and next to Prince Frederick of Orange. The dinner passed off very well; but, to the great astonishment of the company, both the king and queen, without any apparent cause, were at every moment breaking out in violent convulsions of laughter. There appeared to be no particular joke, but every remark our king made to his neighbours threw them into fits. Prince Frederick questioned me as to what could be going on. I shrewdly suspected what it might be, but said nothing; it turned out, however, to be as I thought. The king had long and intimately known the old stadtholder when in England, whose peculiarities and manner were at that time a standing joke at Carlton House; and of course the object of the prince's mimicry, who could make himself almost his counterpart. At this dinner, then, he chose to give a specimen of his talent; and at every word he spoke, he so completely took off the stadtholder, that the king and queen were thrown off their guard, and could not maintain their composure during the whole of the day. He was indeed," said the Duke, "the most extraordinary compound of talent, wit, buffoonery, obstinacy, and good feeling—in short, a medley of the most opposite qualities, with a great preponderance of good—that I ever saw in any character in my life."

Wednesday, 17*th.*—Came back to town. Cabinet councils are holding daily. Talleyrand is returned to London. Everything looks warlike at Portsmouth.

Thursday, 18*th.*—If we are really drawn by France into hostile measures against Holland, we may thank the Whigs for their weakness in allowing us to be the tools of the French ministry, who are afraid of meeting their own Chambers without having some coup de théâtre to boast of.

Saturday, 20*th.*—The French government has made fifty-nine new peers, to get a majority in that chamber.

Tuesday, 23*rd.*—Some conversation with Matuscewitz this morning. He inveighed bitterly against the obstinacy of the King of Holland. Nothing short of self-interest or self-defence will induce the Three Powers to go to war; even Prussia will not prevent the French troops from marching into Belgium to settle the question; and as they have now made up their minds not to protect Holland, they think it necessary to abuse her. France and England, *under her,* will, therefore, have *les mains libres,* and will probably take their own line; in which, if they succeed, all the credit will be claimed by the former, while without us she never would have dared to move. France has never been in so crippled a state as she is at present, both moral and physical; torn by intestine factions, she could hardly have drawn the sword for her own defence, much less would do so for a foreign cause, unless England's headstrong counsellors had thrown the weight of this powerful country into the scale in her favour. The other powers, then, will look on as passive spectators, **against their will,** hoping that the fire may be kept from their own doors, but well aware that they still may ultimately have good cause to repent of their selfish facility.

Wednesday, 24*th.*—A treaty is signed between France and England for the settlement of the question; Neumann told me that, if this had not been allowed, the French government would have gone to war in another quarter. The whole is a case of *tripotage* on their part, we are to be the catspaw; and if it does not meet with immediate success, if the Dutch can by an extraordinary chance make a protracted defence, it may go far to upset the two cabinets of Grey and Soult. Matuscewitz said to me last night, "My mission is closed, and I may go to Melton."

Friday, 26*th.*—Gurwood [Note *: Colonel Gurwood, the editor of the Duke of Wellington's Despatches.] came to town from Portsmouth this morning, and says there is great difficulty in procuring sailors to man our fleet.

Saturday, 27*th.*—Matuscewitz firmly believes in hostilities, and is convinced that Holland will make no concessions; when driven to extremities she will entirely destroy the town of Antwerp; Belgium will then break her contract to pay eight millions of interest on the public debt apportioned to her, for which Holland will not care, if she can annihilate that city rival to her commerce. He concluded by saying, "I make no opposition; your government are running their heads against a wall, and I would bet, neither they, or the present French cabinet, will be in office this day three months." Louis-Philippe and his court at Neuilly are much irritated at the courteous reception which Charles X. and his exiled family have received on their journey through the Prussian dominions; they are arrived at the castle of Prague.

Sunday, 28*th.*—Glengall, talking at dinner to-day of his countrymen, and the ready wit of the lower orders in Ireland, said, "Old Lord Castlemaine was extremely rich, but a miser. One day he was stopping in his carriage to change horses at the inn at Athlone, when the carriage was surrounded by paupers imploring alms, to whom he turned a deaf ear, and drew up the glass. A ragged old woman in the crowd cried out, 'Fait', an' it's no use;' but, going round to the other side of the carriage, she bawled out, in the old peer's hearing, 'Plase you, my lord, just chuck one tinpenny out of your coach, and I'll answer it will trate all your friends in Athlone.' "

Monday, 29 *th.*—Cooke arrived [Note *: Sir Henry Cooke.] this morning from France. He says that a gendarme arrived *en poste* last night at Calais, with orders for all the troops in that department to march immediately for the army of the north at Valenciennes.

He gives a poor account of all the French regiments he has seen during his journey, which are for the most part composed of young and raw conscripts. At Paris there was no excitation; they did not believe in war, and were very suspicious of the sincerity of this government as to coercing Holland; but there was every reason to think that, if they once got into Belgium, it would be no very easy matter to get them out.

Tuesday, 30 *th.*—Accounts received from Portsmouth that the French fleet from Cherbourg of one two-decker and three frigates was arrived at Spithead; they were received by a salute from the batteries, according to orders given to Sir Colin Campbell, the governor, to treat them with all possible respect. Thus opens the new drama.

Wednesday, 31 *st*—Yesterday morning early a meeting took place at Baron Bulow's, the Prussian minister, which lasted six hours. It was attended by Prince Lieven and Matuscewitz for Russia; by Wessenberg and Neumann for Austria; and by M. Zuylen de Neuveldt for Holland. In the evening couriers were dispatched by them to their respective courts.

Thursday, 1 *st November.*—Cooke said he was much surprised yesterday morning by a message from the King to come to the palace. On entering the antechamber at St. James's, he met Lords Grey and Palmerston, who showed evident surprise at seeing him there; Palmerston recognised him as usual, but Lord Grey took not the slightest notice of him. When introduced, the King prefaced by saying that, as he was just returned from the Continent, he wished to have his opinion of the state of feeling and of the army in France; on which Cooke told him his frank opinion. He said, that France was in a most prostrate state; that she might be said to exist only by the countenance of this country; that her army as to numbers was grossly exaggerated, and chiefly composed of raw recruits; that, as it now seemed ascertained that Gérard's army was to march into Belgium on the 15th instant (which circumstance he assumed on purpose to sound the King, who did not in the least contradict it), his firm opinion was, that they would shortly be exterminated by the climate and the campaign, particularly if the Dutch could prolong their resistance. Here the King interrupted him in a very animated way, by saying, "I have always maintained that this would be the case;" which was proof at once how much he differs from his cabinet. He next questioned him about the South of France, the Carlist party, the National Guards at Paris, and of public opinion on the Continent; to all which he gave the answers that may be supposed to his Majesty. With respect to the latter question he did say, that throughout the Continent the general opinion was, that the admission of French troops into Belgium was a most unpopular proceeding. He took good care, during the whole interview, never to glance at the present proceedings as of our government, but as of France, and many times did the King's countenance change when it struck him how irresistibly the remarks applied equally to both.

The King then said, "I understand that—is a great rogue; that he has appropriated to himself large sums that were voted for the organisation of the army; and that he will be impeached by the opposition on the opening of the Chambers" But when Cooke mentioned the remark of a French general to him, "Donnez nous encore six moisd'une guerre défensive, alors, pourvû que nous n'ayons pas à faire avec Wellington, nous aurons une armée à reconquérir tous les hauts faits de la prémiére révolution," the King seemed rather confused at the mention of the Duke's name.

In the evening Cooke dined with us, and gave me some more particulars of this rather singular interview. On entering the King's closet, Sir H. Taylor, who introduced him, said, "I beseech you not to enter into any political discussions with him!" How all conspire to keep the poor man in the dark!

Saturday, 3*rd.*—I have already mentioned the hurried manner in which the French and English ministers were induced by the Russians to sign the Greek treaty, which placed the crown on the head of Otho. Letters from Bavaria mention that, on scrutinising this document at Munich, so many inaccuracies have been discovered, as to the right of future succession, that the Russian government will have little difficulty hereafter in turning them to its own private advantage.

I was talking the other day to Lady * * *—who has passed the last fifteen years in Paris, and was very well received at court by the Bourbons—about the character of the Duchesse de Berri, whose firmness and courage she extolled beyond all conception. She told me, that at the period of her accouchement of the posthumous child, the Duc de Bordeaux, fully sensible of the peculiar circumstances in which she was placed, and the suspicions which public rumour or malevolence had encouraged, that the whole was a deception, in order to foist a changeling on the nation for the continuation of that dynasty, she made up her mind that every trace of doubt should be dispelled by the publicity of the event when it did arrive. When seized with the pains of labour, the great officers of the crown were, as is usual in France, in attendance, and on being asked if she would permit some of the Garde Royale to be summoned, she replied, "Oui, et la Garde Nationale aussi," from the conviction that their testimony would be considered more unequivocal than that of the hired troops. The Dutch steamboat brings the account of further warlike preparations in Holland; and the British consul at Amsterdam had given warning to the British captains in the trade to be prepared to sail at a sudden notice.

Sunday, 4*th*—This morning died Lord Tenterden, Lord Chief Justice of the King's Bench; and last night, in consequence of the injury which she received by being driven over by a hack cabriolet, while walking in the street, Lady Caroline Barham. She was sister to the Earl of Thanet, and the mother of a large family.

Monday,* 5*th.—This afternoon the *Lightning* steamer arrived with the King of Holland's answer to the ultimatum of France and England. It is generally understood to be that, having accepted the arbitration of the Five Powers, he is determined not to obey the mandate of only two. The combined fleets have sailed for the Downs from Spithead. I received a letter from Greffulhe of the third inst. He of course defends the present measures in France, as necessary to support the new ministry, and avoid their resigning place and power to the violent party, with *la guerre et la propagande,* if not inscribed on their banner, at least probably following in their train. He added: "The news of the breaking up of the Conference has produced little effect here, being looked upon almost as a matter of course; and does not preclude a hope that the powers will again, after the surrender of the citadel (a point now regarded as a sine quâ non), unite for the purpose of imposing another armistice on Holland and Belgium, or otherwise preventing the continuance of hostility. The chapter of accidents is, however, formidable, and the horizon doubtless much overcast; but so intense is the general dread of war, that I cannot help participating myself in the hope that the storm will again this time blow over."

Tuesday,* 6**th.—Sir Thomas Denman kissed hands on being appointed Lord Chief Justice of the Court of King's Bench, and was made a privy councilor. To-day an order in council was agreed upon, laying an embargo on Dutch vessels, though the King of Holland had issued a notice, when our consul Ferrier warned the English ships to leave ***his ports, that it was not intended in any case to molest them.

Wednesday,* 7*th.—Sir Stratford Canning, who is lately returned from his embassy to Constantinople, is now appointed ambassador to Petersburg.

Friday,* 9*th.—Nothing transpires. On their voyage from Spithead the two fleets have been separated by foul weather, and the French have not yet been heard of. It would be rather amusing if the English pilots, who detest the tricolour flag, should have run them aground.

Saturday,* 10*th.—Cooke wrote the account of his interview to the Duke, and showed me his reply, in which he says, "I do not think it possible now to establish a system of terror in France, such as heretofore produced the effects which we all witnessed in the late war, particularly in its commencement and up to the eighteenth Brumaire. Neither are the powers of the Continent comparatively so weak now as they were from 1792 to the year 1800 inclusive. But, mind, I do not form an erroneous notion of the comparative resources of France and the powers of the Continent. What I say is, that the danger is not what it was in the former war. It is of a different character, not the same in magnitude; and there are many, very many ways of meeting it which did not exist in the former period. Our wise rulers prefer the course which faction suggested forty years ago to that of wisdom, of experience, and reflection. God knows what will happen to the world." Alluding to the Conference, I said to Neumann to-day at dinner, "Votre vocation est finie." He replied, "Oui, ma vocation est finie, mais la provocation reste." This speaks their feelings.

Sunday, 11*th.*—The French fleet have made their appearance at the Downs, and a part of the combined have sailed for the coast of Holland. The Duchesse de Berri has been taken at Nantes. She was found concealed, with Madlle. Kersablie and MM. de Menars and Guibois, in a secret recess behind a chimney, in which the guards sent to apprehend her had by accident lighted a fire. They were all nearly suffocated by the heat, to which they were exposed during eight hours, before they would discover themselves.

Monday, 12*th.*—I saw M? this evening, who is always consistent in his opinions, and deplores the state to which we are come. There is no doubt that the French troops will march on the fifteenth; "But," says he, "what point is gained? The citadel of Antwerp may be taken, blood may be shed; but what is the advantage to Belgium in obtaining that small spot of ground which the King of Holland has pledged himself peaceably to give up, when the more serious parts of the treaty are fulfilled to his satisfaction? Will it give to Belgium the mainspring of their future existence— the passage of the Scheldt? Will it give them the adjustment of their national debt? Will it gain them the recognition of Leopold's crown from Holland? No: all these points will still remain in abeyance, still more and more difficult to be arranged; and if, then, these points are attempted to be conquered by the sword, then will a general war become more imminent than ever. The powers then will not go to war for the citadel of Antwerp, but they will fight for the integrity of Holland to a man."

Tuesday, 13*th.*—This morning, at the London Tavern, we had a meeting of merchants to memorialise the King against the war with Holland. I had very much contributed to promote this idea with the Barings, and it succeeded amply. From 1000 to 1200 respectable individuals attended the invitation; and each resolution deprecating a war, so foreign to British interests, was carried unanimously; and if the manufacturing towns, which have suffered already by the embargo more than London, follow the example, it must create a great sensation in the country. I proposed the second resolution; Mr. T. Baring moved the first, in a very eloquent speech.

The French troops will march into Belgium the day after to-morrow, at five in the morning, as just announced by Talleyrand; but the next question is, When will they retire? Matuscewitz said to-night, "It is the exact fable of the Stag and the Horse, in Lafontaine. The stag wounds the horse to revenge his wrongs. He asks the assistance of man, whom he bears on his back, to kill the stag; that being accomplished, he requests him to dismount, but the man then rides him for his own purposes."

Thursday, 15*th.*—A large Prussian army is said to be moving upon Aix-la-Chapelle to watch the course of events.

Friday, 16*th.*—It has been thought by certain people that the Duke, notwithstanding his sound Tory feelings, was still rather too much inclined to a near connection between this country and France. I even remarked it myself during my conversation with him on 24th July; but, judging from a letter which he has written two days ago to a friend of mine, it is now evident that later circumstances have tended very much to change that opinion. I transcribe the passage:—

"Walmer, Nov. 14.

"It is quite true that France and England united are too strong for the rest of the world; but what are the objects of this union? Are they French objects exclusively? or English objects? or European objects? The answer is obvious: 'French objects exclusively.' Look abroad at this moment,—Holland, Portugal, Spain, Italy, the Mediterranean,—all tending to the establishment, not of French influence, but of French rule and supremacy. But, it is said, we may stop. When, where, and in what manner? We may stop; but it must be at the risk of war, and at an expense equal to that of the last war, and without a chance of ultimate success. We have no objects in Europe, excepting the independence and tranquillity of all, and particularly their independence of France. The object of France is dominion, dominion to be acquired anyhow, but particularly by domestic disturbance. How can two such powers with such different objects continue in alliance? A step cannot be taken which is not inconsistent with our interests, and anti-Anglican. The peace, then, which this alliance gives us, is hollow, and must terminate suddenly by a state of hostility, the most extensive, the most expensive, and disastrous, because the least expected and prepared for, that the annals of this country have known."

I took leave of Matuscewitz this evening, who departs for Melton. His opinions are noways altered. Holland will remain firm, and blood will be spilt; the citadel will probably fall, but the question will then be even more difficult of solution. Will the French government then have the power, if they still have the wish, to order home their army? And, in such a case, what will Prussia do? He said he was disgusted, and wished to be out of the way.

Much cavilling has been made by the Whigs on the late City meeting, which they affect to despise; but the more they cry out the more it proves that they are annoyed. They say it was too late; but our answer is, "We did not complain till the embargo embarrassed and injured our trade; and then no time was lost in calling the meeting, which was purely commercial, and nowise intended to be political." No news as yet from the *seat of war*. The funds remain firm.

Saturday, 17*th.*—On comparing these two letters from the Duke, in as far as they relate to a fresh war, to its extent and importance, they may appear not only difficult to reconcile with each other, but almost contradictory; they appear to me to have been written each under a very different impression of what that war in its nature would be. The first alludes to a war undertaken upon the principles of the last,—a great alliance of the monarchical powers, headed by England, to repress the aggressions and encroachment of France. Such a war would certainly, as he says, from the comparative strength gained by the nations, not be the same in magnitude or character as the last, and would be more easily met. The war to which he alludes in his last must be a war ultimately to be apprehended, after our alliance with France, at that point where we shall *begin to stop;* where, on finding at last the alliance has only produced advantage and aggrandisement to one side, and has alienated all the other European powers from us, we shall then be forced into a struggle with revolutionary France, aided by all the liberal principles which she, through our sanction and protection, shall have been able in the meantime to disseminate through the discontented spirits in Europe. This must be the war, which he says will be the most expensive, the most disastrous, we ever incurred, and without a chance of ultimate success.

The first act of the drama has commenced. The French army under General Gérard has crossed the frontiers, and marched into Belgium. On the other hand, a large Prussian force, under General Muffling, is assembling on the Rhenish frontier, and the state gazette of Berlin announces, that the king openly disapproves the measures of coercion adopted against Holland.

Sunday, 18*th.*—I received this morning the following letter from the Duke, who is just come to town:—

"I did not receive your letter of the 13th till yesterday morning, upon my road from Walmer to Eastwell Park.

"I am very much obliged to you for it.

"I was delighted with your address. It will do a great deal of good. It will open men's eyes to the mischief of the transaction to which it relates; and their minds to the reflection upon *much more*.

"Believe me yours most faithfully,

"Wellington."

The other day Alvanley asked M. de Talleyrand to explain to him the real meaning of the word nonintervention. His reply was, "C'est un mot metaphysique, et politique, qui signifie à peu prés la même chose qu'intervention." His politics have proved it so.

Colonel Caradoc, son of Lord Howden, is sent out as English commissioner to the French armies in Belgium. The circumstances of his appointment are rather singular. He applied to the Government, and was refused, as Lord Grey, thinking it would be agreeable to the King, wished to give the preference to Lord Frederick Fitz-Clarence; but his Majesty would not hear of it; probably because he thought it would be too decided a sanction from him personally of the present measures. Lord Grey then gave orders for the immediate departure of Caradoc; who left town on Friday so suddenly, that Lord Hill, the commander-in-chief, was uninformed of the appointment even this very morning, and seemed naturally hurt at the neglect.

Monday, 19*th.*—The first feat of our united squadron in the North Sea is announced in this evening's paper. The English man-of-war *Talavera* has run foul of a French frigate in a fog, and both have sustained so much damage, that they were obliged to return to port to repair. The capture of Dutch ships continues, to the great injury of our trade with Holland; but the Dutch king still refuses to retaliate in any way. A noble conduct, which we in no manner deserve.

Tuesday, 20*th.*—The public funds begin to fall: they are eighty-three.

Wednesday, 21*st*—The speech of the French king is arrived, as the Chambers opened on the 19th. It is very unimportant, and says nothing that bears on the great question now at issue in Europe. An attempt to assassinate Louis-Philippe was made by an individual in the crowd, who fired a pistol at him, as he proceeded from the

Tuileries to the Chamber of Deputies, without effect. The numerous troops and police which attended the ceremony were unable to detect the offender, and no trace of the bullet could be found in any direction.

The Prussians are increasing their armaments. The greatest activity prevails in all the military departments at Berlin. The French frigate, which became entangled with the *Talavera,* was the *Calypso.* She had an English pilot on board, who, foreseeing the imminent danger of both vessels, jumped from the French to the English deck, saying, "If I am to be drowned, at least I will go down with my own fellow-countrymen!" Notwithstanding the unnatural alliance between the two cabinets, the old national antipathies still prevail, and more particularly in the naval service.

Thursday, 22*nd.*—On the arrival of the French troops before Antwerp General Chassé has published a proclamation to his garrison, exhorting them to hold out to the last.

I received a letter to-day from Greffulhe. He describes the ministry in France as very unsettled, anxious to get out of the Belgian question, and that their only object is to meet the Chambers, get up an address, and scramble through the session as they can, à la merci des événemens, *and then* "alors comme alors, à la garde de Dieu for the future." Everything unhinged and unsettled; the king unpopular in the extreme with all; and the capture of the Duchesse de Berri producing daily fresh embarrassments. If Dupin should join the opposition, he thinks the ministers would very soon be overthrown.

Saturday, 24*th.*—Received a letter from the Duke, in reply to the opinion that the conduct of the French ministry is a consequence of that of their predecessors in office as to the Belgian Conference. He says, "This is a very easy justification! But when the day of trial comes it will be found to fail altogether. Their conduct is to be attributed to neither more nor less than ancient faction fifty years old, fears of the French, and a desire to bolster up an administration for Louis-Philippe, by conniving at and aiding in the national passion for domination. That is the truth." Sir

Howard Douglas, one of the first engineer officers in our service, was sent over to Antwerp by the Duke of Wellington in 1815, to confer with the Dutch government as to the most efficient means of defending that city and fortress in the event of a future attack from France. All the plans were shown to him, and every confidential communication made to the representative of an allied and friendly power. I understand that a request has been made to him by this Government to contribute his information and advice to assist the present object of the French armies in Belgium, and that he has positively refused to betray as an enemy that which was confided to him as a friend.

This night died, of a rapid decline, Colonel Francis Russell, son of Lord William Russell. He had served in Spain as a distinguished officer, and was much liked in society in London. He was nephew to the Duke of Bedford, and member for his borough of Tavistock. He was colonel in the Guards. His mother was sister to Earl Jersey.

Tuesday, 27*th*—This day the bombardment of the citadel of Antwerp was destined to commence.

Lord Lansdowne arrived on Saturday from Paris. Much speculation has been attached to his visit there at this moment. I hear from a good quarter, that our Government wished, on account of the season, to avoid the naval expedition to the Scheldt, and to limit the operations of the treaty to the military force by land; but the French minister, sensible of the advantage which they gained by the junction of the *two flags,* refused to accede. Now the public feeling against the Dutch war has been generally ascertained here, and the British cabinet, bon gré mal gré, is determined to withdraw its support to the treaty with France as soon as its object is accomplished by surrender of the citadel, and then to insist on the immediate evacuation of Belgium by the French army, in accordance with the pledges given to that effect. Marshal Gérard now says to Leopold, that the attack ought to be made on the city side, from whence the citadel may be taken in three to five days; whereas from the country side it will require fifteen or twenty days, and he may lose five or six thousand men, which will exasperate his army, and render it difficult to prevent a collision with the Dutch. Leopold knows that in the former case Chassé will not fail to burn the city if attacked from thence, and refuses to accede to the proposal, which thus at least creates delay.

Wednesday, 28*th.*—No news from the *seat of war.* We had a House dinner of Tories at the Carlton Club, which went off very agreeably. The party consisted of the Speaker, Sir Robert Peel, Lords Glengall and Stuart de Rothesay, Sir James Scarlett, Sir Alexander Grant, Sir Henry Cooke, Messrs. Herries, Bonham, Theodore Hook, Pemberton, and Holmes. They seemed in high spirits at the progress of the elections. Sir Robert Peel remarked that he had seen a very good picture of General Chassé that morning, and a most *unsurrendering* countenance it was.

The incipient elections under the new bill are beginning now to verify the predictions which were made when it first passed, and that power of which Lord Grey availed himself for his own purpose of retaining office is now beginning to show itself independent and in defiance of his authority. He has sown the winds and must reap the tempest. Westminster has taken the lead in this demonstration, and the Radicals in other places are following the example by exacting pledges from the candidates as to their future conduct in Parliament. The mask is thrown off, and we henceforward shall see three instead of two formidable powers struggling for mastery in the state! The Whig party thus becoming the *juste milieu,* will finally be absorbed in the other two. I say finally, because I do not contemplate the downfal of this Whig government, notwithstanding their numerous blunders, as likely to occur immediately; that power which they have conjured up as a tool, and is gradually becoming their master, has still much to exact from them. The Church, the Bank, the India Company, the ballot, the Triennial Parliaments, the taxes, the debt even, are all to be successively revised, and pruned, and lopped, under the specious name of reform. But, as there is a point where *even Whigs* must *stop,* it is only then that their unrelenting taskmasters will turn upon and overwhelm them.

Thursday, 29*th.*—An express arrived from Brussels this evening with the news that the Belgian ministers were left in a minority in their Chambers on the 26th, and had given in their resignations the following day. The *embarras* which this must occasion will not be confined to Belgium.

Friday, 30*th.*—No news. Lord Beresford was married last night to the widow Mrs. Hope; they are cousins.

Saturday, 1*st December.*—No summons made to the citadel on the 27th, *ergo no bombardment* commenced. Baron Tuyll is just arrived from Holland. He says nothing can equal the unanimity displayed by the Dutch, and he fears a collision between them and the Belgians; the French officers write that they are disappointed and discontented with their reception in their new quarters. The late stormy weather has obliged Sir Pulteney Malcolm to quit the Dutch coast with his squadron, and return to the Downs. Since the blockade of Oporto, by Don Miguel, the cause of Don Pedro becomes hopeless, notwithstanding the reinforcements that have been received from hence and from France.

On Wednesday last, at our Tory dinner at the Carlton Club, the earliest arrivals were Lord Glengall, Sir H. Cooke, Messrs. Herries, Hook, and myself. We were reading the evening papers, wherein it was mentioned that a British sailor, who had served in many engagements abroad, had been carried before Mr. Justice Conant, charged with being drunk in the streets, with having abused the ministers, and with swearing aloud, that the British flag was disgraced by sailing in company with the French tricolour. The poor wretch, having no respondents, was fined by Mr. Conant thirty shillings, or, in default, to two months' imprisonment in Coldbath Fields. On hearing his doom, he only replied, "Sir, you may send me to prison, but the British flag is not the less disgraced."

Our natural impulse was immediately to subscribe the trifling fine to liberate him, which Sir H. Cooke transmitted the next morning; but even this early interference was too late, the committee of Lloyd's Coffee-house had already anticipated our feelings, and rescued the poor drunken patriot. I need not add, that this coffee-house is the resort of all the great underwriters, and the donation was merely an act of strong public feeling.

Sunday,* 2*nd.—How strikingly alike are the respective situations of France and England at the present day. Each country torn by faction and party spirit, each making the same experiments for liberty or democracy, and each equally failing in their object; the one collapsing towards despotism, the other towards confusion. These evils arise from confounding personal with political liberty. I call personal freedom the right to dispose without molestation of one's person and estate, and be secure that neither the one nor the other will be disquieted without your consent. That liberty may be carried to the utmost extent that society can permit. The other species of liberty, called political liberty, consists in the right of taking a part in the government of the state. This kind of liberty should be restrained within narrow limits, for experience proves it cannot be widely extended without destroying the other.

To produce the greatest amount of personal freedom and security with the smallest degree of political power in the lower classes, to combine the maximum of liberty with the minimum of democracy, is the great end of all good government, and should be the great object of every true patriot in every country. This distinction between individual and political freedom, between liberty and democracy, is the great point of separation between the Whigs and Tories. The Conservatives strive to increase personal freedom to the utmost degree, and to effect that they find it indispensable to restrain its worst enemies the democracy. The Whigs affect to attend only to the augmentation of popular power, and in so doing they trench on civil liberty; as we have lately seen in the flames of Bristol, the conflagration of Jamaica, and the dreadful tithe murders in Ireland; nothing of which nature we had ever witnessed in this country from 1815 to 1830, the days when democracy was restrained. In France we have a parallel case. The revolutionists saw their despotic rule impossible under the sway of the Bourbons, and therefore they inflamed the public mind till they got their government overthrown; for the ordinances themselves were no more the cause of that catastrophe than the storming of the Bastille was the cause of the revolution in 1789. Then despotism of one kind or another instantly returned, that of the National Guard, the Parisian émeutes, or Marshal Soult's cannoniers, and liberty has been destroyed by the demagogues who raised the people in its name.

Monday, 3*rd.*—The King came up to town from Brighton, and signed the proclamation for dissolving the present Parliament, and assembling the new on the 29th January, 1833. From this day commences a new era for England.

On the 30th ult., at twelve o'clock, the first cannon shot was fired by General Chassé against his French invaders, and hostilities are begun between the contending parties. The private letters mention that the French troops are much in want of provisions, as no preparations were made by the Belgian authorities against their arrival.

In a preceding page I have alluded to the remark, that this war with Holland originated in the acts of the former government, and copied the Duke's reply to me on that very point; but I have just read such a clear definition of this question in a periodical paper of this month, that I transcribe it: viz.—

"The pretence that we are involved in all this through the diplomacy of the Tories is such a monstrous perversion of truth as cannot blind any but the most ignorant readers.

"1. When was the treaty which guaranteed Leopold's dominions signed by France and England?—In July, 1831; eight months after the accession of the Whigs to office.

"2. When was the treaty, giving Antwerp to Belgium, signed by the Five Powers?—In November, 1831; a year after the retirement of the Duke of Wellington from power.

"3. What treaty did the Duke of Wellington leave binding on his successors, in regard to Belgium?—The treaty of 1815, which guaranteed to the King of the Netherlands his whole dominions.

"4. What incipient mediation did the Duke leave them to complete?—That of the *Five* Powers for the *pacific* settlement of the Belgian question.

"And yet we are told *he* involved Great Britain in a hostile aggression on Holland, and was the author of a measure of robbery by two of the mediating powers.

"The pretext on which France and England have attacked Holland is openly avowed. Let us see the justice of their case!

"It was stipulated by the treaty of the 15th November, 1831, signed by all the allied powers, that the evacuation of the provinces to be mutually ceded on both sides should take place *after* the exchange of the ratification of a final peace. Of course Antwerp was held by Holland, and Venloo by Belgium until that event; and on that footing they have been held for the last twelve months.

"But what do France and England now require? Why, that Antwerp should be ceded by Holland *before* the treaty is either signed or agreed to, and when weighty matters are still in dependence between the contracting parties. The advantages which the King of the Netherlands holds—the security he possesses by holding that great fortress—is to be instantly abandoned; and he is to be left *without any security* for the settlement of this treaty. The two revolutionary powers have also summoned Leopold to surrender Venloo. Is the one a compensation for the other? Venloo is a fortress of thirds rate importance, situated on the right or German bank of the Meuse, and it never belonged to Belgium; while Antwerp is a great and magnificent fortress, the key of the Scheldt. As absurd would it be to speak of Harwich as compensation for London. But the worst feature for England in this case is, that we are inveigled into a war to support a private treaty between Louis-Philippe and Leopold, signed at Compiègne in August, for the object of getting Antwerp."

Tuesday, 4th.—We have no news, except that Saturday and Sunday have passed without any serious hostilities at Antwerp. The French are proceeding in forming their entrenchments uninterrupted, except by a few occasional shots from the citadel, which have hardly molested them. Only two men killed.

Thursday, 6th.—The French, having completed their batteries on Tuesday, began their cannonade on the citadel, which was answered by General Chassé with vigour. The siege is now begun in form, and the eyes of all Europe are fixed on this important struggle. The weather has hitherto been very unfavourable to the besiegers, and their new-made trenches are said to be full of water; but their army has been increased to an extent which would cause apprehension that their object is not limited to this single operation.

Hyde Villiers, nephew of Lord Clarendon, and secretary to the Board of Control, a young man of very superior talents, died on Saturday last at Sir C. Lemon's house in Cornwall, where he was staying on a visit previous to the elections. Lord Howe has never resumed his situation of chamberlain to the Queen *officially*. He has been in constant attendance upon Her Majesty at Windsor and at Brighton, but he has positively refused to be reinstated. His reply to Lord Grey was, that he had been wantonly dismissed by him, and would receive no favour at his hands.

I hear from those about the King that he never was in better health: he lives very temperately, seems to enjoy society, is much more tranquil and collected in his manner than formerly, and seems determined to allow no political anxieties to prey either on his health or his spirits. The fact is, his feelings were never very acute, and he resigns himself to his fate.

Friday, 7th.—The address to the King of the French has been carried in the Chambers by a large majority; and as Dupin, the new president, has in this instance thrown the weight of his party into the scale of the ministry, it appears that the movement party must, for the present at least, be thrown into the background.

Admiral Sir George Cockburn has been appointed to the American station in the room of Admiral Colpoys, deceased. When Sir James Graham sent for him to announce his appointment, he told him that he was indebted for it *solely* to the earnest wish and interference of the King; that, with all the respect which they felt for his talents, the continued opposition which he had made to the Government would have rendered it impossible that they could ever have employed him. It is believed that this condescension on their part to the King may be traced to a wish to get rid of Sir George in the House of Commons.

The bombardment of Antwerp citadel continues with little intermission day and night; but it does not appear that hitherto many lives have been lost.

Saturday, 8*th.*—The news this evening from Antwerp mentions the prosecution of the siege with more loss of life, but no particular advantage.

Sunday, 9*th*—It would appear now that a proposal had been made by France and England to the Prussian government to occupy Venloo with their troops till the adjustment of the Belgian question, in order to give a colour to their unjust attempt to possess themselves of Antwerp. The answer arrived last night, being a flat refusal to take any part in their proceedings, or to sanction by such a step those coercive measures against Holland which Prussia had never ceased to deprecate from their commencement.

A very intelligent officer in the engineers is now at Antwerp, and in constant correspondence with Lord Hill. His letter received to-day mentions that Colonel Caradoc requested leave of Marshal Gérard to bring with him two or three English officers to walk through the trenches, which was flatly refused. He adds, that our allies seem to hate us cordially Perhaps they do not wish the real state of the besiegers to transpire Chassé continues to defend himself with great judgment.

Monday, 10*th.*—This day the elections have begun in the metropolitan districts, and in some other places also.

An additional proposal has been made by Prussia to occupy Venloo, Luxemburg, and Limburg, on her own account, independent of the Conference, to be restored to Holland when certain securities have been given for her own Rhenish provinces. This, if true, would place France and England in still greater embarrassment. Sir S. Canning has been ***ad interim*** appointed to a special mission to Madrid, the object of which is supposed to be an attempt to arrange the protracted quarrel between the two brothers in Portugal.

Tuesday, 11*th.*—Marshal Gérard, finding that his attack on the citadel has hitherto proved abortive, and foreseeing the disasters which must occur to his army from the prolongation of the siege, has formally proposed to Leopold the occupation of the city by French troops, in order to secure his object, although contrary to his original stipulation of respecting its neutrality. Leopold has referred the question to Louis-Philippe; and if no interference is made at Paris by the representatives of the other powers, we may expect to see the citadel taken, but the city laid in ashes.

Wednesday, 12*th.*—A fresh creation of peers. Last night's Gazette announces four new peerages; viz., Marquis of Tavistock as Baron Howland of Streatham; Earl of Uxbridge, Baron Paget of Beaudesert; Lord Stanley, Baron Stanley of Bickerstaffe; Lord Grey, Baron Grey of Groby. All elder sons. The news from Antwerp still favourable to the Dutch.

Thursday, 13*th.*—Duncombe has lost his election at Hertford, which has returned two Tories, Lords Ingestre and Mahon. The ***conversazione*** at White's rather amusing on the Belgian question; Sefton and Byng, as the Whigs, maintaining that the French had only lost 200 men as yet during the siege, and their conviction that they would retire as soon as the citadel was taken; Sir R. Wilson and the Tories fully impressed with a contrary opinion.

Friday, 14*th.*—The elections are going generally very much against the Tory interest. What are called the Reformers ***seem*** to be the most successful; and though the Government plumes itself mightily on this popular feeling, as an evident sign of its strength, it is by no means to be argued as a certainty that these new members will become blind adherents of the ministry on any other point than the continuation of reform in its various branches. They may wish, indeed, to carry that point to a greater extent than is contemplated by their leaders; they may also have a very different opinion on the subject of our foreign policy.

I was rather amused to-day at White's with Sefton's description of his visit this morning to Prince Talleyrand. He is very intimate with him, and is received at all hours; a privilege which he avails himself of very frequently at present, to hear the latest intelligence from Paris and Antwerp, now so generally interesting.

This morning he was ushered into the dressing-room of this celebrated octogenarian, who was under the hands of two **valets de chambre,** while a third, who was training for the mysteries of the toilette, stood looking on with attention to perfect himself his in future duties. The prince was in a loose flannel gown, his long locks (for it is no wig), which are rather scanty, as may be supposed, were twisted and crêpus *with the curling-iron, saturated with powder and pomatum, and then with great care arranged into those snowy ringlets which have been so much known and remarked all over Europe. His under attire was a flannel pantaloon, loose and undulating, except in those parts which were restrained by the bandages of the iron bar which supports the lame leg of this celebrated* cul-de-jatte.

Saturday, 15*th.*—One of the effects of the Reform Bill is, that the bone-grubber, W. Cobbett, is returned for Oldham, while, on the other hand, the notorious Mr. H. Hunt has been turned out of his seat at Preston. The new borough of Brighton, under the very nose of the Court, has returned two most decided Radicals, Wigney and Faithfull, who talk openly of reducing the allowance made to the King and Queen. The famous pugilist and better at Newmarket, Gully, has been returned for Pontefract. In short, the new Parliament will produce a curious medley.

Sunday, 16*th.*—On the morning of the 14th, at four o'clock, the French having blown up the counterscarp of the lunette fort S. Laurent, sent into the breach a detachment of **voltigeurs** and grenadiers, who took this little appendage to the citadel and made sixty-two prisoners of war.

Monday, 17*th.*—Montrond, who is just come from France, repeats the same réfrain, *that there will be no war; that the French troops will retreat from Belgium as soon as the citadel is taken. All the foreigners likewise affect to hold the same language; and yet there is a declaration from Prussia to the Diet just published, under date of the 10th inst., which not only disapproves the coercive system of*

England and France, but speaks openly of its armaments and of two corps d' armée having passed the Rhine.

Tuesday, 18*th.*—The elections in Ireland seem to have gone with hardly an exception against the Government; the returns are all either Conservatives or Liberals.

Wednesday, 19*th.*—It is evident that the government of Lord Grey wishes to stop and induce the Tories to join with them in putting down the rising radical power; this they will hardly be able to accomplish, so strong is party feeling at present. Every government, in fact, whether Whig or Tory, must eventually, in self-defence, become conservative; with this difference indeed, that in the case of the former it can only be done at the expense of former professions and at the risk of alienating their chief supporters; while in that of the latter it is merely the result of their acknowledged principles and those of their followers.

With the Tories this is consistent and natural, with the Whigs it is inconsistent and unnatural Consistency, however, is one great source of strength in government.

Lord Grey has based his power on the advocates of revolutionary principles. Should he at last find it expedient to disappoint their hopes, must not his inconsistency be his fall? A despatch is arrived this afternoon from Colonel Caradoc, before Antwerp, stating that General Sebastiani had just informed him that the Dutch army was concentrating rapidly, and he thought would advance.

Thursday, 20*th.*—Only a fortnight ago I was talking at White's to Admiral Sir Henry Blackwood, who was on the point of going to Ireland to visit his son, then dangerously ill with the typhus fever; accounts were received yesterday that he had caught the infection and was dead. He was much respected in the navy. The French, though they mystify their returns of killed, are losing many men daily in the trenches before Antwerp. Gérard has called up the reserve.

Friday, 21*st.*—The Marquis de Choiseul, whom I met yesterday evening at Macdonald's, was colonel in the Garde Royale of France, under Charles X. At the time of the Révolution de Juillet, in 1830, he followed the fortunes of his master to Holyrood House, and is now living in London with his wife and family. She is an English woman, and a daughter of Lord Southwell.

Saturday, 22*nd.*—The French ministry appears to be predominant in the Chambers. They are proposing and carrying the most despotic measures, in the shape of laws, to repress tumults, and always with a servile majority. The key to this is, that the public money is employed to bribe the deputies.

Two important state papers have been published to-day; the one is the correspondence between M. Van Zuylen, the Dutch minister to the Conference, and my Lord Grey, previous to the commencement of hostilities; the other is the speech of the Dutch premier, Baron Verstok de Solen to the States General assembled, in which the grievances of Holland are fully stated and her steady determination to resist them. He sums up the whole by saying, "We are oppressed because it is known that our population is numerically small and our territory is comprised in a very limited compass; but the time may come when it may be proved that the importance of a nation is not a mere question of arithmetic." The accounts from Antwerp are highly satisfactory; the French are said to have lost, in killed, wounded, and sick, near 3000 men. Major Jones, of the engineers, who was employed by the Duke in 1815 in repairing the fortresses, and absolutely built the lunette of S. Laurent, and that of Kehl, has said that the siege of the citadel may last for five or six weeks more.

Matuscewitz is come to town for a day. He thinks that no one can foretel what may happen, as to the duration of the siege or the advance of the Dutch army. The plans of the King of Holland are fixed, but known *only to himself*.

Sunday, 23*rd.*—Sefton came into White's this afternoon about five o'clock full of news from Prince Talleyrand. His excellency has just received the Independent newspaper from Brussels, dated yesterday, which announces that the French had begun to battre en brèche **on Friday, and with great success; it likewise adds that the total loss on their side,** tous compris, **was not more than 550.** Sont ils bons, les Belges!

Monday, 24*th.*—The Government has got into fresh trouble in Ireland; after promising to support Mr. Boynton, a Protestant, they have suddenly turned round and supported a Repealer, which want of good faith has so irritated the party, that they have threatened to join O'Connell.

At dinner at the Carlton Club the conversation turned upon Scotch marriages. Grant mentioned the instance of a Mr. M—, a man of very large fortune, who kept a mistress, and had an illegitimate daughter; he invited a large party of friends and relations to dinner, the glass circulated, and he took the opportunity of proposing the health of the lady as Mrs. M—, requesting at the same time the whole party to bear testimony that he publicly acknowledged her as his wife; in a few minutes afterwards he made some pretext to retire to his room, and without any further ceremony shot himself through the head. That daughter became by this act legitimate, according to the Scotch law; inherited his property, notwithstanding the claims of his near relations; and having since married, her husband has obtained with her about 10,000*l.* per annum landed property.

Tuesday, 25*th.*—Christmas day. The firing and battering at Antwerp continued during the whole of Saturday with great vigour and great loss of life, particularly to the besiegers, when early on Sunday morning, a breach having been nearly effected, Chassé, wishing to avoid the carnage attendant on assault, despatched a flag of truce to the French head-quarters, with an offer to capitulate. Marshal Gérard has summoned a council of war to discuss the propositions. Since the above, Talleyrand has received a telegraphic despatch, which states that Chassé and his garrison are to remain prisoners of war till the surrender of the forts Lillo and Liefkenschöek. The citadel is to be occupied by the Belgian troops. Every one here is surprised at the suddenness of this event, though it was known in the end to be inevitable.

A good deal of interesting conversation on past politics with Sir H. Cooke and

Sir A. Grant, who dined with me. Grant has been very intimate with Sir Robert Peel, and related several anecdotes of him. When the Duke had made up his mind that he could no longer refuse Catholic emancipation, without endangering the loss of Ireland, he told the late King, who was decidedly averse to the measure, that only one of three alternatives remained to him, either to reconquer Ireland, to make the concession, or to resign. Constituted as the army then was, the first was impossible, the choice must then fall on one of the other two. The King demanded time to consider. In the meantime the Duke applied to Peel for his concurrence in carrying the measure, to which, though equally convinced of its necessity, *he* could not bring his mind to consent; it was a departure from principle which he thought no circumstance, however strong, could justify, and he preferred the loss of place to the loss of consistency and public character. On the following day the King sent for Peel to Windsor, and stated the circumstances which had passed in his interview with the Duke. Sir Robert allowed the validity of the arguments, but at the same time expressed his own determination to abide by his first decision. The King then asked his advice how *he* ought to act himself in such an embarrassing position. Here Peel took a different line, and, viewing the case in all its bearings purely as a state measure, strongly advised his Majesty to yield to the suggestions of the Duke. The King's reply was, that he could not conceive how any man could counsel his sovereign to do that which he would refuse to do himself; and thus they parted. The King gave a decided negative, and the ministers resigned. But Peel was so much staggered by this retort of the King, so personally addressed to him, that he vanquished his scruples, and gave in his adhesion to the Duke. The secession of the ministers did not last for a day, and was little known at the time; on the following morning the King sent up an express to town with his assent to the proposal, and the bill for Catholic emancipation was immediately brought forward, and carried by a government which condescended to allow that it only was actuated even then by an impulse of fear. Hinc illœ lachrymœ!! In May last, when Lord Grey in pique gave in his resignation to the present King, the charge of forming a new administration devolved again on the Duke, who proposed to Sir Robert to join him, with the pledge of bringing in an ample measure of reform. The latter perhaps saw, that in the then temper of the times it was impossible; but, warned by the past, he resolved not to make another sacrifice, and gave to the proposal a flat refusal His answer was, that if such a ministry could be formed by his grace, he would give it every kind of support in his power, but as to joining it in any shape the thing was totally impossible. We know the sequel, and the coolness that ensued between the parties.

Another subject that we discussed was the death of the late Lord Londonderry. His mind had been kept too intensely on the stretch by the important events which occurred in his time, and by late sittings in the House and great press of public business. At last it gave way. The first public indication of this malady occurred at the Regent's court at Carlton House, where he had been to take leave previous to his departure for the Congress at Vienna. Sir John Beckett, the judge-advocate, found him waiting on the steps of the palace for his carriage. He said to him, "So, I hear that you purpose leaving us on Tuesday next to join the Congress?" "Purpose," said Lord L——; "what, are you in the conspiracy against me? are you, too, joining with the others to prevent my journey?" Sir John was so astonished, that he knew not what to say, and left him. When he was introduced afterwards to the presence of the Regent, his Royal Highness informed him, that Lord Londonderry's manner had been so flighty, that he thought he must be out of his mind.

His friends took him down in the evening to his seat at North Cray, and sent for Dr. Bankhead, who found him quite deranged. He returned to the conspiracy against him, and talked of his enemies having brought his carriage to the door with post-horses to drive him to a prison.

There could be no doubt as to his real state, and the necessary remedies, but the doctor only took a slight quantity of blood from him by cupping, which the attendants remarked was of the colour and consistency of treacle. He then allowed him to go to bed, ***without any precautions or attendance***. The next morning he cut his throat with his razor, severing the carotid artery. Such was the death of this very distinguished and fortunate man, owing to the culpable neglect of Dr. Bankhead, who after the event demanded a fee of 100*l.* for his visit, while all the family at North Cray were plunged in the deepest grief.

Wednesday, 26th.—The conversation at dinner to-day turned on the present

King of Sweden, formerly General Bernadotte, to whom, when Prince Royal of Sweden, Cooke in 1813-14 had been sent as British commissioner; and he mentioned several particulars of him. Notwithstanding his promotion to the royal dignity, he particularly piqued himself on having risen from the station of a private in the ranks of the French army, in which he had served in India and elsewhere before the Revolution. In corroboration of this, Captain Yorke mentioned an anecdote which occurred while he himself was in Sweden.

General Sir Alured Clarke was making a tour of pleasure on the Continent, and arrived at Stockholm, when he wished to be presented to the king. A private audience was granted, as a matter of course, to an English general officer. When presented to Carl Johann, Sir Alured was very much astonished to find that the King of Sweden, instead of a formal reception, folded him in his arms, and kissed him on the cheek. He was confounded at this distinction, and more so when the king asked him if he could not recollect him. In this, as his memory was quite defective, he could only express his regrets. To which the king replied, "I am not surprised that you do not recognise in me the Corporal Bernadotte, who became your prisoner at Pondicherry, when you commanded the English army in India, to whom you showed the greatest kindness while in your power, and who now is most anxious to return the obligation in every way that may be most agreeable to you during your stay in his dominions."

Captain—recounted a curious anecdote that had happened in his own family. He told it in the following words:—

"It is now about fifteen months ago that Miss M—, a connection of my family, went with a party of friends to a concert at the Argyle Rooms. She appeared there to be suddenly seized with indisposition, and though she persisted for some time to struggle against what seemed a violent nervous affection, it became at last so oppressive, that they were obliged to send for their carriage and conduct her home. She was for a long time unwilling to say what was the cause of her indisposition; but, on being more earnestly questioned, she at length confessed that she had, immediately on arriving in the concert room, been terrified by a horrible vision, which unceasingly presented itself to her sight It seemed to her as though a naked corpse was lying on the floor at her feet; the features of the face were partly covered by a cloth mantle, but enough was apparent to convince her that the body was that of Sir J—Y—. Every effort was made by her friends at the time to tranquillise her mind by representing the folly of allowing such delusions to prey upon her spirits, and she thus retired to bed; but on the following day the family received the tidings of Sir J—Y—.having been drowned in Southampton River that very night by the oversetting of his boat, and the body was afterwards found entangled in a ***boat cloak***. Here is an authenticated case of second sight, and of very recent date.

Thursday, 27 *th.*—There is chuckling at Brookes's, and great exultation among the Whigs, at the fall of Antwerp, which, after all, was inevitable; and the defeat of 4000 Dutch by 70,000 French is not very wonderful. Still the success does not render the aggression less an act of the grossest injustice. We must now wait the answer from the King of Holland as to the ceding Lillo and Liefkenschöek.

Friday, 28 *th.*—This morning died the Marquis of Conyngham, K.P., for many years the favourite of George the Fourth. He married Miss Denison, daughter of the rich Joseph Denison in St Mary Axe. He is succeeded by his son the Earl of Mountcharles, married to Lady Jane Paget, second daughter of the Marquis of Anglesey.

Saturday, 29 *th.*—The King of Holland will not give up the two fortresses, and the garrison will therefore remain prisoners of ***war,*** although Lord Palmerston said to his electors there is ***no war,*** it only exists in the lively imagination and exuberant fancy of those who raise the cry.

Sunday, 30 *th.*—Wortley is come home from Antwerp, where he had been during the siege. He went over the citadel on Tuesday last, which was nearly destroyed; it was not possible for Chassé to have defended it more than a few hours longer, and even then the breach would have been practicable, the assault would have commenced, and the carnage must have been dreadful. This for the sake of humanity he has avoided by a surrender, which in no way detracts from the glory which he has acquired by the defence. The conduct of the Belgians has been in every way contemptible. The mob in Antwerp attacked a party of unarmed Dutch prisoners with stones, and would have murdered them if the French had not interfered. A Dutch wounded officer, seated on a *fourgon,* was met on the Berchem Road by a Belgian officer, who, heedless of his unprotected situation, began to abuse him, and call him *cochon,* &c.; but a French officer rode up, and, with every sign of contempt, struck the Belgian with the flat of his sword. The latter affected to demand satisfaction, but the other told him he was beneath his notice.

Monday, 31*st*—The King has given to Lord Munster the place of Governor of Windsor Castle, vacant by the death of Lord Conyngham. William of Holland has given to General Chassé the first class of the order of William, and sent him the star which he wore himself, in testimony of his high approbation of his courageous defence.

JANUARY, 1833.

Wednesday, 2*nd..*—A dinner has lately been given to Mr. Thomson [Note.*: Mr. Charles Poulett Thomson, Vice-President of the Board of Trade, afterwards Lord Sydenham, and Governor-General of Canada, where he died in 1841.] by the electors of Manchester on the occasion of his return as member for that city. His speech is to be seen in all the papers; its principles are radical and sweeping; that was to be expected; but so arrogant, so abusive of others, so self-conceited an address to the public, was never before made by so young a man. The marked point, however, of the speech was, its conclusion; after promising *monts et merveilles* to his constituents, he expresses his confidence that, at their next meeting, on the termination of his labours in their cause, they will all greet him with a well-known sentence, "Well done, thou good and faithful servant."

Count Pozzo di Borgo, Russian ambassador at Paris, arrived here this afternoon from France, on a special mission, which attracts general attention.

Thursday, 3*rd.*—I have just received the following account of the present state of Ireland, in a letter from Lord Glengall, dated Cahir, 31st ultimo:—

"The state of this country is too horrid. The Reform bill has given O'Connell and the priests uncontrollable power. Society is totally disorganised. We believe that no jury, whether that of the assize courts, or of the coroner, will convict a prisoner; while we are sure that they will find the magistracy, military, and police guilty. Consequently justice and safety is at an end for the gentry. Nothing but the suspension of Habeas Corpus and making the repeal question a misdemeanour will prevent the loss of Ireland."

Friday, 4*th.*—A letter from Lord Hertford at Naples tells me that Mademoiselle Herbelè, the dancer, is married to Falconnet the banker. The Earl of Denbigh is appointed chamberlain to the Queen. On the peaceable appearance of affairs on the Continent, and the retirement of the French troops from Belgium, the funds have risen up to 873/4.

Saturday, 5*th.*—The Government is meditating severe measures against Ireland, and trying to sound the Tories whether they will give their support to accomplish this object, which they will probably concede, if the evil is attacked with vigour. Lord Althorpe, as leader of the House of Commons, has written to Mr. Manners Sutton, offering him the Government interest to be re-elected speaker; making a merit of necessity, as he well knew that they could not bring in their new candidate Mr. Littleton [Note.*: Now Lord Hatherton.], and at the same time were glad to neutralise Mr. Sutton's vote and power in the House. He has accepted.

Sunday, 6*th.*—The other day a large party dined at the Pavilion. Among the guests was the American minister. The King was seized with his fatal habit of making a speech; in which he said, that it was always a matter of serious regret to him that he had not been born a free, independent American, so much he respected that nation, and considered Washington the greatest man that ever lived. Lord F. Fitz-Clarence succeeds his brother Lord Munster as Vice-constable of the Tower, and Lord Adolphus Fitz-Clarence is made Lord of the Bedchamber *vice* the Earl of Denbigh, now chamberlain to the Queen.

Wednesday, 9th.—Fresh troops are under orders for Ireland; two regiments of heavy dragoons are gone this week.

Thursday, 10th.—Last week died at Paris, at an advanced age, the Princesse de Loraine Vaudemont. She was of the family of the Counts Horn, who were distinguished in the Revolution of the Netherlands; one of whom, notwithstanding his high birth, was broken on the wheel at Paris for murder during the regency of the Duke of Orleans. She was of the senior branch of the House of Montmorency, and before as well as since the Restoration in 1814, her house has been the resort of all the best society in Paris: Prince Talleyrand, among others, always passed his evenings there, and was one of her oldest friends. Madame de Vaudemont assisted in the escape of Lavalette from Paris after the return of Louis XVIII. She is much regretted. At supper Montrond observed how much M. de Talleyrand was affected by the death of the princess; he could talk of nothing else, and added, "C'est la première fois que je lui ai vû verser des larmes."

Upon this Alvanley said, that he had likewise once seen him melted into tears, and the occasion of it was rather curious. A little more than a twelvemonth ago in the House of Peers, the Marquis of Londonderry, in the heat of a violent attack on the foreign policy of the present Whig administration, made some very personal allusions to the private character of Prince Talleyrand, which as ambassador to a foreign court he might have omitted. There was only one opinion on this subject in the House, and the Duke of Wellington rose immediately to protect his veteran friend, finishing his speech with many handsome compliments to the prince on his great talents, and the eminent services which he had performed on many occasions for the good of Europe.

Alvanley went to visit the prince on the following day, and found him perusing the debates of the preceding night, and, though much hurt at the attack of Lord L., still more affected by the friendly intervention of the Duke. He expressed his gratitude, in the warmest terms, while the tears ran down his cheeks, and then added: "J'en suis d'autant plus reconnoissant à M. le Due, que c'est le seul homme d'état dans le monde qui ait jamais dit du bien de moi." The confession was rather ludicrous.

Stuart De Rothesay mentioned another anecdote of Talleyrand yesterday. The prince was unwell, at Paris, some years ago, but wished to take a journey into the country. Stuart called upon him, and strongly advised him to defer the journey; which he fortunately did, and in two days afterwards he was seized with a fit, from which he only recovered by severe bleeding. After a few days Stuart paid him another visit, and found him quite well, eating some soup, when Talleyrand said, "C'est bien heureux que je ne sois pas parti pour la campagne; je calcule que je serois arrivé à Chartres le jour de ma maladie, j'aurois de suite envoyé chercher des sangsues chez mon ami l'Evêque; il est très dévot, il ne m'auroit envoyé que l'extrême onction, et je ne serois pas sûrement içi à manger ma soupe aujourd'hui."

Friday, 11*th.*—The King of Holland, since the departure of the French from Antwerp, has stopped an Austrian vessel, being the first which came down the Scheldt, as a proof that he means to keep the river closed.

Saturday, 12*th.*—General Solignac, a French officer of the Napoleon school, with 400 Poles, is arrived at Oporto to join Don Pedro, who has made him a major-general in his service. Great complaints are made from thence of want of money and provisions, and the cause does not seem to prosper. Louis-Philippe and his family are gone to the frontiers to meet Leopold and his Queen, and to greet the French army on their return. The spirit of innovation and revolution, which fifty years ago was imported into Europe from America, and has fructified so widely here, has now started back across the Atlantic, to impart some of its blessings to the original mother of the evil. The state of South Carolina has announced its opposition to the tariff, and its consequent intention to secede from the Union. The President Jackson's manifesto is arrived, which proclaims his determination to maintain the integrity of the Union by force.

Sunday, 13*th.*—Lord Dudley, who has been residing at Norwood ever since his illness without much improvement, has last week had a serious paralytic attack, which may prove fatal.

Tuesday, 15 *th.*—G——returned last night from Ireland, where matters seem fast coming to a crisis. The unpaid tithes are to be collected by the army, and the ***Habeas Corpus*** Act suspended. Lord Anglesey is now only anxious to try his last resource, military force, and to reconquer the country. Montrond says that Madame de Vaudemont has died without making any will, and leaving behind her a vast collection of private letters, which she had carefully preserved.

Wednesday, 16 *th.*—The Gazette of last night contains the following creations:—

George Granville, Marquis of Stafford, K. G., to be Duke of Sutherland; William Henry, Marquis of Cleveland, to be Duke of Cleveland; Charles Collis Western, to be Baron Western.

The latter is the defeated Whig candidate for Essex, and is made a peer as a recompense for his unsuccessful exertions.

The French ministerial "Journal des Débats" is full of the most fulsome adulation of Louis-Philippe's tour with his family to Lisle; and describes the meeting of the queens of France and Belgium as so affecting, that they regretted it could not be witnessed by all France. "Le Corsaire," in reply, pleasantly observes: "Que le journal se console, nous voyons tous les jours dans la cour des Messageries des exemples d'amour filial de cette force là."

Saturday, 19 *th.*—The King of Holland has announced that the Scheldt is now open to the ships of all nations, except those of England, France, and Belgium; who from their late proceedings merit the exclusion; still it must tend to embroil the question more and more.

Friday, 25 *th.*—The only news of the day is that Ibrahim Pacha has defeated the Sultan's troops, under the Grand Vizir, at Konieh, and was on his march to Constantinople. Russia seems preparing a fleet in the Black Sea, to attempt, under the pretence of assisting the Porte, something for her own advantage. The Belgian question remains still unsettled, and the last reply from Holland throws no new light on the subject.

Yesterday died Admiral Lord Exmouth. He served many years with bravery during the French war, and commanded the attack on Algiers; he entered the navy as Mr. Pellew, was made first a baronet, and then a peer.

Saturday, 26th.—Last Wednesday week died General Sir Banastre Tarleton, aged seventy-nine. He had served in the American war, where he commanded the Tarleton dragoons; and is nearly the last remnant of that school of military men.

Lord Grey was very anxious to give Tarleton's vacant regiment to Frederick Ponsonby; but Lord Hill went down to the King at Brighton to remonstrate: in consequence of which, the regiment has been given to General Sir William Keir Grant.

They have hired a French cook for the Carlton Club from Paris, who lived formerly with the Duc d'Escars, premier maître d'hôtel *of Louis XVIII., and who probably made that famous* pâté de saucissons *which killed his master. It was served at breakfast at the Tuileries to the king, who with the duke partook so voraciously of it, that the former was attacked with a dangerous fit of indigestion, from which he with difficulty recovered, and the latter absolutely died from the excess on the following day. One of the French journals, remarkable for its* facéties, announced the event in the following terms: "Hier sa Majesté tres Chrétienne, a été attaquée d'une indigestion, dont M. le Duc d'Escars est mort le lendemain."

Louis XVIII was not only a great epicure as to the *recherche* of his dinners, but had also a surprising appetite; he has been known at table, in the interval between the first and second courses, of which he always partook largely, to have a *plat* of little pork cutlets, dressed in a particular manner, handed to him by one of the pages; and he would take them up one by one in his fingers, and before the second service was arranged the contents of his little *plat* had disappeared.

The poor duke emulated his royal master in this respect fatally for himself. In consequence of his office he presided always at a large table served for him in the palace, the *menu* of which was precisely the same as that served to the king. I remember once to have seen him in that time with his old duchess, and sundry other emigrants returned with the Restoration, who still retained their powdered heads and their *ailes de pigeon,* and who would eat almost to suffocation. When the coffee was announced, here and there one of the old pursy gourmands would sputter out to the lady, "Madame la Duchesse, veut elle bien me permettre de prendre un instant de sieste;" and then he would recline in his armchair, and throw his napkin over his head, and slumber for a few minutes, till nature was a little relieved.

With all his gastronomy, Louis XVIII. was a man of superior tact and intellect He steered through the difficulties of his reign with great address; and never was a throne surrounded with more jarring and discordant materials. I was in Paris at the time of his death in 1824, and witnessed all the funeral honours of his obsequies. Previous to the body lying in state it was exposed to the public view on a bed the very day of his decease, though the mortification which caused his death had changed the colour of the face to a deep green and the body must have been already in a state of decomposition. His mind retained its vigour to the end, and in his last parting interview with *Monsieur* he tried to impress on his mind those salutary lessons of future government which he so unfortunately neglected. He was perfectly aware of his approaching fate, and met it with firmness, though he had no religious feelings on the subject. He always professed himself an *esprit fort* My friend General Clari told me that, on the Sunday preceding his dissolution, the officer on guard at the Tuileries came to him as usual in the evening to receive the parole and the countersign to be given to the troops. It is customary on these occasions to give the name of a saint for the one and of a fortified town for the other. Louis, with a significant look, gave "St. Denis and *Gyvet*" (J'y vais). He might be said to have died with a *calembourg* in his mouth.

Sunday, *27 th.*—Lord Douro's regiment, the 60th foot, has been lately quartered at Dover. When the Duke his father went to make a short stay at Walmer Castle the officers all rode over to pay their respects, and left their cards at the house as a matter of form. Shortly after came an invitation from his grace to dinner, including all the officers excepting **Lord Douro**. The major who received the note, quite confused, knew not how to act, and showed it to Lord Douro, who was equally puzzled, though he knew it must have some meaning. To solve the difficulty, he went forthwith to see the Duke at Walmer, who with great good humour told him: "I make no distinctions in the service; those gentlemen who paid me the compliment of a visit I invited to dinner; you were not of the number, and so I omitted you in the invitation."

Monday, 28*th.*—The object of Pozzo di Borgo's mission to this country is unveiling itself. Russia, irritated and mortified by the cavalier treatment which she has experienced from France and England in the Conference on Belgium affairs, and the subsequent hostilities at Antwerp against Holland, has now made known her intentions of taking her own line as to Turkey; and a new question is coming forward in Europe, which will be much more difficult to solve than the last. The emperor has begun by positively refusing to receive Stratford Canning at St. Petersburg from private motives.

Tuesday, 29*th.*—This day the curtain drew up, and discovered the Reformed Parliament assembled. The first object which presented itself was Mr. Cobbett seated on the Treasury bench with the ministers; from which he refused to move, as he said he knew of no distinction of seats in that House. The point of electing a speaker was brought forward, when Mr. Manners Sutton was proposed by Lord Morpeth and seconded by Sir Francis Burdett; in opposition to whom, Mr. Hume, to the surprise of the House, proposed Mr. Littleton, which was seconded by Mr. O'Connell. The feeling of the House was too general in favour of Mr. Sutton to admit of a doubt; still the Radicals were too headstrong to give in, and divided the House, when the members for Sutton were 241 and for Littleton 31, leaving a majority for the late speaker of 210.

From some preliminary remarks of Cobbett, Faithful, and others of the new

Radical members, it may be inferred that the Government will not find them so easy to deal with as they have imagined.

Some very indelicate allusions were made as to Mr. Sutton's retaining the pension of 4000*l.* per annum, voted by the last parliament on *his retirement,* in addition to his salary on resuming the chair, which being in itself impossible, could only be looked upon as a gratuitous insult.

Wednesday, 30*th.*—There is no news, except the rumours that the Government is preparing a bill for the emancipation of slaves in the West Indian colonies, by which 160,000,000*l.* of property will be swamped. I believe it to be impracticable, but the idea seems to produce a great panic in the West Indian proprietors.

Having nothing for my diary, I fall back on my recollections of the past; and no subject recurs to my mind so readily as that of his late Royal Highness the Duke of York, who died about this time six years ago. What reminiscences are attached to that name! His agreeable dinners in the Stable-yard, St. James', and constant hospitality at Oatlands, must always be recollected with pleasure, though past and never to return. The *entourage* of their Royal Highnesses the Duke and Duchess of York was indeed a little court, but blended with all the ease and comfort of private life. It was perhaps a rare circumstance to see, on one hand, the uniform kindness and condescension of this amiable prince and princess to all around them, and, on the other, the unceasing respect, and I may say affectionate deference, which even in the gayest moments (and no house was more gay) constantly pervaded the manners and conduct of every individual in that society; more particularly as the men who composed it, generally speaking, were at that time rather spoiled by the world, living on terms of the greatest familiarity with each other, and perhaps distinguished by a more *bruyant ton* among themselves than the young men of the present day. There were many visitors at Oatlands while the family was established there; but in my time those generally invited to go down from Saturday till Monday were Alvanley, Brummell, Cooke [Note *: Sir Henry Cooke.], Foley [Note †: Late Lord Foley.], Yarmouth (now [Note ‡: The late Lord Hertford.] Lord Hertford), Worcester [Note §: Late Duke of Beaufort.], Craven, Armstrong, A. Upton, W. Spencer,

Berkeley, Page, C. Greville, De Ros [Note ǀ: Late Lord de Ros.], Anson [Note ¶: General George Anson, now commander-in-chief in India.], &c.: and at times the elder set, of Lords Lauderdale and Erskine, Sir Herbert Taylor, Duke of Dorset, Warwick Lake, Torrens, &c. The hour for leaving London was generally about five o'clock; and so many chaises often started from White's, that post-horses were not always to be obtained on the road, and I have often gone by Hounslow to avoid the run. The duchess seldom had any other ladies in the house but Lady Ann Culling Smith and her three daughters, the eldest of whom was afterwards married to Lord Worcester and cut off in the prime of youth and beauty—an untimely fate. When assembled under this hospitable roof every one did as he pleased, and if any exception could be made to such an agreeable existence, it was that sometimes we had rather too much whist. It was indeed the Duke's passion, and he never would get up as long as he could make an excuse for another rubber.

Few characters in any situation of life could be placed in competition with the late Duchess of York; she was not only a très-grande dame *in the fullest sense of the word, but a woman of the most admirable sound sense and accurate judgment, with a heart full of kindness, beneficence, and charity. The former was proved by the adroitness and. tact with which she so successfully avoided any collision with the cabals and* tracasseries which for so many years unfortunately ruled in various branches of the Royal Family; and the latter was attested by the constant attachment of her friends and dependents, the gratitude of her poor neighbours during her life, and the undisguised grief of all at her death. Whatever clouds (if indeed they ever existed) obscured the earlier period of her marriage were, in later times, completely dispersed, and nothing could equal the respect and attention with which she was treated by the Duke on all occasions. I have heard him myself express the highest opinion of her good sense, and I believe he rarely failed to consult her opinion on most questions of importance to himself.

The duchess was particularly fond of animals, and curious in their selection also. There was a large menagerie in her flower-garden filled with eagles, macaws [Note *: Two of these favourite birds the duchess left to Mr. Raikes as a *souvenir,* or were given by the duke at her death in remembrance of her Royal Highness.], and various creatures; a little colony of monkeys on the lawn before the windows of her boudoir; a herd of kangaroos, ostriches, &c., in the paddock; but her ruling passion was dogs. There were sometimes from twenty to thirty of different sorts in the house; and many a morning have I, to my annoyance, been awakened from an incipient slumber, after a long sitting at whist, by the noisy pack rushing along the gallery next to my bedroom, at the call of old Dawe the footman to their morning's meal. In death even these favourites were not deserted; around the pool which joins the well-known grotto in the park at Oatlands may still be seen the gravestones and epitaphs of the departed *mignons*. The idea I suppose was taken from her ancestor Frederick the Great of Prussia, as I remember to have seen a similar cemetery at the palace of Sans-Souci in the year 1799. Another custom, likewise of German origin, and now more common, was annually kept up by the duchess at Oatlands on Christmas day. The great dining-room was converted into a German fair, and booths were erected round the sides, stored with various commodities; in the centre was placed a tree, or *mat de Cocagne,* the branches of which were garnished with oranges, cakes, gingerbread, &c. On one table at the end of the room were displayed all the presents which we the guests had brought from town to lay at the feet of her Royal Highness; on the other were placed those which her Royal Highness presented for us as keepsakes. I have still three of those yearly *cadeaux* in my possession; one of which is a morocco pocket-book, embroidered in gold by the hand of her Royal Highness, with a gold pencil-case and amethyst seal. The original intention was, that the presents should be of a moderate cost on both sides; but Brummell, then in the days of his magnificence, was not to be restrained, and I remember he once brought down a Brussels lace gown as his offering, which cost 150 guineas. It threw all our *colifichets* into the background, but it was not thought good taste at the time to make such a valuable present to royalty. It certainly was reversing the maxim of La Rochefoucauld, who says, the proper present to a superior should be something of little value, but difficult to obtain. To return to the fair; all the servants were admitted in their best attire, and also the charity children supported by the bounty of the duchess, who at a given signal flew upon the *mat de Cocagne,* and in a few minutes stripped it of its gingerbread blossoms.

The party then adjourned to the hospitable board. The Duchess of York understood and spoke English perfectly, though in correspondence she preferred writing in the French language. After one of my visits to Paris, before French manufactures had been much introduced into England, I brought with me a pretty **workbox,** or, as it is called, a nécessaire de dames, in which was a musical machine that played several tunes; and on my arrival I begged permission to place it at the feet of her Royal Highness, who was pleased to accept it, and sent me the following note in return:—

"Oatlands, ce Avril 25, 1817.

"Il me seroit difficile de vous exprimer, Monsieur, toute ma reconnoissance pour la plus jolie des boîtes que j'ai reçue hier au soir de votre part. C'est tout ce que j'ai vu du plus nouveau, et du meilleur goût, et je me suis amusée toute la journée à en écouter les sons.

"J'attends avec impatience le moment de vous en réiterer mes remercimens à Londres, et de vous assurer combien je suis sensible à cette obligeante attention de votre part.

"C'est avec les sentimens les plus distingués que je vous prie de me croire toujours,

"Monsieur,
"Votre tres affectionnée amie et servante,

"F."

The duchess, in her morning walks at Oatlands, often visited the farmyard and amused herself with noticing the different animals and their families, among which was a sow that had lately farrowed some beautiful pigs. A few days afterwards at dinner some persons asked her if she would eat some roasted pig. Her answer was; "No, I thank you, I never eat my acquaintance."

During the latter years her health grew more precarious, and she seldom visited London for any time. At Oatlands she never appeared till the hour of dinner, and always retired from the drawing-room at twelve o'clock; but not to sleep, as I have always heard that her attendants read to her till four or five o'clock in the morning before she would compose herself to rest.

Her demise was gradual; and her slight frame, being exhausted by the complaint, which at last showed itself by a suffusion of water, she sank to rest in the spring of 1820, and was, by her own desire, buried in a private manner in the parish church of Weybridge. A few days previous to this event Lord Lauderdale, who had long been ranked among her friends, went down to Oatlands to inquire after her health. She could not see him, but sent him from her bed the following note:—

"Mon cher Lord L.,
"Je fais mes paquets, je m'en vais incessamment. Soyez toujours persuadé de l'amitié que je vous porte.

"Votre affectionnée amie,

"F."

After the lamented death of her Royal Highness the Duke never returned to live at Oatlands, and in the course of two or three years it was sold for 180,000*l.* to Mr. Ball Hughes.

The duke then lived almost entirely in London, and his chief amusement was planning and building that splendid palace in the Stable-yard, on the site of his old residence, which he never lived to inhabit himself, and is since become the property of the Duke of Sutherland. The Duke was always very fond of collecting curiosities of every description, jewels, books, bronzes, &c.; and spent considerable sums in purchasing old chased plate, with which the sideboards in his dining-room were loaded, like altars in a Roman Catholic chapel: he had also a collection of pictures of military men in curious old uniforms. I sent him one which I had bought in Paris;

it was a painting of Louis XV, when young, riding in the gardens at Marly, dressed in the uniform of that day. The following was his reply:—

"South Audley-street, Wednesday, March 15, 1826.
"Dear Raikes,

"I cannot sufficiently thank you for the picture which you have been so good as to send me.

"You do not do it justice in abusing the painting of it; besides which, I think it is extremely curious, and will, I can assure you, be considered by me as a great addition to my collection.

"Ever, my dear Raikes,
"Yours most sincerely,
"Frederick."

His kindness and good-nature to all around him was beyond expression. When Colonel Berkeley, his aide-de-camp, died, he cried like a child in my presence. As to taking offence, it did not seem to be in his nature. I remember once at Brighton he asked Keatinge, a good-natured Irishman, but not very refined in his ideas, to dine with him, and make up his rubber at whist. Keatinge won, and not having received the money,—being accustomed to punctuality,—he wrote some days afterwards to remind his Royal Highness of the debt, which was immediately sent. Keatinge, in return by way of expressing his gratitude, began his letter with the following quotation:—

"Now is the winter of my discontent
Made glorious summer by the Sun of York."

It was a liberty which would not have suited many princes of the blood, but the Duke only laughed.

In the year 1819 his Royal Highness, being on a visit at Windsor Castle, unfortunately slipped on the floor, fell, and broke his arm. He was confined there for some time. I was then in Paris with Alvanley, and very unwell. On my return to England I naturally wrote to inquire after the duke's health, who replied:—

"Windsor, April 24, 1819.

"Pray accept my best thanks for your kind letter of yesterday and inquiries in consequence of my accident, from which I am recovering very favourably. Indeed, I shall not be surprised if I reach the winning-post before you. At all events, I think I have the best of it, though I do not think either of us is to be envied. I was, indeed, much concerned to hear that you had been so ill at Paris as to have excited the commiseration of even the Persian ambassador, which, from his Excellency's account of Alvanley, may probably ere long be extended to him also. I hope soon to receive a better report of you.

"Ever yours most sincerely,
"Frederick."

These are from amongst several others that I have by me still, and which contain many kind expressions.

In our set, the duke's chief favourites I should say, were Alvanley and Charles Greville; to the latter of whom he gave the management of his racing stud at Newmarket after the death of Mr. Warwick Lake; and two more amiable and agreeable men are not to be found in society. It was also a peculiar quality in the duke, that he never was known to desert an old friend. Tom Stepney, I believe, tried him as high as any one, but still they were never entirely estranged; and though Brummell, on his departure from England, had given too much cause to the world, and indeed to his friends, to speak harshly of him, and remarks even of this nature were at times by some people brought forward at his Royal Highness's own table, I never knew or heard of an instance in which he did not immediately check them. It was not in his nature to speak ill of those whom he had once liked, neither could he bear the feeling in others.

The duke took at all times much pleasure in the amusements of the turf, and had at one time a string of very good race-horses at Newmarket under the management of Mr. W. Lake; but I never heard of his deriving much profit from those speculations; owing perhaps to that strictly honourable feeling by which he was guided in this as well as in every other transaction of his life. When he left the Stable-yard he removed to Cambridge House in South Audley-street, and many were the pleasant hours we have all spent in those days at dinner at that house. Ude was then the maître d'hôtel, which says everything for the delicacy of the fare. With those of us who then kept house, Yarmouth, Alvanley, Foley, Worcester, myself, and others, he would always readily come and dine without any ceremony as a private individual; but in London we by common consent avoided the whist table amongst ourselves. Other hosts who were more anxious to flatter the taste of his Royal Highness were kept up probably till four in the morning. His constitution at last began to give way; and though his disorder at first appeared to be asthma, from the difficulty of breathing in bed (which increased to such a degree that he latterly slept in his arm-chair), it was at length pronounced to be dropsy. His private surgeon MacGregor, who attended him from first to last with the greatest attention, has often told me, that he imputed the complaint of his Royal Highness not only to late hours, but to the want of necessary rest, which ultimately exhausted him. Hence his tendency to sleep after dinner, and in travelling the instant he was in his carriage, which arose from pure lassitude and exhaustion. He always rose early, at whatever hour he might have gone to bed; and that constant sedentary position tended to cramp and check the circulation of the blood, particularly in one of so gross and full a habit. In other respects he was by no means given to any excess; and had he allowed himself that proper wholesome sleep which nature requires, he might have been alive at this day. What between his vigils at night and his early attendance as commander-in-chief at the Horse Guards in the morning, he sacrificed a life most valuable to the country and his friends. His last illness was not painful, except from the punctures in his legs to relieve the accumulation of water; and he sunk quietly, without a struggle, in his arm-chair, at the Duke of Rut land's house in Arlington-street (which was lent to him), on the 5th January, 1827. The body was removed to St. James' Palace, where it lay in state, and on the 20th January following was interred with the usual funeral pomp in St. George's Chapel at Windsor. It was a mournful ceremony. The night was cold in the extreme, and the whole scene very affecting to those who felt *really* on the melancholy occasion. It is not for me to write the character of the Duke of York; his rank and his services claim for him a page in history. In his politics he was a Tory; in his religion a High Churchman; in his profession a most assiduous commander-in-chief, and of unblemished courage; in his public life a warm supporter of the British constitution; and in his private life a staunch friend, a kind master, and a most amiable, good-hearted man. Had he lived to the present day, his firmness would have guarded us from many of the visitations which have since been inflicted on this country.

Saturday, 2nd February.—An armistice has been concluded between the Sultan and Ibrahim Pacha, which may obviate the interference of Russia in the quarrel. My friend Matuscewitz writes to me from Melton as follows:—

"I am looking forward with great anxiety to the King's speech. Meantime I fancy no war will arise out of the Belgian question, or out of the storm which threatens the superannuated empire of Constantinople. In both cases some compromise, even temporary, will and must be devised and agreed upon, as all the leading powers in Europe are determined to maintain peace. In this pacific policy Russia fully participates, you may depend upon it notwithstanding all the absurd statements to the contrary, in which newspapers abound. Therefore, however circumstances may appear menacing, my opinion is that a general war will be avoided."

Sunday, 3rd.—Sir Robert Peel said to me, that he was very much struck with the appearance of this new Parliament, the tone and character of which seemed quite different from any other he had ever seen; there was an asperity, a rudeness, a vulgar assumption of independence, combined with a fawning reference to the people out of doors, expressed by many of the new members, which was highly disgusting. My friend R——, who has been a thick-and-thin Reformer, and voted with the Government throughout, owned to me this evening that he began to be frightened.

Monday, 4*th.*—The Government has been much alarmed at the effect caused by their rash project of emancipating the slaves in the West Indian colonies, and have given assurances to-day to the deputation of proprietors, which have in some degree calmed their fears for the present.

The King came to town this morning, and the cabinet council has been sitting till five o'clock, to compose the King's speech for to-morrow. There are many reports in circulation, but sufficient for the day is the evil thereof. Amendments will certainly be made by the Radicals.

Tuesday, 5*th.*—The King went in person to open the Parliament. The speech from the throne, though long, is in no way satisfactory. It allows that the Belgian question remains unsettled, and that the embargo will continue; that rigorous measures must be used against Ireland. It mentions Church reform, but omits entirely West Indian projects.

Wednesday, 6*th.*—The address from the Lords was presented to the King, that from the Commons is not yet carried, owing to the amendment moved by O'Connell on the subject of Ireland, on which the House adjourned to-night. He called it a brutal and bloody speech, for which Lord John Russell moved that his words should be taken down. There was much personality against Mr. Stanley during the debate. The stocks fell to-day in consequence of the speech.

Thursday, 7*th.*—The debate on the amendment carried on in the same strain, and the House again adjourned. The chief Tories have now formed their plan; they will take little part in the debates, except on two or three momentous questions, leaving the Government to fight their own battles with their Radical opponents, in the hope that either the Government may be obliged to dissolve the Parliament, or to be turned out themselves. The power which the Whigs have raised for their own purposes now begins to act without them, and they must follow in its wake. Ireland is become the first stumbling block. Lord Anglesey returns to his government on Saturday, with full powers. Lord Milton, in opposition to the wishes of Lord Althorpe, has given notice of a motion on the corn laws, and Mr. Grote, the new Radical City member, for one on the ballot.

Friday, 8*th.*—Last night Sir Robert Peel made an excellent speech in the sense as above, which gave much satisfaction. This night the House at length divided on the address, which was carried by a majority of 388. The King has been detained in town to receive it, and much annoyed at the delay in carrying it.

Saturday, 9*th.*—Notwithstanding the pacific attitude which the Duke and Peel and the leaders of that party are now disposed to take towards the present Government, I can see clearly that the less influential members are determined to vote without that moderation, and to oppose the Whigs on all occasions. Many of these are in straitened circumstances, anxious to regain their places, and aware that, if their conduct creates future troubles, they will embarrass the chiefs and not the subordinates. They will keep only one object steadily in view, that of obtaining a majority on any terms against the Government.

Monday, 11*th.*—The Jamaica packet has been stopped from sailing by Government, as they are apprehensive that fresh insurrections will arise in Jamaica and Demerara, when they hear that the question of emancipating the negroes has been again agitated here.

Tuesday, 12*th.*—This evening the Irish Church Reform Bill was introduced into the Commons by Lord Althorpe. It reduces two archbishops and ten bishops, abolishes the vestry cess, &c.

Thursday, 14*th.*—There is one thing which appears to me very striking in the present new aspect of affairs; and that is the important position to which Sir R. Peel seems now to direct his views. In his opening speech, which was highly applauded, he has shown considerable address. He went down to the House that night with the public feeling certainly against him; he returned home with the tide of popularity running fully in his favour, even from the *ministerial* benches, the members of which seemed grateful for his forbearance. He has declared himself to belong to no party; but his object is insensibly to make *one* of which he shall be himself the centre and the chief. He is an ambitious man; and to this great object his endeavours will invariably tend. Now, when we consider his talents, his knowledge of business, his eloquence, and, above all, his twenty years' experience in the forms and usages of the House of Commons, joined to that **guarded conduct** which his present new position forces upon him, a position quite different to his former triumphant post, where the confidence in an obsequious majority might at times have rendered him more buoyant, less cautious, and less sensitive as to public opinion:—I say, all these circumstances considered, and, on the other hand, looking to the complexion of this new Parliament, a large proportion of which consists of men really and **de facto** bound to no party—of loose Tories, loose Whigs, loose Conservatives, and loose Radicals, acknowledging no head, but wishing to become influential by some means or other not yet ascertained by them,—it is not very rash to anticipate that to his talents it may be given to unite their discordant interests, and that, under the plausible character of a liberal Tory, the conviction may imperceptibly steal into the House of Commons, that **Sir Robert Peel** is the fittest man to govern this country. In this object he must be very much assisted by the inconsistent conduct of the present Government, which has enraged the Conservatives and disappointed the Radicals, who, if ever they were to coalesce, which is not improbable, might eventually run them very hard.

Friday, 15*th.*—Earl Grey brought forward his coercive measures for Ireland, which are strong and effective. Sir Robert Peel in the Commons brought on the question of the Dutch embargo, when Lord Palmerston allowed that the Belgian question was as unsettled as ever. O'Connell, having heard the speech in the Lords, came back to the Commons boiling with rage, and said to a friend of mine that he could not bear to hear sentiments to which he dared not reply.

Sunday, 17*th.*—O'Connell had a meeting with his party last night, in which they determined to oppose the bill of coercion, by delaying its progress through the House by every artifice.

Tuesday, 19*th.*—Talleyrand is going to leave us; his health begins to break, though his intellect remains unimpaired. Madame de Dino is anxious to go; and she will gain her point. They talk at present of going to Roche-Cote, a country seat given her by Talleyrand. The Lievens, too, are in perplexity; the Emperor Nicholas has positively refused to receive Sir Stratford Canning as ambassador at his court, Lord Palmerston is equally obstinate, and will not make another appointment; in which case chargés d'affaires *must transact the business of each court, and Prince Lieven must be recalled as a matter of course. Talleyrand has a very bad opinion of the state of affairs here; he thinks we are going gradually to ruin. When the Reform Bill was first proposed by the Whigs he said it was* la convocation des États généraux à Paris in the commencement of the Revolution; and it must at least be allowed that he has experience to guide his judgment in these matters.

Wednesday, 20*th.*—The West Indian proprietors are in great alarm; they hear that the bill for the emancipation of the slaves is drawn up, and will be made public in the next week. A meeting on this subject is to be held at Apsley House on Tuesday next.

Friday, 22*nd.*—Received a letter from Paris, which says, "The great rise in the funds here is owing to the fact, well ascertained by the Antwerp expedition, of the disinclination or the inability of the other powers to go to war; by the higher attitude assumed in Europe by this government—*thanks to that dash;* but chiefly to the dread shown by the majority of the Chambers and of the great middle class for the *mouvement parti* and doctrines, and the consequent determination to rally round the government *tel quel, faute de mieux, crainte de pis;* which motto Louis-Philippe might well inscribe on his banners and *armoiries*. In a cooler moment that eternal nightmare the Dutch question will occur again; for I heard only yesterday from the present chargé d'affaires that he considered matters less in a train of arrangement than at any former period!—his king showing the same determined spirit, and being prepared for the worst; *i.e.* the extremity of another attack, which the high tone of ministers here, and the treatment of his colleague in London by Lord Palmerston, lead him to view as by no means improbable. But the remarkable circumstance is, that Austria and Prussia are now most urgent for submission on the part of King William; so much so, that Appony and Werther use violent language to him whenever they meet. The communications from Vienna and Berlin must of course be of the same effect to the Hague. Then, what is the look-out at the latter place? what is the secret of such great obstinacy? The ministry draw but indifferently together, and the old warlike Marshal (Soult) was in great jeopardy the other day, when those foolish duels fortunately turned up and reseated him. If M. Carrel [Note *: Armand Carrel, at that time chief editor of the "National," the great organ of the liberal party. He had just been severely wounded in a duel arising out of the Duchesse de Berry's conduct, then keenly canvassed by the press. In 1836 he was killed in a duel which he fought with M. Emile de Girardin.] had died, a second edition of General La Marque's funeral was apprehended; in which case the army and its commander might again have been wanted."

Sunday, 24*th.*—The conversation at White's and Brookes's solely engrossed by the speech of O'Connell at the meeting of the Political Union last night, which is beyond expression violent, not to say treasonable. The Whigs are enraged, and talk of expelling him from Brookes's; but they may thank themselves for it.

Monday, 25*th.*—The Political Unions at Birmingham, &ac., are beginning also to meet and oppose the coercion bill for Ireland. Lord Althorpe said this morning, that the Government would stand or fall by its success. This day the Queen's birthday was kept, but the drawing-room was very thinly attended. Lord Frederick Fite-Clarence has resigned his place at the Tower, from the conviction that this Parliament would not vote the money for the salary.

Tuesday, 26*th.*—The West Indian deputation went up to the Government by appointment at one o'clock. They returned bound to secrecy as to the nature of the emancipation bill, which will not be divulged for two or three days.

Wednesday, 27*th.*—Whatever may be in store for this country, whether it work for ultimate good or ill, none can foretel; but that a great revolution in the state is advancing none can deny. The democratic power is raising its fearful head, and, as the "Times" paper says this morning, let the present Government resign or not, the march of affairs will continue, and defy all opposition; no sooner is one innovation accomplished than a fresh inroad is proposed, as if increase of appetite had grown by what it fed on. The aristocracy are hourly going down in the scale; royalty is become a mere cipher. I was walking the other day round the Royal Exchange, the *enceinte* of which is adorned with the statues of all our kings. Only two niches now remain vacant; one is destined to our present ruler, and that reserved for his successor is the *last*. [Note *: In one respect the omen was fulfilled, the Royal Exchange having been burnt in 1838, within six months after the accession of her present Majesty.] Some people might say it was ominous.

Thursday, 28*th.*—Van Zuylen is recalled in consequence of his disagreements with Lord Palmerston, and a new Dutch envoy, M. Dedel, is coming in his place.

Friday, 1*st March.*—The French "Moniteur" contains a letter from the Duchesse de Berry, announcing that she had been for some time privately married. This accounts for the apparent anxiety shown lately by the French government about her health, when they with great publicity sent two physicians from Paris to report on her state. Reports were circulated then that she was *enceinte,* which have unfortunately proved too true, and, instead of endeavouring to conceal the frailty of a poor, weak, defenceless woman, Louis-Philippe and his ministers would not let slip such an opportunity of disgracing the Bourbons and mortifying the Carlist party; they have, therefore, compelled her, as it were, to make this exposure to the world, in hopes that it may tend to strengthen his throne and render the claims of the other family more precarious; but every generous mind must see that they have cruelly abused their power over one who had no hope but in their delicacy and clemency. There is some little reaction in public opinion in the city; Lyall, the Tory candidate, has been elected by a large majority in the room of Alderman Waithman.

Saturday, 2*nd.*—The Speaker said to me at White's this morning: "It is the fashion to compliment me on my knowledge of the forms of the House and the rules in debates, but all my past experience in Parliament is positively good for nothing; the business of the House is carried on so differently from the former system, that I am, in fact, as great a novice as any of them. The cry for adjournment from a particular party generally followed after a convincing speech from their own side; now they are clamorous for adjournment when their adversaries have just carried the palm in argument against them."

Sunday, 3*rd.*—The news of the day is, that Don Miguel has succeeded in raising a loan at Paris, which will render the cause of Don Pedro nearly hopeless; that Châteaubriand, notwithstanding the unfortunate situation of the Duchesse de Berry, has been unanimously acquitted by the jury on the prosecution instituted against him for his pamphlet in her favour, which openly advocated the claims of Henri V.; that accounts have been received from Vienna stating the submission of the Pacha to the Sultan; that our fleet off Lisbon has been ordered to proceed to the Mediterranean, where we had not one line-of-battle ship left; that the fresh despatch arrived from Holland is more unaccommodating than the last.

Monday, 4*th.*—Irish coercion bill still adjourned.
Tuesday, 5*th.*—Bill carried by 466 to 89.

Wednesday, 6*th.*—This morning, died, at Norwood, the Earl of Dudley, aged fifty-two. A relation, the Rev. Mr. Ward, succeeds to the title of Lord Ward, with 4000*l.* per annum, and about 80,000*l.* per annum is left to his son.

Friday, 8*th.*—The plan of emancipation in the West Indies, though not yet divulged, engrosses much conversation. There seems little doubt that compensation is intended to the proprietors, the funds for which can only be raised by a loan. The Government asserts that the country demands the abolition of slavery. If it can be done at the cost of one unfortunate class, well and good; but I believe the philanthropist has very little inclination to contribute any part thereof out of his own pocket:—

"Sur le sort des pauvres nègres avec larmes il s'explique,
Sans pouvoir chez lui garder un seal domestique."

Saturday, 9*th.*—There are various reports of difference in the cabinet on the subject of this Irish bill; but they seem to lead to no serious change. The King has given to Sir P. Sydney the place of surveyor-general of the duchy of Cornwall, worth 2000*l.* per annum.

Thursday, 14*th.*—Lord Durham resigns his place in the Government, and is to be made an earl. M. Dedel, the new Dutch ambassador, arrived in London. Schimmelpennich, his brother-in-law, writes to us thus: "On attend monts et merveilles de son apparition chez vous; je ne partage pas cette opinion, je pense qu'on ne veuille pas effectivement le paix."

Friday, 15*th.*—This night's Gazette announced the earldom of Lord Durham. The King came to town, it is said, about some differences in the cabinet. Van Zuylen took leave, but Dedel was not presented. The run for gold in Ireland is becoming more serious, and the value of property there is falling.

Saturday, 16*th.*—The Russian fleet with troops is arrived from Sebastopol at Constantinople, in consequence of the Sultan's demand for assistance to resist the Pacha, much to the annoyance of France and England, who wished to have the éclat of terminating the hostilities themselves, and are now most anxious for the withdrawal of the Russians. This event recals to my mind the words which Matuscewitz used to me about a fortnight ago. He said, "With regard to the East, we will not allow any power to dictate to us; it is our natural field. We are there close at hand, and can always take our measures before any other interference can clash with our views."

Monday, 18*th.*—Our Government has been properly duped by our friends the French at Constantinople. Admiral Roussin has been on the alert; he has made a tool of our chargé d'affaires *Mandeville for his own purposes with the Porte, and then, keeping him in the background, has signed a treaty on* his own responsibility *with the Sultan for the Pacha, claiming* for France *the whole merit of the interference. Lord Palmerston is biting his lips with vexation; Neumann is vexed* à outrance; *and as to Russia, as the peace is made,* it is supposed that their fleet must return to Sebastopol.

Tuesday, 19*th.*—The election for Marylebone, in the room of Mr. Portman, closed to-day. There were three candidates, Mr. Hope in the Tory interest, Mr. Murray in the Whig, and Sir Samuel Whalley in the Radical. As the Whigs would not give a vote to a Tory, nor the Tories to a Whig, Mr. Murray having resigned last night, the Radical has come in. I received a letter from Paris thus: "I thought some clue might perhaps occur to the strange mystery at Blaye; but the various circumstances still remain unexplained, though the main fact admits, I fear, of no doubt, malgré *the obstinate disbelief of some* very staunch Legitimists. I believe the plan now is to set her (the Duchesse de Berry) at liberty after her recovery, and then to grant a general amnesty for political offences, which would include the four prisoners at Ham. [Note *: The Prince Polignac and the other ministers of Charles X., who had advised him to violate the "Charte," an act which issued in the July Revolution of 1830.] Such a proceeding would in some degree tend to wipe off the disgrace attaching to the government for its loud and official proclamation of that poor woman's avowal. Louis-Philippe's sole prop is the negative dread of what might succeed him. That feeling of course grows fainter as internal alarms subside; which you may collect from the debates in the papers of the deputies, where the ministry meet daily checks and rebuffs. The *tiers parti,* with skilful management, might soon turn them out; but the leader of that set, M. Dupin, the president, wants political weight, talent, and consistency for the part. Therefore they will jog on, I suppose, *tant bien que mal,* some time longer. I have just heard that a courier from Constantinople brings an account that the Russian fleet from Sebastopol, having made its appearance there, the French Ambassador, Admiral Roussin, who was just arrived, demanded its being *sent back* in very peremptory or rather threatening terms, which, after some discussion, was agreed to by the Sultan; whose application to that effect to the Russian minister produced a rather reluctant promise that they would sail back the first fair wind. I have not heard whether Admiral Roussin acted in concert with the English embassy. How will this be liked by the autocrat, whose ill humour is already so manifest?

Wednesday, 20*th.*—A letter from John King at Paris says, "Some event or other occurs daily to discredit this government. They have been defeated within the last day or two on more than one important question in the Chamber of Deputies. The procès du coup de pistolet is the subject of universal derision. The dissensions in the cabinet are so strong, that a speedy change is contemplated by everybody."

Thursday, 21*st.*—The Court of Assize in Paris has acquitted the two men accused of firing the pistol at the king.

Friday, 22*nd.*—We went this evening with Sir H. Cooke to see the oratorio at Covent Garden. It is a new spectacle this year, being the representation of the Israelites in Egypt, with the passage of the Red Sea; the singing by the first professors. The orchestra and the decorations are all excellent, but it is too much like a real opera to be repeated in Lent another year.

Saturday, 23*rd.*—Don Carlos is banished by King Ferdinand from Madrid, and the liberal party in Spain seems gaining ground.

Sunday, 24*th.*—I had a letter this morning from the Duke of Wellington in reply to the news I had sent him about Constantinople, &c. He writes thus:—

"I am afraid that Count Matuscewitz is mistaken, and that the emperor will find his fleet returned to Sebastopol. Where is old England, with all her interests in the Levant and in Asia, in all this!"

Cooke likewise had a letter from his grace the same day, in which he also writes as follows:—

"We are going, but I think that it will be gradually. There will be no catastrophe; we are not equal to one. We shall be destroyed by the due course of the law, unless the Virgin of the Pillar or some miracle saves us."

It is interesting to record the sentiments of such a man in such times; his presentiments of the future are indeed gloomy, but not unfounded.

My brother, as governor of the Bank, was yesterday with Lord Althorpe, who expressed strongly the determination of the Government to resist the motion for the alteration of the currency by a fresh circulation of paper money. His expression was, "A gross robbery on the public was committed by Mr. Peel's bill in 1819, and we will not sanction a similar robbery in 1833 by repealing it." To-day I hear that the party are becoming so strong in the House of Commons that they will forcibly carry their point.

Monday, 25*th.*—A general court of proprietors was held at the India House to consider the proposal of the Whig government for reforming the East India Company:—

1. That the China monopoly should cease.

2. The company to assign to the Government the whole of its territorial possessions; that the government of India should be retained by the company; that the dividends be continued to the proprietors as before, but secured only on the territorial revenues of India, redeemable at 200*l.* for each 100*l.* capital, with other innovations, which had been declined unanimously by the directors, and were now referred to the proprietors, who are to meet again at a general court on the 15th April, to discuss this very important question.

It is singular that the Right Honourable Charles Grant [Note *: Now Lord Glenelg.], son of the late Mr. Grant, who was so long chairman of the East India Company, and so warmly attached to the interests of that body, should, in his situation of President of the Board of Control, be the instrument of thus annihilating the very existence of this splendid and powerful establishment. His correspondence with the chairman is now before the public, and has excited much animadversion from its testy and unstatesmanlike style. The English government is now raising the whirlwind in the eastern and western hemispheres; not satisfied with domestic commotion, it seems determined to shake the very globe itself to its centre. To predict is futile! Who can tell what even to-morrow may bring? But every one may now observe in society the marked contrast which exists at this crisis between the two great clashing parties in the state; the one agitated by fear and apprehension, faint-hearted and panic-struck at the evils which they see coming on the world; the other sanguine, reckless, exulting, and, as Lord Lyndhurst said of Lord Brougham in the House of Lords, making their sportive gambols on the surface of a whirlpool.

Dedel had a stormy interview with Lord Palmerston last night, leaving little hope of a settlement thus far.

Tuesday, 26th.—India stock rose ten per cent. this morning, on the prospect of the dividend being continued as before; but the speculators seem to have taken a superficial view of the question. The Russian emperor is highly offended at the French Admiral Roussin's interference at Constantinople, and requires a serious explanation from that government, which has already approved of the conduct of its ambassador. This last insult, added to the previous causes of irritation, will probably bring the point to an issue whether the autocrat will dare to go beyond a *war of words*.

Wednesday 27th.—The Duchesse de Berry is alarmingly ill in her prison at Blaye. M. Clermont Tonnerre writes from Paris to a friend of mine: "We are occupied in observing the progress of affairs in England, where a great revolution seems to us inevitable." Mr. Robinson's motion in the House last night for a sweeping repeal of taxes, and the imposition of a property tax, though opposed firmly by ministers, still found 155 adherents. To give some idea of the tone of the French journals at present, the following is a quotation from the "Corsaire" of last week: L'état de l'atmosphère, mélange de neige, de vent, de pluie et de chaleur, est absolument celui de notre situation politique. Salmigondis d'arbitraire, de violence, de peur, de men-songe et de lâcheté."

At this day's levée Lord Goderich was made privy seal in the room of Lord Durham.

Thursday, 28th.—Mr. Stanley [Note *: Now Earl of Derby.] is made colonial minister instead of Lord Goderich, and Sir J. C. Hobhouse [Note †: Now Lord

Broughton.] secretary for Ireland, in his room.

Friday, 29*th.*—The "Petersburg Gazette" takes no notice of Admiral Roussin's interference. It merely states that affairs look more peaceable in the East; in which case their fleet may retire to the neighbouring port of Sizeboli, where *it will be joined by another fleet and an army by land.*

Saturday, 30*th.*—No news. Matuscewitz will leave us on Tuesday for Petersburg.

Tuesday, 2*nd April.*—There is mutiny in Don Pedro's fleet off Oporto. Admiral Sartorius has refused to act till the arrears due to him and his crew are paid. Sir John Milley Doyle was sent on board to place him under arrest, and Sartorious immediately ordered him to be detained as a prisoner till the grievances are redressed.

Wednesday, 3*rd.*—Last night, in the House of Commons, ministers had only a majority of eleven on the question of continuing the system of flogging in the army, and still many Tories voted with them.

Thursday, 4*th.*—House adjourned for the recess.

Saturday, 6*th.*—The removal of Lord Goderich from the colonies has been compulsory, and sorely against his will. He stated to Earl Grey, that to remove him at such a moment, when the emancipation question, with which he had been so long officially occupied, was on the eve of settlement, was an act of great injustice to him; that, if the result was satisfactory, his successor would reap all the credit of his labours; but if, on the contrary, the project should be a failure, all the obloquy would still devolve upon him. The premier remained inflexible. He was convinced of the necessity of the change, which had met the approbation of his Majesty; he could enter into all the feelings of Lord Goderich on the subject, but where the public welfare was at stake he could not allow them to bias him, and he finally trusted to his good sense to subscribe without further difficulty to the wishes of the cabinet.

He assured him that the King would be happy to give him any compensation; that his advancement to an earldom would be easily accomplished; and that he himself (Lord Grey) would be anxious, when affairs became more settled, to offer him any further promotion. To all these observations Lord Goderich remained firmly inaccessible, till at length Lord Grey, resorting to his usual last resource, informed him that he would instantly go and place his own resignation in the hands of his Majesty. Resistance then became useless, and Lord Goderich yielded.

Sunday, 7th.—There has been very little foreign news this last week. The new tariff has passed in America, which will probably pacify the Carolinians. Dedel's negotiations go on but slowly in Downing-street. The Russian fleet remains immovable before Constantinople, in spite of Admiral Roussin, which will not tend to make the King of Holland more tractable. I affected to joke last night with young Lieven about the return of the Russians to Sebastopol His reply was, "Rira qui rira le dernier."

A reaction has taken place at Madrid; the liberal party are confounded, and Zea Bermudez is more firmly established than ever.

Monday, 8th.—The news from the East becomes more serious. Ibrahim Pacha refuses to stop the march of his Egyptian troops, and the Russians are marching through the provinces to assist the Sultan, who invokes their aid, to the great disgust of the French and English envoys at Constantinople.

Tuesday, 9th.—The news from Jamaica is very bad. Lord Mulgrave, the new governor, has been publicly assailed in the streets. Everything seemed to announce a serious insurrection in the island.

The feeling of jealousy which might have existed between Austria and Russia last year seems to have completely subsided; and the union of France and England, for their so-called liberal objects, has only drawn closer the ties of amity between the three other great powers. Neumann, who is not in general communicative, openly asserted at dinner that Austria acquiesced in the proceedings of Russia at

Constantinople, and was equally convinced of the moderation of her views in that quarter.

Wednesday, 10*th.*—The Irish Coercion Bill being now a part of the law of the land, Lord Anglesey has begun to put it in force by placing the county of Kilkenny under martial law. The Government has received a smart hint as to the change of public opinion. Captain Berkeley, who has been made a lord of the Admiralty, has been defeated at Gloucester by Mr. Hope, a Tory candidate, on trying for his re-election. At Sunderland Lord Grey's son-in-law Captain Barrington has been compelled to resign, and Alderman Thompson is elected in his room. Edward Ellice has been gazetted secretary-at-war *vice* Hobhouse.

Thursday, 11*th.*—The Russian fleet in the Bosphorus was, on the 5th ultimo, reinforced by several frigates, containing more troops and artillery.

Although we have not been visited with the cholera this year, yet a species of influenza, which attacks the lungs more or less violently, has made its appearance, and the medical men say that they never witnessed at any season so much serious illness as at present.

An insurrection has taken place among the students at Frankfort. Much blood has been spilt, and a ducal palace has been burnt It is supposed to emanate from the propaganda in France, where everything seems to announce that the liberal party are preparing to make a great movement against the government of Louis-Philippe. My friend General Stopford is just arrived from Calais, and says that the language of the Mouvement party becomes daily more menacing.

Alvanley has been spending a week at Lord Sefton's at Stoke. He says that the chancellor and Lord Melbourne, who were of the party, seemed in very low spirits at the aspect of affairs and the increasing difficulties which pressed on the Government. The liberal press begins to assail them with abuse and predicts their fall. The handwriting on the wall for them is "Go on, or go out!"

Friday, 12*th.*—Lord Goderich has been made an earl by the title of Earl of Ripon in Yorkshire. His original wish was to have taken the name of Harold; but some allusions in "John Bull" of last Sunday to **Childe Harold** have probably altered his intention.

Saturday, 13*th.*—It is now well known that the persons ridiculed by Molière in his comedies were living in France at the time he wrote. The original of Tartuffe was one Roquette, who was much more of a polisson than a priest, and who belonged to the diocese of Autun. This circumstance has suggested the following epigram on Talleyrand:—

"Roquette dans son tems,
Talleyrand dans le nôtre,
Furent évêques d'Autun.
Tartuffe est le surnom de l'un,
Ah! si Molière eut connu l'autre."

In the passing events in Belgium the name of Count Vilain Quatorze is often mentioned. The origin of this title is curious: his grandfather was made a peer by Louis XIV., and when the monarch asked him if he wished to change his name, he merely asked for the numeral addition, that his family might never forget the creator of their title.

Tuesday, 16*th.*—A sad, melancholy day. At seven o'clock this morning died my deeply-regretted friend Lord Foley. One short week's illness has carried him to the grave. For twenty-five years have I lived with him in the closest intimacy, and never knew a kinder or more friendly heart than his. The unbounded hospitality of his nature brought him into pecuniary difficulties, which embittered the latter years of his life; and I very much fear that anxiety of mind contributed to render his last illness fatal. He was of a noble and princely disposition; a kind, affectionate parent, and a warm friend. He married the sister of the Duke of Leinster, and has left eight children. He was lord of the bedchamber, and captain of the band of Gentlemen Pensioners to the present King.

Wednesday, 17*th.*—This evening the first reading of the bill for the emancipation of the Jews, moved by Mr. Robert Grant, was passed without a division in the House of Commons. If it had been Turks and heretics it would have been just the same thing; indeed, Mr. Hume did make some allusion to the Parsees in India as worthy of the same distinction. It has been pleasantly said of this Whig government, that it is impossible to ravish them, because they concede everything. A communication has lately been made to the Bank for the renewal of their charter, which expires in August next. The original proposal made by Lord Althorpe is, that the charter be extended for only ten years; that the 250,000*l.* annually paid by the Government to that establishment for the management of the public debt, &c., shall be conceded; that one half of the capital, being 7,300,000*l.*, shall be repaid by the Government and distributed to the proprietors; while the dividend on the remaining half shall be raised from 8*l.* to 10*l.* per cent, with the stipulation that all future profits made by the Bank exceeding that 10*l.* per cent on 7,300,000*l.* shall accrue to the Government This proposition has met with a flat refusal from the court of directors, who have in return submitted a plan much more favourable to their own interests, to his lordship's attention, and comprehending much greater immunities than he had contemplated. Their proposal is this:—

(1.) That the exclusive privileges be continued for *twenty-one years*.

(2.) That no joint-stock bank be chartered for issuing paper money within sixty-five miles of London.

(3.) That a weekly return of liabilities and assets be returned confidentially to the Chancellor of the Exchequer, in the form as delivered to the commissioners, to be dealt with as he may deem proper. If the Government determines on the publication in the Gazette, it is proposed that such shall be made quarterly, containing the average of the three preceding months.

(4.) That 25 per cent of the capital now held by the Government be returned to the proprietors.

(5.) That the Bank do deduct 100,000*l*. per annum from the present charge for management.

(6.) That the Bank be permitted to divide 9*l*. per cent. on the remaining capital held by Government, and to accumulate a cash surplus of 3,000,000*l*. prior to any further allowance being made to the public, stipulating at the same time that the cash surplus shall not be reduced below 2,500,000*l*.

(7.) That, after payment of the dividend of 9*l*. per cent. and accumulation of cash surplus as above, half any further profits acquired by the Bank shall be annually deducted from the sums payable by the Government to the Bank.

(8.) If, in lieu of participation by the public in future benefits, a private compensation is preferred, the company propose the further sum of . . . . . . *l*. to be deducted from the prior charge.

Thus the matter stands at issue at present; but it is probable that no answer will be returned till after the currency question, to be moved by Mr. Attwood on Friday next, and which excites great attention, shall have been decided.

Thursday, 18*th.*—Died Henry Herbert, Earl of Carnarvon.

Saturday 20*th.*—Last night Lord Althorpe took precedence of Mr. Attwood's motion for the distresses of the country and a change in the currency, by producing unexpectedly his budget, which consisted in retrenchments producing about 1,400,000*l*. and taking off taxes for 1,100,000*l*. The result seemed to give no real satisfaction, as it would produce no real relief to any class in the country.

Monday, 22*nd.*—Attwood's motion for a committee on the distress of the country, combined with a plan for a depreciated standard, came on this evening in the Commons.

Tuesday, 23*rd.*—The House divided on Attwood's motion, ayes 139, noes 331; being a majority of 192 for ministers.

Thursday, 25*th.*—A riotous meeting at the Crown and Anchor for the repeal of the assessed taxes, at which the sitting members for Westminster were violently abused for their votes on Attwood's motion. The Government is becoming daily more unpopular.

Friday, 26*th.*—A deputation of fifty from the unions, headed by one Gough, waited on Lord Althorpe at the Treasury, to represent their grievances; who, on the plea of engagements, begged to decline receiving them. They sent him word that they would recommend him, for *his own* convenience, to admit them, as at four o'clock they should pay him another visit to the number of 5000.

At night, in the House of Commons, Lord Althorpe, having been taunted with neglecting the agricultural interest in his late budget, announced that he should move for two committees to inquire into the causes of distress, one of the agricultural, the other of the trading interests. Sir W. Ingleby then proposed his resolution for reducing one-half of the malt tax, which would amount to about 2,000,000*l*. It was carried, to the manifest confusion of Government, by a majority of ten against them, many Tories joining the number; among whom was Mr. Baring, the member for Essex (a barley county), who did not dare to vote against the will of his constituents.

The revolution so long predicted seems to be approaching. No real government can henceforward exist in this country. We must own no other rule than that of the House of Commons, which is now beginning, as in the time of Charles I., to refuse the supplies. Another motion comes on upon Tuesday for the repeal of the assessed taxes, which will also be carried; making a further deficiency in the revenue of 2,800,000*l*.

Lord Grey has positively refused to lay on a property tax.

Saturday, 27 *th.*—The ministers are at their wits' ends. Lords Grey and Althorpe have been to the King to offer their resignations, which he could not receive; nor were they justified in offering to desert him. A cabinet council then was called, which lasted several hours; but the result was not known. Neither the Duke nor Peel would consent to come in at such a moment. They must see too well the dangers and difficulties that would await them. At night the public mind became more tranquil, on the idea that the ministers would make a great effort on Monday night to rescind what they call the surprise of Friday; and that, if unsuccessful, they would then allow the repeal of the malt and of the assessed taxes, replacing them by a property tax; but constituted as this House of Commons now is, who can calculate on its being carried?

Sunday, 28 *th.*—The same state of uncertainty all day: nothing decisive known, but cabinet councils sitting to a late hour."

Monday, 29 *th.*—This evening the House was in breathless anxiety for the ministerial decision, when Lord Althorpe rose, and said, that he meant, on the proposal of the motion to-morrow for the repeal of the assessed taxes, to move as an amendment, "That the repeal thereof and the reduction of the malt tax would occasion such a deficiency in the revenue as could only be supplied by the substitution of a general tax on property and an extensive change in our whole financial system, which would be inexpedient at present."

Tuesday, 30 *th.*—I never saw so much dismay and anxiety generally pervading all parties as to the result of this night's debate and the consequent feelings it may excite in the country. There is a fearful conviction of the weakness of the Government gaining ground, even among their own partisans, which makes all thinking men apprehensive for the future. They would now gladly resist the clamour of the people; but, as the Duke said, the real danger is when they begin *to stop*. To get into power they have promised all their boons, and the bond will be exacted. At night there was a call of the House; and, from a dread of the impending danger, and the threat of resignation on the part of ministers, Lord Althorpe's amendment was carried by a majority of 154. Thus the matter is arranged for the present; but the same dilemma may easily occur again. Hobhouse has resigned his place and his seat.

Wednesday, 1*st* May.—A temporary calm; but the late measures have destroyed the little remaining popularity of the Whig government; and even this new Reform Parliament comes in for its share of abuse from the public press.

There are meetings of the unions and murmurs of refusing to pay the assessed taxes. In the meantime Russia, aware of the embarrassments which absorb the attention of the European powers, is quietly prosecuting her own views in the East, and gradually entangling the Sultan in her meshes.

Thursday, 2*nd.*—Sir John Hobhouse is to be reinstalled, and put up again as a candidate for Westminster. Sir J. Malcolm died this morning. The undertakers here have more work than they can accomplish. Lord Roden is just returned from Brussels. He told me that the country was quite paralysed,—no trade, no society, no energy; the policy of the King of Holland is quietly making its way towards a restoration.

Friday, 3*rd.*—Accounts have been again received by telegraph, through France, from the Mediterranean, announcing the death of Admiral Sir Henry Hotham, commanding the English squadron on that station. He was an excellent officer, and a most valuable man. He married Lady Frances Rous, sister to the Earl of Stradbroke, and has left her a widow with three boys. In the navy it will be difficult to replace such a man, particularly at the present crisis in the East.

At a meeting of the council of the Birmingham Political Union the following resolutions were adopted unanimously:—

(1.) That his Majesty's ministers,—

First, By violating the constitution and destroying the liberties of Ireland;—

Secondly, By denial of the general distress amongst the productive classes and refusal of all inquiry into the means of its relief;—

Thirdly, By refusing to make any perceptible reduction in the present overwhelming load of taxation; by persisting in the continuation of the partial and unjust taxes assessed upon houses and windows, notwithstanding the relief which was imperatively demanded by the depressed state of trade; and especially by their absolutely forcing upon the country the odious and oppressive malt tax, without any diminution, although its partial abolition had been deliberately resolved upon by a vote of the House of Commons only three days previously;—

have betrayed the confidence of the people and turned their sanguine hopes into despair.

(2.) That, in this frightful situation of the country, it is the opinion of this council that public meetings ought to be held ***with the least possible delay*** in every ***county town*** and ***village*** throughout the ***United Kingdom,*** to implore his Majesty to dismiss from his councils men who have proved themselves utterly unworthy, unable, or unwilling to extricate the country from the dangers and difficulties with which it is surrounded.

(3) That for this purpose the council deems it expedient that a public meeting of the population of this district should be held at Newhall Hill, &c.

Friday, 10*th.*—The election for Westminster is decided; the Whig and Tory candidates, Hobhouse and Escott, are defeated, and the Radical Colonel Evans [Note *: Now General Sir De Lacy Evans] has gained the day,—a type of the dominant feeling.

Monday, 13*th.*—A public meeting held in Coldbath Fields to form a National Convention. The Government having previously issued a proclamation declaring such assemblage illegal, the numbers did not amount to more than 2000 or 3000; but the language held and the banners exhibited on the occasion proved that their object was nothing short of revolution. They were ultimately dispersed by the police; but not till three or four of that body had been stabbed by concealed daggers; one of whom died on the spot. Some of the ringleaders are now in custody.

Tuesday, 14*th.*—Mr. Stanley produced this evening in the Commons the Government plan for negro emancipation; which, if carried into effect, must threaten the ruin of the West Indian proprietors. It is so complex in its machinery, that none think it practicable; and as it is not sufficiently decisive for the Abolitionists, and much too severe on the West Indian interest, it gives equal dissatisfaction to both parties. In the meantime it paralyses the trade with the colonies; spreads fear and anxiety among those interested in it; and, as a question now mooted, but long to remain undecided, will unsettle immediately the minds of the negroes and probably create rebellion and confusion throughout the islands. Thus do difficulties daily-increase. The discussion of this bill is now adjourned to the 30th instant.

Château de C——, near Orleans, August 29.1833.

The state of politics at home and abroad remains unaltered; the Belgian question is still unsettled; civil war continues to rage in Portugal. The Russian troops, it is true, have quitted Constantinople, as pledged to do, on the retreat of the Pacha into Asia, but not till a treaty offensive and defensive was signed between the Emperor and the Sultan, unknown to the other powers; by which the influence of the former in Turkish affairs is rendered more decisive than if a Russian army of occupation had attempted to prolong their stay in the Turkish capital. Stratford Canning is returned from Madrid to England, his mission to the Spanish court having proved abortive. Otho is established as king in Greece, and little attention is excited by his proceedings. Austria and Prussia remain in ***statu quo,*** watching with a jealous eye the proceedings of France and England in Portugal, and alarmed at every movement which takes place in their German and Italian provinces.

At home the Whigs, ***faute de mieux et crainte de pis,*** remain in the Government. The session of Parliament is just expiring, and the two great questions of the East and West Indies yet unsettled. Party spirit remains as strong as ever. Death has been busy in the higher circles since we left England. The Duke of Sutherland has not long survived his new dignities. The Earl of Plymouth has died of apoplexy on board his yacht in the river. Lord Dover, whose health has been for some time declining, died a month ago in London. Sir Harry Goodricke, who inherited the immense property of his uncle Lord Clermont, is just dead in Ireland, much regretted by all who knew him, but particularly by the society of Melton.

Wednesday, 8*th October.*—I was in Paris the last week. The state of affairs begins to change. On Sunday week, the 28th September, Ferdinand King of Spain died. The news arrived in Paris on Thursday morning, and on the Friday a courier was dispatched by the French government with the formal recognition of the young princess as queen, to the exclusion of Don Carlos. Orders have been given to form an army of observation on the frontier of the Pyrenees, and French troops are already on the march thither. The Spanish funds have fallen in consequence 15 per cent, and the French 3 per cents. to 71.60. I called on Count Pozzo di Borgo, the Russian ambassador, by appointment, at his hotel in the Champ Elysées, who spoke very openly on the aspect of affairs. He seemed much irritated at what he called the hypocrisy of the French government as well as of the English, against whom he expressed himself almost equally hostile. He said that, contrary to all diplomatic etiquette, which requires that each nation should carry on its own correspondence *direct* with foreign powers, France and England had sent a, *joint note* to Russia, on the subject of her interference in Turkey, couched in terms which he knew they would not dare to maintain. He said that Russia, Austria, Prussia, and Holland were all united in sentiment, and understood each other perfectly; that their armies were never so well appointed; and that 600,000 men could be brought into the field at any notice. As to Louis-Philippe, his opinion was, that little dependence could be placed on him, he was consistent only in one point, and that was his determination to remain king; if he could not reign with the *bonnet gris,* he would condescend to reign with the *bonnet rouge*. All his questions seemed to tend to what means could overthrow the Whig government in England. He desired C——, who was with him during my visit, and who is going to England, to tell the Duke that, if ever he returned to office, all the Four Powers were unanimous to abide in everything by his instructions; that if he wished any particular object to be accomplished for the good of Europe, they would follow it up hand and heart; in short, that in such a case their counsels should be guided by England: but, added he, "if she is still to be governed by her present rulers, let her beware of the consequences. Our plans are laid. We shall attack her in her most vulnerable point,—in her commerce. We have means in our power to destroy her: we will prohibit every species of manufacture or produce that can in the slightest degree affect her interests; we will shut up the Sound against her; we will offer such advantages to America her rival, that the whole carrying trade of Europe shall come into her hands; and we will do everything to accelerate that ruin which her own mad rulers are already eventually bringing on her head." He then adverted to Poland. He said that the great fault the emperor had committed was giving her a constitution, a mild government, and a national army. Those things would now no longer exist; all the fortresses in that country were now rebuilt, and strengthened with such impregnable works, such immense batteries of artillery, such numerous garrisons, and such a system of police throughout the country, that though it was true the expense had been enormous, yet all idea of insurrection had been set at rest for ever.

The news from England is of little importance, except that the spirit of resisting payment of the assessed taxes gains ground more generally, and the people are taking counsel's opinion as to the legality of that resistance.

George Villiers is arrived as minister at Madrid just in time to witness the death of Ferdinand.

Tuesday, 5th November.—I have a letter from C——, In which he says: "I wish that when you arrive in Paris you would see P. di Borgo, and inform him that I had a very long and confidential communication with the Duke, and told him all that I was desired to say. He says, in reply, that matters seem in a worse state than they were before the recess of Parliament. It is requisite that P. di Borgo should know and comprehend, not only that we have less prospect than ever of any change of Government, but that the faculty of resistance is daily diminishing by the supineness of those who have rank or fortune to lose. The Duke, it seems, could have turned out the ministers on the Irish Church Bill in August last; but during the progress of the debate Peel sent the Duke word that, if his grace was successful, he wished it to be distinctly understood that he would be no party to any new Government; but that he would give his cordial support to any administration formed on Conservative principles. The Duke, then, feeling he was deserted and working only for others who would run no risk, abandoned the plan, and he now thinks that no administration could be formed that would last two months if the Whigs were ejected. Financial difficulties indeed may any day bring them to a *standstill;* and he then thinks that, unless the King publicly appeals to the nation at large to support his throne, the country itself will be lost and ruined for ever. Till some such great crisis has arrived, no Conservative government can now ever be formed.

"Great care should be observed by all foreign powers, especially Russia, to avoid any measure that can lead to a popular war. The ministers would take advantage of it, and France and England combined would not only sweep every sea, but destroy the commerce of all the world. A popular war would be a most dreadful scourge to all the sovereigns of Europe; even such a war, if England remained neuter, would enable France by her propaganda to set the subjects of all Europe against their sovereigns, and create universal desolation."

*Monday 11*th.—We arrived at Marly-le-Roi.

Wednesday, 13*th.*—I went to Paris this morning, where I called upon Count Pozzo di Borgo. He expressed himself very much interested with Cooke's communication, and begged to take a copy of it. He then proceeded much in the following manner:—

"When I was lately in England I had great reason to foresee that things were approaching their present state, which is certainly not only ominous to yourselves, but to all Europe. Your union with France will produce no benefit to England; they will make no treaty of commerce, they will only use you for their own purposes.

"Russia is your old ally, and under the Duke's government, convinced as we are of the rectitude of his intentions, there are no facilities to commerce, no sacrifices, that we would not make to cement that alliance; but under your present rulers we are everywhere held up to odium and suspicion, as if the conviction that you had unjustly deserted an old friend only made you more anxious to injure and traduce her for your own justification. We (meaning the Three Powers) are not so much at the mercy of you propagandists as you may think; Austria has no apprehensions for Italy, and the Prince [Foot note *: The present King of Prussia, who, whatever other good qualities he may possess, has certainly displayed neither the "courage," nor the "daring" with which he is credited in the text, since his accession to the throne.] Royal of Prussia has lately made a tour in the Rhenish provinces, where he has been received with great enthusiasm and loyalty, the people being much pleased with the new commercial regulations.

"He (*par exemple*) is an excellent man, strongly attached to the good cause, with more courage and daring than his father; who, though a most amiable character, has suffered so much misfortune through his long and stormy life, that one cannot be surprised if his vigour and energy should in a certain degree subside at the conclusion of his career.

"We are now on the eve of important events; a civil war is established in Spain, and though the cabinet of Louis-Philippe are not anxious to cross the Pyrenees, yet the Carlist party are exerting themselves with so much assiduity and vigour to up-set the throne of Queen Isabella, that the military interference will probably take place. What then, will you say, will the Three Powers do? They will look on quietly, will not only not oppose, but perhaps inwardly applaud the measure; and these are our reasons:—'It will occupy at least 100,000 men; it will cost a serious sum of money,' which will have the double effect of preventing France from interfering with us, while it must inevitably weaken her and impair her financial resources at home. We all know what a war in Spain really is. It is not like an invasion of Belgium, where you may march in and fix the day of your return.

"Let the French troops go into Spain on a revolutionary errand, and become well mixed up with the clashing party spirits of that country, who then shall say when and how they will be able to tirer leurépingle du jeu? Napoleon might date his fall from that rash undertaking, why not another individual who has not one-tenth of his resources?

"As to the observation of England and France united destroying the commerce of Europe in the event of war, it would be setting fire to a neighbour's house, which must communicate destruction to your own. The United States would become first the carrier and then the mistress of the world."

Nothing can equal the veneration which Pozzo di Borgo professes for the character of the Duke, and the anxiety to learn his sentiments on all political subjects, which he said would have the greatest weight with the Russian cabinet; but recollecting, as I do, the feeling which prevailed in Petersburg in 1829 on the subject of his Grace's policy at that period, when he stopped their march to Constantinople, and the bitterness then expressed against him, I must rather impute the present change to a sense of impending danger from the state of Europe, and a wish to gain partisans in any quarter that may be useful. Their intrigues in London were directed against the Duke prior to Canning's administration. They assisted *then* in giving the *first* check to *his power,* and in laying the first stone of *that* bridge over which, aided by unforeseen circumstances, another party has since stepped into office; whose influence, opposed as it is to their own, they will have double cause to rue, from the conviction that they may have, though unwittingly, contributed to raise it, and are now utterly powerless to overthrow it.

Saturday, 16*th.*—This villa [Le Chenil-Marly], belonging to General Sir A. Mackenzie, was formerly the residence of the Grand Venuer of the kings of France, when the palace of Marly was the scene of much splendour, in the reigns of Louis XIV. and XV. The park and the domain of the old palace still form a striking feature in the country, but every vestige of the buildings was destroyed at the time of the Revolution. One magnificent *abreuvoir,* as it is now called, but which, in those days, was a fine *jet d' eau* in the royal gardens, is at the gate of these grounds, and seems alone to have survived the desolating hand of the "*sans culottes*" and the "*bande noire*" Summary vengeance, indeed, was taken by the mob on these scenes of royal luxury and prodigality, whose neighbourhood still recals to the mind some anecdotes in the Memoirs of St. Simon or Dangeau. It is two leagues from Versailles and one from St. Germains, with the Seine winding below, through a beautiful country studded with châteaux, villages, and campagnes. The drive from Paris may be accomplished in two hours.

I met to-day a French officer who had served in the campaigns of Napoleon, and related many little traits of his character, and anecdotes which proved how completely he knew the way to rouse the enthusiasm of the French soldier. On the morning of the battle of Leipsic Napoleon advanced to harangue the whole line. He addressed himself first to the Saxon and other German auxiliaries, who still remained with him, in a speech that lasted twenty minutes, translated to them by an interpreter, in which every argument was used to excite their ardour and animate their courage; but it was evident with little effect, as they seemed to listen without much interest. Piqued at this result, and at the failure of his eloquence, he galloped up to the French line, who were waiting his arrival. His only words were, "Français, je n'ai rien à vous dire, vous avez juré de vaincre ou de mourir, faites votre devoir;" and the air resounded with acclamations of ***vive l'empereur*** from thousands who were ready to die in his cause—a cause which had already sent so many millions in the other world.

Monday, 18*th*.—I was amused by hearing an account of the balls now given by Louis-Philippe, at the Tuileries, which are very splendid as to decorations, but not very select as to company. In order to gain popularity a certain number of tickets are sent to each of the ten legions of the National Guard. Great part of the society is, therefore, composed of the shopkeepers of Paris, who, even in this scene of festivity, do not lose sight of their own interest It is said that a lady happened to complain the other night that her shoe pinched her, when her partner immediately presented his card of address as ***cordonnier du roi,*** and offered to wait upon her the next morning.

There was a grand review the other day at Paris, and it must be allowed that the French troops are very much improved in appearance within the last twelve-month. Their cavalry is not so well mounted as ours, but the regiments of infantry were composed of good-looking young men, generally short in stature, but active, well disciplined, and all seemed animated by a good spirit, and cheerful.

Wednesday, 20*th.*—I went to Paris, and dined with J. King. It appears that a division exists in this cabinet as to the military intervention in Spain. It is advocated by Marshal Soult and Thiers, but opposed by the Duc de Broglie, who is apprehensive of the consequences; owing perhaps to the readiness with which the Three Powers have seemed to accede to the measure. It is now generally known that, when the subject was proposed to them by France, their answer was, "You may do as you please." At the same time this permission has been coupled with a decided notice that *arrive qui voudra,* they will not suffer another military interference in Belgium. I understand, likewise, that one or two other points have been stated, on which they have now made up their minds—to declare war in case France should attempt to go counter to their wishes. They are united and agreed in their policy, and the period is arrived when they mean to make a stand. The reference to Belgium at such a moment is worthy of remark, and, as the King of Holland still shows no disposition to come to a final accommodation with Leopold, should he once see the French armies well entangled in a Spanish war, he will probably avail himself of that opportunity to create a ferment and revive his claim on his lost provinces.

My letters from England are gloomy; both parties seem apprehensive of a crisis. F. Byng said to Cooke, "The Tories have brought to pass all that may happen; we have merely delayed it" The cabinet is divided on one question among themselves,—Shall Lord Durham come into power again? shall E. Ellice have a seat in the cabinet? They have decided not to touch the Corn laws or the malt tax, but who shall say they have the power to maintain their decision?

Sunday, 24*th.*—Received this morning from C——the Duke's opinion on my communication of the interview with Pozzo on the 13th. He writes thus to C—:—

"Strathfieldsaye, 20th November.

"I return the enclosed which is very curious.

"You recollect what I told you about Spain. The truth is, that the war in Spain suits nobody. It is weakness to France. Louis-Philippe will not engage in it if he can avoid it. The moment he does the Continent are more than a match for him, even with England on his side. But I think that Pozzo has left one element out of his calculation, that is Portugal.

"In Napoleon's time Portugal was not only sound, but, with our assistance, formidable. It was the basis on which the machinery was founded which finally overturned the world. Portugal is now in a state of revolutionary confusion. But wait a moment! We shall presently see the sale of the estates of the church and nobility in Portugal; loans negociated upon that security; revolutionary armies raised in England, France, Belgium, and Poland, and paid with that money; and, I fear, the whole Peninsula revolutionised by the aid of these means, and by following this example in Spain. This is the result to which our revolutionary Government is tending!"

Wednesday, 27 *th.*—The park of Marly is an object of curiosity, if only as a record of past magnificence; but the avenues, the drives, the woods, the lakes, the hills, and dales alone have survived the hand of the destroyer. The grand entrance to it was from the Versailles road, and must have been very striking. From the great gate you enter into what was once a vast circular court, the walls of which still in part remain. Here were the barracks and stables of the French king's body-guard; from thence you descend by a straight, broad avenue into the vale, surrounded by woods, where formerly stood the palace; a mere mass of rubbish now alone remains to mark its situation. It consisted of one large pavilion, the offices of which were detached, but so numerous that they extended to a great distance. In the front was a lake containing an island, now choked up with high grass and weeds, but in those days ornamented with ***jets d' eau*** and waterworks. On each side of this lake a triple avenue of lime trees, which was a favourite drive of the old court, and served as a screen to six smaller pavilions on the right, and six on the left, ranged in a straight line, and appropriated to the reception of the court. Here one may stand, amidst heaps of broken stones, and picture to the mind what may have been the scene in the beginning of the last century:—the magnificent apartments, the royal retinue, the sumptuous banquets, the smooth lawns, the gay parterres, and the princes, the ministers, the courtiers; while, on the brow of the hill, the guard, drawn out, salutes the ponderous coach, with eight horses, containing Louis and the Widow Scarron, which rolls down the broad, paved avenue, followed by a clattering train of gorgeous satellites.

Hardly one stone now remains upon another to mark the spot where luxury and splendour held their reign.

Whenever I make my inquiries in the neighbourhood I am pleased to observe a general feeling of regret at the surrounding ruin. Some indeed still exist who witnessed and perhaps assisted in this work of desolation and havoc; but the intoxication is passed, the resentment against the aristocracy of the land has subsided, and the national pride now regrets the lost monuments of former grandeur which revolutionary madness has levelled with the dust as a froward child cries for a toy which a fit of passion has destroyed. Would that England at her present crisis could take warning from her neighbours, and reflect for one instant in this her ardour for constitutional innovation and destruction, that a time may come, and that not very distant, when she may rue with bitter tears "the ruin it has left behind."

Friday, 29*th.*—The English papers announce that Mr. Daniel O'Connell has recommenced his system of agitation in Ireland since the recess, to enforce the repeal of the Union. The following character of him appears in the Post: "There is one man in Ireland whom neither Whig nor Tory loves or esteems or trusts. Gifted with powerful talents, he has almost made us forget his talents in the profligacy with which they have been exerted. Possessing extensive influence, he has employed that influence in fomenting the mischief which it ought to have been used to allay. He has been successively the rancorous enemy of every administration, the slanderous reviler of every public man. He has made the King and the Parliament by turns odious and contemptible; he has defied their authority, and derided their indulgence. He has invented a legal resistance to the law, and organised a system of anarchy. From him the noon-day assassin and the midnight incendiary derive, if not their guilt, at least their impunity. Professing patriotism, he has made patriotism a profit to himself; professing religion, he has made religion a curse to his country. To receive praise from him is degradation; to covet support from him is guilt. Strongly as we express ourselves, we write only what all honest men know and feel. Upon the principles and the purposes of the man we describe there is no difference of opinion. Censure is unvaried by one phrase of apology; detestation is unanimous. Lord Grey condemns with the Duke of Wellington, and Mr. Stanley denounces with Sir Robert Peel.

"This man, who, if he cannot be visited with judicial vengeance, ought at least to be distinguished with moral reprobation, the Whigs have courted ever since their accession to office with a laborious sycophancy which would have been despicable even if it *had not failed*. Promotion is offered to his ambition, and pay to his cupidity; the loyal are affronted at his bidding, and the guilty are pardoned at his intercession; Lord Grey sues for his assistance, and Mr. Littleton invites him to his table.

"When we see the offers made which have been rejected, the compliments paid which have been mocked, the favours granted which have been scorned,—when we find noble lords and right honourable gentlemen labouring to persuade into virtue, or to conciliate into forbearance one of whose tried depravity they judge as we judge, and speak as we speak,—we despair of experience, and think that history has been written in vain."

Saturday, 30*th.*—Was in Paris, and saw Pozzo. Notwithstanding the gasconade of entering Spain, this Government becomes apprehensive of the consequences, and is no longer anxious to interfere. Affairs in that country are taking an unfavourable turn for the Legitimist party. M. de Cruz has been dismissed, and the fall of M. Zea seems probable. The exertions of Don Carlos seem paralysed; he is living the life of a monk, and his followers are disheartened. Many of the nobility have been made captains-general of the provinces by the queen; which, being offices of considerable power and emolument, have secured their allegiance to the new order of things. Saw Lord Granville, who says Durham is expected here; he, therefore, is not returning to office.

The other day we drove over to Versailles. Here are again all the scenes of St. Simon's reminiscences, and here is, as it were, the history of the last three monarchs previous to the revolution in 1789.

This palace was the seat of their grandeur, the scene of their pleasures, and the witness of the downfal of their race. Here fortune smiled on the long and splendid reign of Louis XIV.; here the *parc aux cerfs* and Madame du Barry stigmatised the luxurious reign of his successor; and from hence the unfortunate Louis XVI. was hurried away by a relentless mob to pay the forfeit of his life on a scaffold for the prodigalities and faults of his predecessors.

While I was still in the great court before the palace, a bystander, who remembered and seemed to regret the splendour of former days,—probably an inhabitant who had been ruined by the departure of the court,—told me that he had stood on that very spot the day of the first convocation des États généraux. Early in the morning all the princes of the blood were assembled round the king, and in that court he had seen thirty-six carriages, each with eight horses, waiting for their respective owners.

Under the present régime *Versailles has been found to require an establishment too expensive for a* Roi citoyen; it is, therefore, now in contemplation to convert this pile of building into a suite of museums for works of art and antiquity, which it is thought, by attracting an influx of curious strangers, may in some measure indemnify the inhabitants for the loss of a royal residence.

Tuesday, 3rd December.—On the 29th ultimo died, at Brighton, the Marquis of Funchal, while on a special mission from Don Pedro and now from Donna Maria to the court of London. He was seventy-five years old; had passed many years in England formerly as Portuguese minister, where his grotesque little figure and animated manner had made him very notorious in society. He was then succeeded in his functions by the younger Count Souza, now Count Villa-real, who since the revolution has taken as decided a part for Donna Maria, but opposed to Pedro.

Wednesday, *4th.*—To those who persist in holding out the hope that our Whig government will obtain a commercial treaty from France, in return for the concessions already made by them to French commerce, and the promotion of free trade principles, the following article in the-papers this morning may show the fallacy of their opinion:—

"The councils general of agriculture, manufactures, and commerce assembled together yesterday for the opening of their sittings by the minister of commerce. M. D'Arblay, in defending the agricultural interests, having expressed a hope that the government would not enter into any treaties with other countries which might prove ruinous to those interests, the minister of commerce declared that no engagements whatever had been entered into with any foreign country, and that the councils and chambers were at full liberty to stipulate for the interests of France in such manner as should be most suitable to their views. He added that neither his journey to England nor the tours of Dr. Bowring and Mr. Villiers on the continent had led to any conclusion whatever."

Monday, *9th.*—We went to Paris for a few days, at the Hôtel Bristol, and found several friends. The only political news from England is, that a serious misunderstanding exists between our cabinet and Russia: the latter holds high language, even warlike, and Lord Palmerston finds he dares not hector in the Turkish as he did in the Belgian affair.

Tuesday, *17th.*—Mr. Hume, M. P., has been here: he fell into the society of the *journalistes,* and is gone away to England with the impression that the present order of things cannot last. He was to have been presented by Lord Granville, but was obliged to leave Paris the day preceding. Louis-Philippe, who had seen the list, was disappointed, and said, "Où est Mr. Hume?" He wished to have got a word said for him in the House of Commons. The trial of Raspail and his associates, ***les amis des droits de l'homme,*** is going on daily, with little prospect of a verdict against them: they have much more wit and talent than their accusers, and treat the king's advocate with great levity. This government will not take lesson from past acquittals, and still persists in these frivolous accusations which only turn to their own disparagement.

Talleyrand set off on Monday night, to resume his post at the English court. The papers say he had an interview of six hours previously with Louis-Philippe.

The weather all this week uncommonly tempestuous, and interrupting the communication with England.

Paris, Hôtel de Breteuil, Rue Rivoli.

Sunday, 22*nd.*—The trial finished to-day, with the acquittal of all the prisoners. The president made some severe animadversions on the counsel for the accused, and proposed to take down the words of M. Dupont as treasonable; upon which all the other advocates, twenty-five in number, rose up and desired that the words might be registered also as the opinions of all. The court broke up in some confusion.

Monday, 23*rd.*—The king went, **but with no state,** to open the chambers. There was no crowd in the streets, nor any demonstration of interest. The speech said nothing.

Tuesday, January 7*th.*—"Bertrand and Raton," at the Théâtre Français, which everybody goes to see, is a play by Scribe, alluding to the late revolution, and full of point The character of Talleyrand is drawn with humour, and his impassible manner is well represented by Samson; the position of Laffitte, as Raton, employed as a tool and gaining no advantage from his exertions, is described with some *finesse*.

Wednesday, 8*th.*—The club here, in the Rue de Grammont, is established on the same footing as those in London, with the exception that no games of chance are permitted. The society is composed of half French and half foreigners, but in attendance the latter predominate.

Thursday, 9th.—There was a grand ball last night at the Tuileries; near 4000 persons were present, the apartments were splendidly illuminated, and the supper very magnificent. To give an idea of the company, Yarmouth said that he called in the morning on his coachmaker, to desire that his carriage, which required some little repair, might be ready at night, as he was going to the ball. The coachmaker said, "That puts me in mind that I am also invited, and I must get my own carriage ready likewise."

Saturday, 11th.—Stratford Canning has resigned his post as ambassador to St. Peterburg. Russia stood firm and would not receive him, and Lord Palmerston has been obliged to bow to the will of the autocrat.

A pert note given in by the French chargé d' affaires at St. Petersburg to Count Nesselrode, on the subject of the Turkish treaty with Russia, has received a most decided answer, which, after repelling the right of any other power to interfere in the matter, concludes thus:—"It is under this conviction, and guided by the most pure and disinterested intentions, that His Majesty the Emperor is resolved, the case occurring, faithfully to fulfil the obligations which the treaty imposes on him," acting thus, as if the declarations contained in the note of M. Lagrenée did not exist.

Wednesday 15th.—I called this morning at the Hôtel du Rhin, Place Vendôme, to inquire after Lady Lyndhurst [Note *: Lady L. early in life was married to a Colonel Thomas, who was killed at Waterloo,] who has been dangerously ill for the last three days. The reply was, that the case had become desperate, and the physicians had prescribed morphine as a last resource. At four o'clock this day, after much suffering, she died.

The civil war in Spain is raging with great violence, and the Carlist party is rising in the scale. Their partisans are becoming so numerous and so powerful, that the Cabinet messengers cannot proceed on the public roads without strong military escorts, which in some instances have been unable to preserve them from violence, and their despatches from plunder.

Lord Grenville is dead, after a long lingering illness; his place of Auditor of the Exchequer is given to Lord Auckland *pro tempore,* and, it is said, without salary, till some new arrangements are made in that office. Earl Grey has given his son, Lord Howick, the place of Under Secretary for the Home Department, *vice* George Lamb, deceased.

Monday, 20*th.*—Letters from England. The Ministers have been on the totter: serious differences arose in the Cabinet, on the question of sending troops to Portugal to assist Don Pedro, and Lord Grey, who was opposed to the measure, was left in the minority. He went down to Brighton to consult the King, who sent him back with orders to arrange the matter with his colleagues, as no troops should be sent. The Whig emissaries at the clubs now disclaim, on the part of their principals, any intentions of the sort.

The Duke of Wellington, it is thought, will be Chancellor of Oxford, in the room of Lord Grenville.

Tuesday, 21*st.*—Zea Bermudez, the Spanish minister, is dismissed by the queen, and Martinez della Rosa appointed in his place.

Thursday, 23*rd.*—The Duke of Orleans gave a ball on Sunday night at the Tuilleries, at which the English ladies declined going on account of the day; but, as some of their husbands accepted the invitation, the question was naturally asked, What is the English religion, which forbids the women and permits the men to go to balls on a Sunday?

Wednesday, 29*th* .—This day a duel took place, in the Bois de Boulogne, between General Bugeaud and M. Dulong, members of the Chamber of Deputies, in consequence of a dispute arising out of the debate on Saturday, on the limits of military obedience. The parties were placed at forty paces. They were advancing and taking aim at each other, but had scarcely moved two paces, when General Bugeaud fired, and M. Dulong fell. The ball entered the forehead a little above the left eyebrow, and remained in the head. He was still living at midnight, but unable to speak.

Thursday, 30*th.*—M. Dulong died this morning at six o'clock, and the funeral takes place on Saturday. There is some idea that the Liberals will make an attempt to disturb the public tranquillity.

Saturday, February 1st—The funeral of M. Dulong took place without any disturbance, as 20,000 men were under arms, and cannon placed in different quarters of the town. The cortége itself was followed by troops, and two pieces of artillery with matches lighted—such are the precautions of a Citizen King.

Sunday, 2*nd.*—The Due de Mouchy was seized last night with an apoplectic and paralytic fit, and lies in the utmost danger. He was formerly well known in England, before the first revolution, as Charles de Noailles.

Monday, 3*rd.*—The Due de Mouchy is dead; and the papers mention that my old friend Mrs. Orby Hunter died in Grosvenor Place on Thursday last.

Thursday, 6th.—The King's speech arrived, as Parliament opened on the 4th. It is not otherwise important than as it betrays an evident wish, on the part of Government, to stop in their revolutionary course.

Tuesday, 11*th.*—Being *Mardi gras,* and the conclusion of the Carnival, the whole town was in movement; the Boulevards and principal streets were crowded with carriages; and processions in masques,—that of the bœuf gras attracted the chief attention.

Wednesday, 12*th.*—M. de Bourrienne, ex-minister of the Emperor Napoleon at Hamburg, and author of the Memoirs which bear his name, died on the 7th inst of apoplexy at Caen, in Normandy. The loss of his fortune and the revolution of July deprived him of his reason, and the latter part of his life was spent in a maison de santé.

Thursday, 13*th.*—Count Kergolay and M. Dieudé, the responsible editor of the ***Quotidienne,*** were tried this day before the Court of Assize for libels on the Government of Louis-Philippe, and expressions of devotion to Henri V. M. D'Aglées, substitute for the Procureur du Roi, concluded his speech for the prosecution with the following appeal to the jury:—"If you deliver a verdict for acquittal, you will have thrown the elements of disorder and anarchy into society." The jury retired, and, after an hour's deliberation, pronounced a verdict of "Not guilty," in favour of both the accused.

Monday, 24*th.*—We hear that last week the English Ministry had only a majority of eight on the division about the Pension List, in which they reckon fifty Tory votes, who sided with them to preserve the King's prerogative; and on O'Connell's motion to arraign Baron Smith (which in their mean, truckling spirit they supported), they were left in a minority of six.

Auteuil.

Tuesday, 25*th.*—The peculiar state of this government, and the position of Louis-Philippe, are very obvious to all. Heaven knows if they will last, but both are unnatural, and grounded on false principles; both are highly unpopular, because they seek for their support in resources which are essentially unnational, and opposed to all the principles which caused the revolution of July, to which they themselves owe their existence. There exists in no country in Europe a government so little respected abroad, or a king so little respected at home, as is the case in France at the present moment. The government of the *juste milieu* only ventures to act openly, when sure of the connivance or approbation of England to their foreign policy; Louis-Philippe only trusts a garrison of 60,000 men near Paris, to gradually undermine the liberties of the nation. Strange as it may appear, and anomalous in the extreme, the one, with the high-sounding watchword of liberal principles, would gladly, if it dared, join with the Holy Alliance; and the other, with liberty and the charter in his mouth, would go any lengths, as far as his own safety would permit, to establish a military despotism. But public discontent is a warning to which both must lend an unwilling ear. At this present moment, under the reign of the Citizen King, above 100,000 troops are occupied to keep in awe only three cities in this kingdom, Paris, Marseilles, and Lyons.

Here indeed it seems the policy, when pretexts are wanting, to create artificial excuses for additional rigour. The town has been infested for the last six weeks with wretched itinerant vendors of the most disgusting trash, and abuse against the royal family,—the lowest species of caricatures. I have watched them in the street; no one noticed them, none purchased their wares: it seemed indeed a most unprofitable trade; but still it was continued, without check on the one side, or encouragement on the other. I at last expressed my surprise to a friend at their impunity. "Oh," said he, "it is an *attrape;* they are agents paid by the police, to sound the feelings of the multitude." In a week afterwards came out a bill of the most sweeping nature against the public criers, interdicting them from selling even the public journals. Since that has appeared an *ordonnance* requiring the theatres to close their doors at eleven o'clock, which has been treated with contempt; and yesterday was brought into the Chambers a most arbitrary law against associations of every description, on which the *National* makes the following remark:—"The law which shall destroy open associations, will found secret ones. Every political association will henceforth have subversion for its aim: it will conceal its existence only to march more resolutely and surely to its end."

There have been some trifling appearances of discontent shown by the people on the Boulevards and on the Place de la Bourse; but the military are always on the alert, and the sober *bourgeois* who thinks only of preserving his shop from pillage dreads a *mouvement*.

Wednesday, 5th March.—The meetings on the Place de la Bourse have been put down with much severity, and several people have been wounded by bludgeon men employed by government, just as it happened with our policemen in Coldbath Fields. It is singular to observe how events in the two countries respond to each other. M. Salverte made a motion in the Chamber of Deputies to investigate the conduct of ministers on this occasion, but it was overruled.

Sunday, 9th.—There is a club established here [Note *: Le Cercle, Rue de Grammont.], on the same footing as White's or Brookes's, where the dinners are moderate as to price and quality. One half of the members are foreigners, chiefly English; and now that the ballot is general, the admissions are become difficult; but the French character does not seem formed for such establishments. Whenever a general meeting of the club is called to frame any new resolution, the noise and clamour preclude all rational discussion: political feeling interferes likewise too much at these meetings, and prevents either party from introducing their friends. The chief advantages of living here are, that the climate is better, the living is cheaper, and you may regulate your expenses on any scale you please without remark or reference to your neighbours, which we all feel in England is hardly practicable.

Tuesday, 11th.—Mr. Hume's long expected motion for the repeal of the Corn Laws was rejected on Friday (7th) by a majority of 157, being 312 to 155. The most curious incident in the debate was, that two members of the Government, Sir James Graham and Poulett Thomson, were violently opposed to each other on the subject; and the latter was not a little personal in his attacks on his colleague.

Sunday, 16th.—While sitting with Lady Julia L——, the Prince de Bauffremont came in, who had lately heard from Naples, that Lady Strachan had bought a palace in that city, and the patent of a title of Marchesa Salza; and that she was married to an Italian named Piccalillo.

The conversation turned to the frequency of poisonings in Italy. M. de B. said, that he last year remarked to a certain Cardinal at Rome, how much fewer assassinations were heard of now than formerly. His Eminence replied, "Oui; il est vrai que le chocolat noir a fait éviter de grands scandales dans les familles."

Monday, 17th.—Two remarkable divisions have just taken place in our House of Commons: a Mr. Cuthbert Ripon moved that the archbishops and bishops should be deprived of their seats in the House of Lords, which was negatived by 125 against 58, neither the Government nor the Tories taking any share in the debate. This minority may still be considered formidable. The other motion was by Major Fancourt to abolish flogging in the army; negatived by 227 *versus* 98.

A commercial treaty has been made between Russia and the United States. This circumstance, combined with the new commercial regulations organising in Russia and Austria, and the secret negotiations now pending in the Congress at Vienna, corresponds perfectly with the confidential avowal made to me in October last by P. de B. of the retaliations meditated by the Three Powers against England, in the point where she would be the most vulnerable. The foreign policy of our Government has gained us many bitter enemies, and at best only one very doubtful friend. All will be unveiled at last; but Louis-Philippe, who in the hour of danger clung to England for protection to maintain him on his throne, could he now see an opportunity of identifying himself with the hostile system, and consolidating his royalty by a closer union with the Holy Alliance monarchs, would be restrained by no ties of gratitude from leaving us to struggle alone against the machinations of combined Europe; nay, more, would have little hesitation in joining their ranks against us.

Tuesday, 18*th.*—The French and English newspapers present another instance of the similarity which exists at present between the two countries in this new æra of intellect. They are each entirely filled with the debates in the Commons and Deputies, while a very small space is allotted to the proceedings of the Peers, who seem only to meet and separate, in order that the world may know that they still exist. In England the Peers are gradually losing their legislative influence; but their great wealth, and local influence in the country, will maintain their preeminence in every crisis short of a sweeping revolution. Their brethren here are in a very different position; exhæreditated by the law, and impoverished by various circumstances, they are become mere cyphers in the State, neither objects of respect nor of regard; and what is the result? They have only made way for the upstart aristocracy of wealth, the most unworthy of all distinctions, which has not failed to produce in France its natural consequence,—a *general* and debasing system of selfishness and egotism throughout the country. It matters not who they are, or whence they come,—Jew, Prussian, or Spaniard, Rothschild, Delmar, or Aguado, loan-monger, stock-jobber, or cigar-merchant, it is all one,—their *salons* will be filled with the highest society in Paris, and their smiles courted by the most illustrious sycophants.

"Dat census honores, census amicitias, pauper ubique jacet."

Tuesday, *25th.*—The bill against associations was carried in the French Chamber of Deputies. Mr. Shiel has lately attacked the Government, in our House of Commons, on their foreign policy with regard to Turkey and Russia. Lord Palmerston made a very long defence, resting chiefly on the good understanding which he had maintained with France. The "Standard" makes the following observation:—"Lord Palmerston has but one answer for everything that could be said against the foreign policy of the Government—The French Alliance. True, Russia had obtained full possession of the remnant of the Turkish empire, but then King William and Louis-Philippe are on the best possible terms! True, France had obtained Belgium; true, the French government had converted Egypt, their so long coveted object, into a French province; true, France had laid the foundation of a colonial empire at Algiers; true, France had drawn upon Great Britain the hatred of all the rest of Europe, the most anxious desire for our destruction; true, that if France were to-morrow to propose a combined attack upon England, the ruin of her trade, and the partition of her colonies, all the powers of Europe would most cheerfully attend the feast; but, then, King William and Louis-Philippe are on the best possible terms! Now, this is all very well; but the best things may sometimes be bought too dear, and they are always bought too dear, if they might be had for less than we pay for them. Could we not have had the friendship of France, without surrendering to her Belgium, Egypt, and Algiers; without making it the interest of all Europe to give Turkey to Russia; without drawing upon ourselves the hatred of the whole European family; and without surrendering our own national independence, as we have done?

Friday, *28th.*—Longchamps. An annual procession of carriages from Paris to the Bois de Boulogne, in which the hackney carriages were by far the most numerous.

Sunday, *30th.*—In talking to Ellice after dinner, I told him that our foreign policy was much abused, that we were hated all over Europe, and that his friends the ***doctrinaires*** here would not stand by the Whig Government in England longer than it suited them. I was surprised to find that he did not absolutely deny this. He replied, "*We do not care;* England is powerful enough, and strong enough to stand against them all." I merely rejoined, "You remember the fate of *don't care*."

When he remarked that England never was so flourishing, or the Government so strong, I said, the trial was beginning now; that they evidently wished to *stop*. His reply was, the Government never will *stop*.

Durham is here, in constant communication with M. Thiers on the old topic of a commercial treaty; but there seems little chance of his succeeding better than P. Thomson, Villiers, Bowring and all that party. The prejudice is far too strong against it here.

Tuesday, 1*st April.*—The Chamber of Deputies rejected the proposal of ministers to grant twenty-five millions as an indemnity to the United States for claims during the Empire.

Wednesday, 2*nd.*—In consequence of this defeat, the Due de Broglie and General Sebastiani have resigned their seats in the ministry.

Thursday, 3*rd.*—The very un-Gallican spectacle of a steeple-chase took place in the Vallée dc Biévre, near Jouy. There was as much scrambling and as many falls as might be expected amongst so many novices in such an amusement, and all, generally, very bad horsemen. The race was won by M. de Vaublanc. In the evening, at the opera, some discussion took place amongst themselves, as to the merits of the riders, when M. Manuel observed, that the winner was more indebted to chance than to his skill in riding for success. This immediately produced a personal quarrel on the spot with M. de Vaublanc. A challenge ensued; the next morning M. Manuel was run through the body for making the unlucky observation.

Sunday, 6*th.*—The French ministry is made up by putting Admiral de Rigny in the place of M. de Broglie, and by some other changes. Durham and Ellice went yesterday, under the guidance of the celebrated Vidocq, to see all the prisons in Paris. To show them the process of the guillotine, he had a mannequin of straw beheaded in their presence. Ellice said, "I hope the Tory prints won't get hold of this; they will assert that we are going to introduce the guillotine into England, and are come over here to take a lesson." They both seemed pleased with their journey, and are very good-humoured.

Tuesday, 8th.—There have been riots at Brussels during two days, and much damage done by the mob. A stud of horses which belonged to the Prince of Orange, at Tervuyren, was confiscated, and ordered to be sold by public auction. Some of the Flemish nobility, still attached to that family, and struck by the injustice of the proceeding, had subscribed to purchase the horses, and return them to their rightful owner. This, perhaps indiscreet, determination got wind, and the houses of the authors were immediately singled out for pillage and destruction.

Those of the Prince de Ligne, Marquis de Trasignies, Counts d'Oultremont, de Bethune, de Vinck, de Wert, Wezel, M. de Wusme, and Weerszaels, with many others, were nearly destroyed. The tumult was at last suppressed by the interference of the military; but might with ease have been entirely prevented, if the government had not, for some time, looked on with apathy, perhaps with satisfaction, at proceedings which inflicted such signal vengeance on their own political opponents,—an example which had been previously shown them by Lord Grey's government, during the Bristol riots.

Thursday, 10th.—Fresh disturbances have broken out at Lyons among the workmen, who, under the name of *Mutuelistes,* form the same bands as the trades' unions with us. The town is completely occupied by the military.

Saturday, 12th.—The accounts from Lyons are alarming; and the explanations given by the ministers in the Chamber of Deputies very unsatisfactory. The fighting in the streets with the military force had not ceased up to Thursday night. The rioters had retired into the narrow lanes; and General Aymon had taken up a position which he called *inexpugnable* but is not quite *intelligible*. There is much apprehension of some movement here, and the troops are on the alert.

Sunday, 13*th.*—Force has prevailed; and, after a bloody resistance, the workmen at Lyons seem to have been vanquished. Last night the *rappel* was beating in every quarter of Paris. Some trifling skirmishing took place in the street, and above one hundred *suspects* were privately arrested by the armed force.

Monday, 14th.—Early this morning the rioters were in full conflict with the armed force. Barricades were erected in the small streets near the Rue du Temple and St. Martin. A great carnage ensued. Two or three shots were fired at the Duke of Orleans, as he rode by with his staff; the troops immediately rushed into the houses from whence the attempts were made, and put all the inhabitants indiscriminately to the sword In a few hours all was still: 30,000 troops and 50,000 National Guards soon exterminated the mob; but some officers and men were killed. In the evening, Paris was as gay and as thoughtless as ever.

Wednesday, 16*th.*—The fighting at Lyons continued till Monday night, and several thousand lives have been lost. The following curious fact appears in this day's journal:—"M. Marchand du Breuil, prefect of the Ain, came lately to Paris, and was on the point of being married. On Sunday he accompanied his brother, who is captain of the 2nd battalion of the 11th Legion, to the scene of action, and returned safe; but on Monday morning, as he was hastening to quit his apartment, in order to enter the carriage which was to convey him to the mayoralty with his intended bride, he stumbled against a piece of furniture, and threw down his musket, which he had left there loaded the day before. The piece went off, the contents entered his body, and he expired instantly.

Wednesday, 16*th.*—I dined at Glengall's; met Madame de Flahault, Mrs. Damer, Lady Hunloke, Montrond, Stanley, Sheridan, de St. Marsan, and Lord Francis Egerton. Talking about riots, the latter said, that, some time back, during the struggle between the Whigs and Tories, a mob broke into Downing Street, and approached the sentinel posted at the door of the Foreign Office, crying, "Liberty or Death!" The soldier presented his piece, and said, "My lads, I know nothing about liberty; but if you come a step further, I'll show you what death is."

The Dowager Marchioness of Hertford [Note *: Daughter of Lord Irwin, of Temple Newsam, Yorkshire, sister to Lady William Gordon, Mrs. Meynell Ingram, Mrs. Hervey Aston, and Lady Bamsden, all great heiresses.] is dead. She was married to the late Marquis, 1776,—a well-known beauty in her time, and possessed of vast wealth, which, with the estate at Temple Newsam, reverts to her own family.

Friday, 18*th.*—Durham and Ellice left Paris for London, having given up the plan of going to Brussels.

Saturday, 19*th.*—M. de Fitz-James, son of the duke, has been sentenced to three months' imprisonment, for some childish Carlist demonstrations at Rouen some time ago. He had been acquitted, but the sentence was changed by an appeal to the Cour de Cassation.

Few or no Carlists have been arrested during the late riots. The movement was entirely Republican, and so sudden, that the other party had not time to join them, though it is believed that they furnished money. One Carlist was searched, and epaulettes were found in his pocket. He owned, that if the rising had been deferred only fourteen days, he should have had 10,000 men under his command.

Thursday, 24*th.*—The procession of the Trades' Unions, with a petition on behalf of the Dorchester convicts, to the Home Office, passed off quietly. Much praise is due on both sides;—to the great masses, who conducted themselves with so much order and decorum to the Government, who, well prepared to maintain the public peace, still avoided any irritating display of precautionary force on the occasion. What a contrast, and, indeed, what a satire on the proceedings here. There is something awful in these great assemblages, which seem to have kept London for twelve hours in a state of much anxiety; even their discipline and order bespeak a more formidable resolution and unity of purpose than the efforts of a lawless mob. Lord Althorpe may now begin to find his mistake.

Wednesday, 30*th.*—Lord Wenlock, late Sir R. Lawley, one of the Peers in 1831, died on the 10th July, in the neighbourhood of Florence, without issue.

Paris as a city and as a capital is certainly far superior to London. There is an air of ancient grandeur in the monuments, the palaces, the hotels of the nobility, the long avenues, and the spacious quays, the gardens, and the statues, which must strike every foreigner with admiration, and some with subject for reflection. *Tout est en grand,* and fallen as the nation is from its former aristocratic splendour, the *locale* still remains a sturdy testimony of former magnificence. Paris is now the reverse of the Castle of Otranto,—it is the abode of giants inhabited by pigmies. I do not mean to say that the positive situation of the country is not improved: that, as thinking and independent beings, the French nation generally has not advanced in the scale of rational existence, since the Revolution of 1789, but Paris itself was adorned and beautified with other views, and for another race. It has risen at the nod of monarchs, mighty and despotic, of a nobility wealthy, prodigal, and luxurious. Times are now altered; that system of government is destroyed, and the fortunes of its satellites are scattered to the winds. The privileges of the few are dissolved, and the rights of the many are established; but Paris and Versailles will long tell the tale of fallen grandeur, and the taste of that æra which Louis XIV. has made his own, and which, under the levelling circumstances of the present day, can never rise again.

Thursday, 1*st May.*—Madame Walewski died yesterday morning, having never recovered from her late *accouchement* She was surrounded by her family, as Lady Sandwich, her mother, Mr. and Lady Harriet Baring, and Lord Sandwich, are all in Paris.

A discussion has been going on for several days in the Chamber of Deputies, whether the colony of Algiers shall be retained or abandoned. Many disclosures have been made by the Committee of Inquiry, as to the expenses of this new establishment; and, also, as to the flagrant instances of mal-administration of which the French authorities there have been guilty. To the public discussion of these latter disgraceful transactions, Marshal Soult vehemently objected, by citing the homely proverb, "On doit laver son linge sale en famille." The case, as at present, lies in a short compass. The expense is enormous, and hitherto without advantage:

the surrounding population hostile and irreclaimable. In the event of a war, the naval power of England would easily intercept all communication with France; but Polignac promised the British Government to abandon it, and therefore French pride and obstinacy are determined to retain it. The Whigs dare not insist, and the French, as Dr. Franklin used to say, will pay dear for their whistle.

In England the Commons have been occupied with O'Connell's motion for a Repeal of the Union, which has produced a tedious and tiresome debate for several days, and only places the leader in an even more contemptible light than before.

General Goblet was sent by Leopold as his minister to Berlin; but M. Ancillon declared to him, that the King of Prussia would never receive at his court a man who had quitted the service of Holland, without having obtained his dismissal from King William. He therefore returns to Brussels. General Bourmont and Count d'Haussez are now at Rome, and highly esteemed by the Pope, which has excited the indignation of the French ambassador, who addressed a note to Cardinal Bernetti, demanding the expulsion of the two Legitimists. The reply was, that his Holiness considered General Bourmont as having rendered the greatest service to the church by the conquest of Algiers, and had the most sacred claims on his protection. As to Count d'Haussez, the pontifical cabinet replied, that it could not discover any reason why an asylum in the States of the Church should be refused to him. As soon as this step and its results were known, the representatives of almost all the other powers took a malignant pleasure in going with parade to congratulate the two ex-ministers of Charles X. The most singular feature in the occurrence is, that the French ambassador wrote again to Cardinal Bernetti, requesting that he would consider his preceding note as if it had not been written.

Saturday, 3rd.—O'Connell's motion for the repeal has met with a signal discomfiture, by a majority of above 500.

Sunday, 4th.—Went to St. Cloud, to see the waterworks and dine. There were not many visitors, but the park looked well and in good order.

Monday, 5th.—After all the negotiations and discussions at the Belgian Conferences in London, on the necessity of dismantling the frontier fortresses, they prove to be merely a tub thrown out to the whale. The Brussels paper of the 3rd announces, that there is no longer any intention of demolishing them, as contracts have just been entered into for the military repairs of Mons, Charleroy, Philippeville, Marunberry, Namur, Dinant, Arlon, Tournay, and Ath. A quadruple treaty is signed by England, France, and the revolutionary governments of Spain and Portugal, to put down all opposition in the peninsula. It is meant also as a counterpoise to the league of the Northern Powers: their reply to it is not yet known.

On a fresh loan being made by Austria, it may be inferred that the general disarmament in Europe is less probable than ever. France contemplates the same measure to a large amount. This is the great sore of the states of Europe, but particularly here. Governments begin by making themselves unpopular, and then require large armies to protect themselves; and as these large armies occasion great expenditure and heavy taxes, their unpopularity increases. They thus run round in a dangerous circle, till they fall into an abyss.

Friday, 9th.—The Whigs have had a nervous attack again, on D. W. Harvey's motion for the repeal of the pension list, and the old threat of resignation was held out; but Sir R. Peel and the Tories brought them through with a large majority.

Saturday, 10th.—The Duchesse de Berri is arrived at Vienna, and has been received there in the most distinguished manner, apartments being allotted to her in the Imperial Palace. A body of Spanish troops has marched into Portugal, nominally in quest of Don Carlos, but with a view of intimidating the Miguelite party, between whom and the Pedroites the contest is still maintained with great obstinacy, notwithstanding the secret assistance given by France and England to the latter.

Sunday, 11th.—Don Pedro, in return for the protection afforded him by England, has put all the other Powers on the same footing as to duties in Portugal, as we have hitherto been by favour. Mr. Robinson made a motion for papers on the subject, and during the debate Lord Palmerston's foreign policy was stigmatised with weakness and ignorance, in which the feeling of the House generally seemed to concur.

Wednesday, 14***th.***—A duel took place in Paris the other day, under the following circumstances; Madame de C——has a mother, who wished to make a second marriage with Mr. R——, a gentle man of proportionate age, but the step was highly displeasing to the daughter, who determined to prevent it, and in order to effect this object, she instructed all her male friends in society, to abuse and calumniate the character of Mr. R——. Among the foremost in this cabal was her own lover, Mr. de F. This soon excited the attention of the intended bridegroom, who called upon his assailant to say whether he had really uttered such and such atrocities; the only reply was, that he should not take the trouble of giving any explanation, and that the other might act as he pleased. A meeting therefore took place, and the injured party, as often happens, was wounded in the groin, and lies in great danger: that very night the aggressor was dancing in public with his chére amie, having apparently gained stronger claims on her affections and gratitude, by what was, in fact, little better than the conduct of a brigand. This may be called a trait worthy of the Mémoires de Brantome and the times of François Premier.

Thursday 15th.—Lord Burlington is dead in London: he was brother to the late Duke of Devonshire, and a great patron of the turf at Newmarket; he is succeeded by his grandson, Lord Cavendish.

Friday, 16***th.***—The Duke of Richmond is arrived in Paris, to defend his title to the estate of Aubigny in France, against the claims of his family, who consider themselves legally entitled to share it with him, according to the laws of France. This estate was granted by Louis XIV. to Charles II., and to the first Duke of Richmond, natural son of Charles by Madame de Kerouailles, Duchess of Portsmouth, his mistress. The suit involves a considerable interest, the rental of the estate valued at 2000*l.* a year, and a sum of arrears to be refunded of near 30,000*l.*

The trial will shortly come on in the French courts. The following grants have been voted this year to the royal theatres:—

For the Grand Opera	670,000fr.,
and for the pensions of retired artistes	180,000fr.,
making together	34,000*l.*
For the Théâtre Français	8,000*l.*
Opéra Comique	7,200*l.*
Italian Opera	2,800*l.*
	52,000*l.*

Sunday, 18*th.*—A bill for making parliament triennial was only thrown out by a majority of fifty, when 420 members voted in the House. Colonel Caradoc has been sent on a private mission to Spain, it is said to the head-quarters of the Spanish army under Rodil, on the frontiers of Portugal.

Tuesday, 21*st.*—This morning at five o'clock died General Lafayette, aged seventy-seven. His name has been prominent in the defence of liberty, both in the Old and New World; he was a well-meaning man, but his talents were of the second order, and his career through life has been proportionally unimportant.

Thursday, 23*rd.*—The funeral of Lafayette passed off very quietly; the procession was attended by an immense military force, which had more the air of menace to the living than of respect to the dead. He was interred, according to his own request, in the private cemetry of Picpus, which belongs to a very few families of old date. The following are among the names on the tombs:—Françoise de Lamoignon de Malesherbes; Count Ferrand, Lepelletre de Rosambo, De Gourg d'Arcy, the daughter of General d'Eblè, Count d'Escars, Marie-Françoise de Noailles, Due de Levis, Prince de St.-Maurice, and Princesse de la Tremouille.

Friday, 24*th.*—The King has made Miss S. E. Wykham, of Thame Park, a baroness by the title of Baroness Wenman, in token of old recollections. I well remember the time when, as Duke of Clarence, he was anxious to marry an Englishwoman of large fortune, and made his proposals to this lady, as well as to the Wanstead heiress, the late Mrs. Long Pole Wellesley, with the same unsuccessful result. It proves that he does not bear malice for the refusal.

Saturday, 25 *th.*—Went with the Glengalls and Lockwoods to St. Cloud, and returned at night. This château has been a favourite summer residence with many of the different sovereigns who have reigned over this fickle nation. Napoleon was very partial to St. Cloud: Charles X. took his flight from hence to Rambouillet, and then to the sea-coast; Louis-Philippe, though attached by habit to Neuilly, passed here a part of the season, and there is an air of comfort about the apartments which justifies the selection.

Prince P. Esterhazy, the Austrian Ambassador at London, is arrived here on his way to Vienna, and has been received with the most marked attention at the Tuileries; he had a long interview with the King, who, he says, is in heart a most ultra-conservative: so, indeed, was Napoleon at last. In all the newfangled revolutionary ideas and changes of later days, it appears that what is called the people are the only dupes. They are cajoled, and set in motion by specious prospects of advantage to themselves, and find at last that they have gained nothing but a new master, perhaps worse than the last; they are then laid on the shelf till fresh circumstances, or fresh excitement, may require the puppets to act another drama, with precisely the same results for themselves.

After nineteen years' residence as Russian ambassador at our Court, Prince Lieven has been recalled home by his Emperor. Attached as he and the Princess are to English society, customs, and refinements, not only by habit but by taste, a return to such a country as Russia, however honourably they may be greeted by their imperial master, must be intolerable. No foreigner, perhaps, ever before gained such influential footing in our best English society, as the Lievens have acquired, from long residence, large fortune, and an important political post. The gentlemanlike manners and hospitality of the Prince, combined with the talents and grand air of the Princess, rendered their house, not only the resort of the most distinguished society, but the rival of our own most magnificent establishments,—while the Princess, identified with all our English ideas, and occupied with all the passing intrigues of the day, both in politics and society, created for herself an influential position in the *grand monde* which no foreign ambassadress had ever previously enjoyed in this country. She was deeply engaged in all the cabals with Mr. Canning in the year 1827, which ended in the resignation of the Duke, and the shortlived administration of the other. On his Grace's return to office in 1828, she was anxious to regain his friendship, but the breach had been too flagrant ever to be entirely made up again. That event and the death of the Empress-mother, with whom she was long on the most intimate terms of correspondence, latterly very much diminished her political importance in London. Prince Lieven was always very much supposed to act according to her suggestions. She was a great favourite of George IV., who much admired her musical talents, and in those days she was a constant visitor at the cottage in Windsor Park. I have occasionally seen her at the Duke of York's at Oatlands; but that was seldom, as the duchess rarely admitted female society besides the household. Madame de Lieven is a Livonian by birth, and is remarkable for the distinction of her appearance as well as for her general talents. The reason of this recall is not known. She is the only foreigner who was ever made a patroness of Almack's, into the *tracasseries* of which establishment she entered very cordially, and as her manner at times is tinctured with a certain degree of *hauteur,* she has not failed to make many enemies.

Madame de Lieven is, however, in every sense of the word, a trés-grande dame, and has formed friendships and intimacies with the highest persons of all parties in England.

Monday, 27*th.*—The accounts from London of the King are rather extraordinary; his mind appears to be under excitement; every day is occupied with some fresh scheme or party to visit some place or establishment, which generally, as at Sandhurst, concludes with a speech, not always the most appropriate. At the levee a considerable sensation was created the other day by his insisting on an unfortunate lieutenant in the Navy, who had a wooden leg, kneeling down to kiss hands: it was impossible; but the Sovereign would not concede the point, and the other was obliged to hobble away without going through the ceremony.

Tuesday, 28*th.*—We went with the Glengalls to see the cathedral at St. Denis, the burying-place of the kings of France from the earliest ages. The vaults are full of tombs and monuments from the reign of Clovis, which were repaired and preserved in Paris during the Revolution, after they had been broken open and the mortal remains contained in them scattered to the winds; they are now replaced here and classed in order. The principal vault was constructed by Napoleon for his own family, but none were doomed to become its tenants: Louis XVIII. was buried there, and it will be reserved for the present family, if **they remain**. The church itself is a beautiful structure, and the painted windows very fine: the workmen are now occupied in restoring it upon the ancient plan, A chapel called that of Expiation for the Crimes of profaning this Sanctuary of the Dead, during the first Revolution, is also constructed in it.

Another duel took place yesterday morning between M. Damoreau Cinti, husband of the famous singer, and M. Manuel (whose father was killed in a duel twelve years ago), on account of his attentions to the lady: the husband was the victim, and received three severe coups d épée.

Thursday, 29*th.*—More disunions in the Whig cabinet. A motion in the Commons by Mr. Ward, on the established church of Ireland, is bringing their radical feelings to the test; Mr. Stanley and Sir James Graham are averse to the spoliation proposed, and the result of the debate is expected to produce some resignations. The names of the Duke of Richmond, Earl of Ripon, and C. Grant are also mentioned among the dissidents.

Friday, 30*th.*—The resignations are confirmed, and the discussion on Mr. Ward's motion has been postponed to Tuesday evening, at the request of Lord Althorpe: in the meantime, there is much confusion in the cabinet, and indecision as to the new men who are to be called to office.

The Prussian ambassador, M. Arnheim, is about to leave Brussels, under pretext of family affairs, but in reality to obey the laws of etiquette. The Belgian government, dissatisfied at the non-reception of Goblet at Berlin, appears decided to accredit in that capital only a chargé d' affaires. The Prussian cabinet will imitate this example.

Monday, 2nd June.—The English papers are full of the hesitation and difficulties which occur in patching up Lord Grey's cabinet, and the consequent anxiety expressed by the public. The proposed new appointments of Spring Rice to the Colonies, Lord Auckland to the Admiralty, and Ellice to a seat in the cabinet, seem to give general dissatisfaction, while Lord Brougham's manœuvre to exclude Durham, and create unnecessary confusion, prove his secret ambition
"To ride the whirlwind and direct the storm,"

as head of a government of his own creation.

The Conservatives look on in silence and anxiety for the result, while the Radical party is clamorous for men who will promote the movement by which they may ultimately swim to the top. The Whigs must see the gradual accomplishment of those predictions which they have affected to ridicule and despise.

Wednesday, 4*th.*—The Times is very indignant at the omission of Lord Durham, in the new-fangled cabinet, and vindicates Lord Brougham from the suspicion of being accessory to it. In reply to this, the Globe as the Government organ, says, "We may specifically state, that owing to causes connected more with temper than with principle, no member who has been in the cabinet with Lord Durham is disposed to act with him again, and we defy the best informed journal in existence to prove, that in this respect Lord Brougham is of a different opinion from his colleagues."

Thursday, 5*th,*—The ministers have got rid of Mr. Ward's motion, by the old manœuvre of moving the previous question, by which means they secured the votes of 120 Tories, who of two evils chose the least, and gave them a large majority; at the same time they have issued a commission under the King's seal, as a tub to the whale, for the Radical side of the House,—a proceeding which neither quiets the apprehensions and fears of the one party, nor satisfies the clamour and rapacity of the other.

Accounts have been received from Lisbon, stating that Don Miguel and Don Carlos have surrendered at Evora, and are to be embarked on board an English ship for England.

Friday, 6th.—Letters from England mention that on the late division, the Duke and Feel had come to an understanding with Earl Grey, that they would support a moderate Whig government, provided no further innovating measures were proposed, and Durham, Duncannon, and O'Connell still excluded from any share in the Government. An address was got up at Brookes's signed by a number of members of the House of Commons, expressing their confidence in the present administration, and presented to Lord Grey. His lordship's reply, in consequence of the above agreement, was couched in a very conservative sense, and in almost a plaintive tone deprecates, "that constant and active pressure from without, to the adoption of measures, the necessity of which has not been fully proved, and which are not strictly regulated by a careful attention to the settled institutions of the country, both in Church and State," &c. Thus the Whigs now only hold office by the disinterested influence of their Tory opponents, and owe their very existence to the men whom they have never ceased to revile and calumniate. A more humiliating position cannot well be imagined.

Dr. Doyle, the Catholic Bishop of Kildare, is dead. He was one of the Catholic party whom Lord Anglesey tried to propitiate, but in vain.

Monday, 9th.—An interesting debate took place on Friday night in the House of Lords, on the subject of the Irish Church Bill: Earl Wicklow, in moving for the production of the King's commission, accused the Government of wishing to apply the funds of the Church, under moral and religious pretences, to secular purposes. Earl Grey in reply strenuously denied this intention, but urged the necessity of every Government proceeding in conformity with the spirit of the age, which is the present plea for all fresh innovation. Unfortunately for his Lordship, Earl Ripon and the Duke of Richmond, in stating the reasons of their late resignations, asserted, as openly as Sir James Graham and Mr. Stanley had done in the Commons, that in quitting their seats in the cabinet, they had been actuated by no other feeling but that of conscientious opposition to the measure now adopted by the Government, which, notwithstanding the denial of their late colleague, went to nothing less than destroying the principle on which alone the Established Church existed. He further adds, his noble friend has said that it was not safe to rest. He knew, "That it was in difficult times often very difficult to rest; but if they were to act on that principle, they would rest on nothing; they would still go on to rest nowhere. If this were the consequence, was he not justified in saying that he would take on himself to try if they could not rest here? If they did not here, he knew not where the resting place would be. He had no particular desire to avail himself of the compliment that he and his colleagues had been paid in adverting to their having been described as the 'drags' of the Government to which they had belonged; but he might remark that possibly they had been useful 'drags.' He certainly did feel, with regard to the commission, that if he assented to it, the question as to the appropriation of the revenues of the Church to secular purposes was settled."

This evening we drove to Bagatelle, in the Bois de Boulogne. It is another of the royal residences before the Revolution, or, I may rather say, a retreat, as the house consists only of an entrance-hall, an immense and beautiful saloon, with a dining-room on one side and billiard-room on the other, hardly any bed-rooms above, and those very small, low, and confined. It must have been used chiefly as a banqueting-house. The grounds and park, consisting of forty acres, are laid out with great taste, and form a delightful spot An artificial piece of water, supplied by an aqueduct from the neighbouring Seine, flows through majestic rocks, under Chinese bridges, and round constructed islands, till it appears again in the shape of a cascade, which rushes like a cataract from a rocky precipice into the basin beneath. It is quite a fairy scene; and though the house is fast going to decay, the grounds are still kept up in good order. There are some pretty buildings attached to it, as ***vacherie, laiterie,*** stables, and offices of the rustic order, which give it the air of ferme ornée; ***though frequently mentioned in St. Simon, it was repaired and beautified by Charles X., when he was Comte d'Artois; after the restoration, it was a favourite retreat of the Due de Berri, and now belongs to the Due de Bordeaux, though the new*** régime has appropriated it to the State. Two attempts have been made to sell it by auction; but as the land is bad, and the expenses of repairing and keeping up the place would be very great, no buyers appeared at the set-up price of 300,000 fr. The hay has just been sold, this year, on the ground, for 104 fr [Note.*: Bagatelle is now the property of the Marquis of Hertford.]

Wednesday, 11*th.*—The Church Question, and the late debate on it in the Lords, will render the existence of Lord Grey's Government more precarious; but if there be any force in words, the day cannot be far distant when a motion not merely in form, but in substance, will put the fate of the question, and of the Ministry, at issue together. Lord Winchilsea has published a letter, or rather a manifesto, to his countrymen, calling them to stand up and protect their religion from Popery, scepticism, and infidelity.

The agitation produced by this question will not render the House of Lords, and perhaps the country, more disposed to accede to the continually encroaching demands of the Dissenters.

Thursday, 12*th.*—Our two great Universities present, at this moment, a remarkable exhibition of political feeling, aggravated, no doubt, by the late unfortunate agitation of the Church Reform Bill by the Whig Government; and the effervescence in favour of Tory or Conservative principles is equally striking in both. The inauguration of the Duke of Wellington, as Chancellor of the University of Oxford, has collected in that city as large an assemblage of the highest families, all in the Tory interest, as ever was known on such an occasion. The Duke has been received with the greatest enthusiasm, and as much respect shown by all the colleges to his public political principles as to his high independent private character.

At the same moment, the contest between Mr. Spring Rice and Sir Edward Sugden, to represent the town of Cambridge, has called forth a similar exhibition of feeling from that University, and the Tory candidate appears to be supported with as much eagerness in one seat of learning as in the other. Mr. Abercromby is appointed Master of the Mint, with a seat in the Cabinet.

Lord Grey's answer to the address from Brookes's has enraged his democratical friends, who are afraid that he is trying to slip through their hands. Their abuse of him is unqualified; but, like Faust, he has sold himself to the Evil Spirit, and he must either go on or go out.

Friday, 13*th.*—We went with the Darners and Glengalls to the Faubourg St. Germain to see the Hotel de Cluny, built in the fifteenth century, the old architecture of which is still preserved. Here resided Mary, wife of Louis XII., and sister to our Henry VIII. Mrs. D. showed me a letter from—, which says, "I went, yesterday, with their Majesties to the private exhibition at Somerset House. We were received by the president of the Royal Society, who, among other portraits, pointed out to the King that of Admiral Napier, who has been commanding the fleet for Don Pedro. His Majesty did not hesitate to show his *political* bias on this occasion, by exclaiming immediately, 'Captain Napier may be d——d, sir, and you may be d——d, sir; and if the Queen was not here, sir, I would kick you down stairs, sir!"

Saturday, 14*th*—F. Byng arrived this week in Paris, to look over the accounts of the embassy for the Foreign Office. He is forward in maintaining the doctrine, that a Whig Government should not allow even the subaltern places under them to be held by a Tory; always forgetting, that he himself, though a declared Whig, was always permitted to remain in the Foreign Office, under every Tory Government.

The French government has made some slight concessions as to duties, on a few articles, imported from England, rather to meet the clamour of the nation on these points, than to promote any new commercial intercourse between the two countries.

They are, in fact, unimportant; but Dr. B., delighted, after three years' ineffectual pressing and supplication here, to have obtained even this slight relaxation, is gone over to London with the proposal Of all the men, high or low, whom I ever met in society, this Dr. B. is the most presuming and the most conceited. He is a fit *charlatan* for Whig employment; pushing and overbearing in his manner, and, like other *parvenus,* assuming an official importance which is highly ridiculous.

Some years ago he was arrested by the French government at Boulogne, and his papers seized. Irritated at this embarrassment, he wrote a most violent letter to the police, in Paris, in which, after bitterly complaining of this infraction of the Law of Nations, he concluded by saying, that the Bourbons had committed an act on his person which might hurl them from their throne

Sunday, 15*th.*—Went with Glengall to Versailles. We walked over the gardens of the Petit Trianon, which are kept in excellent order. The Swiss village still remains, where Marie Antoinette and her favourites used to dress themselves up as rustics, and pretend to inhabit the little cottages bordering on the lake, where the blasés inhabitants of the palace at Versailles, under the garb of Maître Jacques le Meunier, or Fanchette la Laitière, &c, found a new zest for their amusements in personating their inferiors. In all these fêtes, Charles X., as Comte d'Artois, acted a principal part; and while the actors in this comedy were pursuing their rural revels, a revolution was brewing under their feet, which already had marked them for her prey.

Notwithstanding the reception of Sir Edward Sugden at Cambridge, he has lost his election by a majority of twenty-nine for Spring Rice. It is feared that the indiscreet interference of the vice-chancellor in favour of Sir Edward did much harm to his cause.

Don Miguel is to go on board a British man-of-war to Genoa; and Don Carlos is shipped in the Donegal, with a numerous suite for England.

In Portugal, the convents, monasteries, and all religious establishments of monks are abolished, and their estates incorporated with the national domains. If a proper use is made of these funds, if they are not destined to excite revolution elsewhere, no one can regret the destruction of these bigoted and corrupt institutions, which, for so many centuries, have tyrannised over the Peninsula and their South American dependencies.

Monday, 16*th.*—The elections for the new Chamber of Deputies are beginning throughout the country, and the government is straining every nerve to preserve the majority in the new, which they obtained in the last. The two parties of the Carlists and Republicans have little weight now, and are little feared; but the main object seems to be the exclusion of those men who profess independent principles and a wish to act as a check on the expenses and encroachments of the present system To this point, all the machinery of threats and cajolery is put in motion by the ministry; and when to this is added the known bribery which takes place when the deputies are assembled, it is not difficult to surmise what will be the result of the present canvass. Louis-Philippe is workingly steadily to bring about a despotic monarchy, the first step to which is now secured by a numerous, well-appointed army, which is attached by flattery and favours to his interest. He has two other powerful engines working in his favour, which rally round him the National Guard, or what may be called the middling classes, and of which he is availing himself adroitly and constantly,—the fear of revolution and pillage with those who have property, and the allurement of favour and patronage with those who wish for advancement. He is carrying everything by degrees; and though by no means increasing his popularity, if no unforeseen event occurs, he may probably succeed in his objects.

He is aiming a bold stroke at Versailles, which the last Bourbons could never accomplish. Permission was given some time back to fit up that palace as a great national museum for works of art, to be brought from the various residences and *gardes meubles* of the civil list, and kept as a public exhibition. This is in part arranged, and will be opened shortly to the public. I was surprised, however, to learn, during our visit on Sunday, that advantage has been taken of this circumstance to fit up the private apartments of Louis XIV. precisely as they existed at that period. The identical bed in which he slept has been repaired and put up, as well as many other fine pieces of furniture which had been laid aside and forgotten. What was wanting has been supplied from other quarters, but all harmonising with the taste of that day; and the effect is said to be really superb. Neither money nor interest can obtain a view of this collection from the guardians, to whom the king has given the strictest orders that no one shall be admitted; indeed, M. Montalivet said to Glengall the other night, that if any one dared to show it, he would be instantly dismissed. I could not help asking my informant, if it was the king's intention to reside in it? He only said, with a significant look, "Not yet!"

The gardens are all kept in excellent order, and the waterworks play on the first Sunday in the month during summer. The exterior and interior decorations of the palace have been restored. Under one pretext or another, furniture may be gradually introduced, till some fine day the monarch of July may find himself installed in that gorgeous abode, the reckless and enormous cost of which contributed much to hasten that series of changes and misfortunes which have at length placed him on the throne of his ill-fated relatives. It is said that the expense of creating this royal residence, which was constructed under the most unfavourable circumstances of nature, on a tract of marshy land, so much exceeded all possible calculation, that even Louis XIV. was ashamed of the prodigality, and ordered the accounts to be destroyed.

But supposing for an instant that Louis-Philippe should succeed in his object, if it is his ambition to occupy the seat of Louis XIV., where will he find the brilliant court, the splendid fortunes, the highbred nobility, which reflected so much lustre on the monarch of that era? Not in the parsimonious, money-loving, self-opiniated, plebeian ranks of lawyers and editors by whom he is surrounded. The days of courtly magnificence are gone for ever.

***Wednesday,* 18*th.*—A curious statement has been published by one of the papers in Madrid, respecting the number and revenues of the Spanish clergy. It appears that the number of buildings appropriated to religious purposes throughout Spain is 28,229: that of the clergy is 159,322; that of the friars and nuns is 96,878. The entire revenue of the ecclesiastical orders is 50,000,000 dollars (300,000,000f.); and of this sum the part consumed by them is shown to exceed the whole revenue of the state by some eight millions of dollars. How many years' purchase is it now worth? Quære, one year?

Earl Grey has **strengthened** his Government by appointing Marquis Conyngham Postmaster-General, and Colonel Byng a Lord of the Treasury. A learned lord, on these appointments being notified to him, is said to have asked, "What is the humour of all this; and in the name of all that is ridiculous, what are we to do with these two geniuses?" It may be thought that Lord Anglesey has been pacified at somewhat too dear a rate, for the production of his letter, by the promotion of his two sons-in-law.

Mr. Cutler Fergusson is made Judge-Advocate-General in the room of Robert Grant, who is to be Governor of Bombay, *vice* Lord Clare.

Thursday, 19*th.*—Went with the Glengalls, Damers, and Lady Sandwich to see the Hotel de Cluny, for the interior of which we had now a ticket of admission. The furniture, though collected at a considerable expense, is more curious than valuable, more suited to the antiquarian than the man of taste. Every broker's shop in Paris seems to have been ransacked for remnants of worm-eaten furniture, to complete the collection with which this old Gothic building is literally stuffed; and as the era of Francis I. was not distinguished by much refinement in the arts of comfort or splendour, the Hotel Cluny is only remarkable as a contrast to modern improvements. There is a profusion of old carving in ebony which does not enliven the picture; one fine cabinet, in *pietra dura,* evidently of Italian manufacture at that period; the bed of Francis I., carved in oak, with tapestry hangings; a chess-board and men in *cristal de roche,* at which two men in armour seem to have been puzzling themselves for the last four centuries; the chapel as it then existed, with a *mannequin* priest in chasuble et étole; *the dining-room, with the buffet, and the table laid with plates and dishes of Dutch* fa?ence; *and in every room a profusion of ancient household furniture, from the massive* armoire with carved pilasters, to the rusty snuffers or worm-eaten bellows which the indefatigable collector could discover in the garrets and lumber-rooms of the broker or the antiquary.

It is said that he has invested a considerable fortune in this burlesque exhibition, which the worms and moths hold in disputed possession with him.

The government are continuing their intrigues to bias the elections; and, as it is asserted that 32,000,000 Frenchmen are bound by the acts of 200,000 electors, their task is not very difficult. The following letter sent from the Ministère de l'Intérieur to an undecided voter has been published in the Courrier Français:—

"Paris, 17 Mai.

"On voit toujours avec douleur un homme de bien, mû sans doute pas des sentimens louables, se mêler à des intrigues qui peuvent compromettre l'avenir de ses *parens*. C'est pourquoi je crois rendre service à M——, en le prévenant que le ministère étant instruit des courses et démarches qu'il fait pour le triomphe de l'élection d'un candidat qui lui sera hostile, il ne doit espérer aucun avancement pour les siens, employés dans l'administration de l'état et peut-être doit il avoir des craintes pour la *conservation* de leurs emplois. S'il continue le même rôle, il doit sentir qu'un gouvernement quelconque ne peut conserver en place les parens d'un citoyen, qui agit ouvertement contre lui."

Saturday, 21*st.*—After some difficulties being started by the English Government, who sent Mr. Backhouse from London to negotiate with Don Carlos on board the Donegal man-of-war at Portsmouth, permission has been given to him and to his family to land. Every attempt to induce him to abdicate his claim to the crown of Spain has been fruitless The King dined with the Duke of Wellington on Wednesday, the eighteenth anniversary of the battle of Waterloo.

The prosecutions against the press are going on with unceasing vigour, and fines and imprisonment are visited on the editors. M. Conseil and M. Carrel, proprietors of the *National,* were to take their trial before the Court of Assizes at Rouen, in pursuance of a decision of the Court of Cassation, on Monday last; but on the preceding afternoon, while taking an excursion on the Seine with some friends, the boat was upset by a sudden squall of wind, and all thrown into the water: M. Conseil was unfortunately drowned, and M. Carrel so severely suffered from the accident, both in body and mind, that the hearing must be put off.

Monday, 23rd.—On Friday the Dissenters University Admission Bill was carried in the Commons by a large majority. Sir R. Peel declared that he regarded this bill as a blow at the security of the Church.

Wednesday, 25*th.*—Clanricarde has resigned his post of the Yeoman of the Guard, from *religious scruples* as to the Church Question.

Quære, Does he think the House tottering?

Thursday, 26*th.*—We drove over to St. Cyr, a large blank white building, like a manufactory: no traces left of Madame de Maintenon and her young élèves; it is become a military school for young cadets, who represent battles and sieges instead of Esther and Athalie. There are only 250 students at present, whose conduct is at times refractory and displeasing to the government; nineteen were cashiered the other day. The distance is not above two miles from the palace.

Friday, 27*th.*—Visited the Grand and Petit Trianon, which are only costly accessories to the grand palace, and are still well kept up. There are some good pictures of the Bourbon family still remaining,—Louis XIV.; Louis XV., and his two daughters, one of whom is playing on the violoncello; some fine views of the palaces, particularly of Marly as it then existed; a scene, on the terrace, of courtiers playing at *cache cache,* in which Madame de Montespan, apparently watching the game, is evidently more occupied by an earnest conversation going on in another quarter between Madame de Maintenon and Louvois. The costume of the time is well represented, and the latter lady is easily recognised by her black *coiffe* and gown. We saw the noble chapel at Versailles with its painted roof and splendid decorations: all these costly monuments of art are gradually resuming their former splendour, and owe their restoration as much to Napoleon as to the later care and attention of the Bourbons on their return.

At night we came back to Auteuil.

Saturday, 28*th.*—The elections are finished, and the government candidates have been generally successful. The opposition has lost strength, and many of its members have not been re-elected.

A meeting took place the other day at Clichy between two professors of the English language, Messrs. Robertson and Glashin, when the former quarrelled with the latter's second on the spot; a duel ensued, and the second was shot: the other party was adjourned.

Sunday, 29*th.*—We went to Versailles to dine and sleep at the Glengalls'. There are various *bosquets* in the gardens, railed in and locked up, to which the public are not admitted, but are privately shown. We saw this morning the colonnade temple, which is a large circular construction of arches and marble columns forming an amphitheatre, with thirty-six recesses, in each of which are marble basins and fountains supplied with water from the great reservoir, which play at the same time with the other waterworks. In the centre of this temple is a fine *groupe* in marble of the Rape of Proserpine, by Girardin; the bas-reliefs on the pedestal are beautifully executed. The whole is without a roof, and open to the sky. Louis XIV. in those days frequently gave concerts to his court in this temple, at which time large crystal chandeliers, with innumerable wax candles, were suspended from the centre of each arch, while underneath, the marble fountains spouted up cascades of water in which the lights were reflected in all directions like streams of diamonds. In another *bosquet* is the bath of Apollo, formed of massive rocks, in the centre of which is seen the marble *groupe* of Apollo with Thetis and her attendants; in recesses on either side are the horses of the god in very spirited attitudes; below is the basin which is fed by waters from the surrounding cascades. The immense mass of rocks was brought from Fontainebleau, and erected here by Louis XVI.

Monday, 30*th.*—Went to Fontainebleau, by a cross road which joins that from Paris, about a league on this side of Fromenteau: we travelled through a pretty country, with occasional views of the Seine, which winds its course to Paris on the left, through all this department. About a league on this side of Essonne is Petit-bourg, a fine château and estate formerly belonging to the Due de Bourbon, now the property of the Spanish banker Aguado, who from being a retail dealer in cigars and sherry at Paris, has made a colossal fortune by speculations in the Spanish funds within the last ten years, which he spends with great liberality. The last stage is through the forest, and the approach to the town very striking.

Tuesday, 1st July.—The town and château *of Fontainebleau is situated in a valley, placed in the middle of an immense forest, consisting of 33,000 acres, spreading over hill and dale, and abounding with gigantic rocky promontories and scattered masses, which diversify the scenery in every direction; at one time looking from the eminences, like distant cities; at another like frightful cliffs, or precipices, hanging over the immense ocean of green shade which is waving below in the valley and curling to the wind. The timber is of the finest description; the most magnificent lofty oaks, beech, chestnut, &c, kept with great care and diligently pruned, present in every direction to the traveller avenues and drives intersecting each other through the extensive* massifs, *and opening at every turn upon the most beautiful pictures of forest scenery, or the wildest views of savage nature. The forest has indeed been called tremendously beautiful. The great desideratum which appeared to me was the absence of game: herds of deer and wild animals roving amid such picturesque scenery, would have completed the* tableau, *but they were all destroyed in the first Revolution, and there are now scarcely sufficient to afford an occasional scanty* chasse. In former times these woods abounded in every species of game. There are several beautiful points of view in this forest, to which the attention is directed by the guides, among which Frenchard, la Madeleine, and particularly Le Rocher des deux Sœurs, are the most striking and attractive. In the whole of this woody tract, equal in extent to some counties, not even a village has been built.

Colonel and Mrs. Damer joined us to-day.

Wednesday, 2nd July.—This day was dedicated to seeing the castle, which, though not so fine as Versailles, is infinitely larger and more curious. It represents, within and without, the different styles of architecture from Francis I. to Louis XVI. The etymology of the name was at one time supposed to be *fontaine de belle eau;* but historians now assert it *fontaine Bliaud,* from an individual of that name, who originally held the property before the time of St. Louis. Long previous to François Premier it had been a royal domain; but he first gave it celebrity as a royal residence, by building the present front, and various other wings, which still attest the founder by the Fs which are let into the brickwork.

The principal entrance is by the Cour du Cheval Blanc, which is extensive, and enclosed by an iron railing: it leads to the great stone staircase (à ***double rampe***), of a circular form, communicating with the principal apartments: this spot is now become historical By this staircase Napoleon descended to take leave of his Guard assembled in the court, while his travelling carriage, and that of the commissioner, waited in a corner to convey him on his journey to Elba in 1814. One side of the quadrangle is a range of small houses which were used for the establishments of the different ministers of state; the other was for various officers. Some idea may be formed of the immense size of this palace when you are informed that it contains 1500 lits de maître. ***Besides this court, there are the Cour d'Honneur, Cour des Princes, Cour Ovale du Donjon, Cour de la Fontaine, and Cour des Cuisines. The apartments, as may be supposed, are innumerable: that which was appropriated to the reception of Pope Pius VII. is very handsome; the principal rooms are hung with fine specimens of the Gobelins tapestry. A small drawing-room is shown, in which Napoleon prevailed on the Pope to sign the famous concordat, which he afterwards was so unwilling to ratify. He was attended by sixteen cardinals, and served by his own attendants, but an establishment of servants and equipages was placed at his disposal, which he declined to avail himself of. He never once during his stay crossed the threshold of his abode. Not so the cardinals, particularly Ruffo, who went to the*** chasse, ***and beguiled the time as well as circumstances would permit. Mass was daily celebrated in the*** Salon, hung with tapestried representations of the banquets of the heathen gods.

Napoleon seems to have been very partial to this residence, which suffered more during the havoc of the revolution than any other; the furniture, glasses, and ornaments of every description being pillaged or destroyed. His hand restored much of the damaged decoration, and he furnished it entirely at an enormous expense; but the furniture, though handsome, is modern, and ill accords with the ancient style and decoration of the walls, much less can it replace those magnificent works of art, with which Louis XIV. and XV. had made it their pride to adorn it. The artists of that time have established their fame; but even in the time of François Premier, who may be called the founder of Fontainebleau, when French ingenuity and industry had made but little progress, his Italian architect and painter, Primatticcio, employed his own countrymen, who were far more advanced in those arts than their neighbours, to decorate this superb château: many invaluable specimens, therefore, of that early period were also destroyed by the ruthless vengeance of the revolutionists in 1792.

The Galerie de Diane has been quite restored, and new gilt, partly in the time of Louis XVIII., who has put up a tablet to record it in. the twenty-second year of his reign. There is a fine picture of Henri IV. on horseback, and several modern paintings of different events in his reign.

The Galerie of François I. is well worthy of remark, as giving a specimen of the architecture of that time, enriched with the Italian painting and decorations, which, though injured by time, still retain a fine and even rich appearance: it is the intention of Louis-Philippe to restore this gallery, the proportions of which are very good. There are pedestals at equal distances, supporting the marble busts of every hero or philosopher in every period,—the medley is rather ridiculous; there is also a fine picture of Louis XIV. on horseback, said to be by Vandyke.[Note *: It could not have been by Vandyke, who died in 1642, four years after Louis XIV. was born.]

The Galerie des Cerfs, so called from the stags' heads with which it was ornamented, has been lately pulled down and converted into private apartments. It was in this gallery that Christine, Queen of Sweden, when residing at Fontainebleau, superintended the assassination of her minister Monaldeschi, who is buried in a small church at a short distance from the town.

The Galerie or Ball Room of Henri II. is in the same style, but far handsomer than that of François I., and had suffered still more from dilapidation. The workmen are now employed in thoroughly repairing all the decorations, repainting the fresco designs, and adding a profusion of gilding: the ceiling alone is just finished with gold and silver mouldings to the compartments, which has a novel and beautiful effect. When the entire gallery is completed, it will eclipse every other room in the palace.

What are called the state apartments, are in the richest style of Louis XIV., and still in very good preservation. La Salle du Trône and the Levée Room are rich in gilding and carving, by the first artists; but the throne itself and the furniture, which were put up in the time of Napoleon, have still a meagre appearance when contrasted with the ornaments of the preceding æra.

The state bed-room is fitted up in the same manner. An immense canopy bed, with ostrich feathers at the four corners, and rich silk hangings, in which formerly Napoleon reposed with his empress, is now occupied by Louis-Philippe and his queen when they visit Fontainebleau.

Adjoining to these, are shown the private apartments of Napoleon, which are furnished very richly; but the most remarkable object in them is a small round mahogany claw table on which he signed his [Note *: Les puissances alliées ayant proclamé que l'Empereur Napoléon était le seul obstacle an rétablissement de la paix en Europe, l'Empereur Napoléon, fidèle à son serment, déclaré qu'il renonce poor luiet poor ses héritiers aux trônes de France et d'ltalie, et qu'il n'est aucun sacrifice qu'il ne fasse même celui de la vie poor l'intérêt ds la France—10 Avril, 1814.] abdication of the French Empire. A brass plate recording this event is fixed in the inside, and an autograph copy of the document is placed in a frame on the console table opposite for public inspection.

There is a beautiful theatre built by Louis XV., which is still in constant use, when the master resides here; and even the citizen King has not hesitated to follow the example of his predecessor. Actors from Paris are sent down as in the time of Napoleon.

The gardens attached to the château are well laid out, but did not present any very striking feature. The repairs, which are carrying on by order of Louis-Philippe, are alike creditable to his taste and his liberality: no expense seems to be spared in giving the old designs their original beauty, while those parts which must be re-made are in strict keeping with the old.

In these late repairs we observed that he has not hesitated to restore the ***fleurs-de-lis,*** which is the more remarkable, as in the commencement of the last revolution he had effaced them from his own arms.

Thursday, 3*rd*—We returned to Auteuil. The papers mention the death of Countess Antrim. She was the heiress of the great Macdonnell property in, the county of Antrim, and widow of Sir H. Vane Tempest, after whose death she married Mr. Phelps; the property goes to her daughter, the present Marchioness of Londonderry. Pozzo the other day was giving a description of the present race of Frenchmen: he said, "Ils sont malhonnêtes, mal élevés, libertins, arrogans et faux; mais ils sont braves, et de cette manière ils s'en tirent, parce que personne n'aime à avoir une affaire avec un mauvais sujet."

The English Government seems much embarrassed with their new guest Don Carlos. He has been permitted to come with his family to a house at Brompton; but though driven from his own country, and left apparently without resources, no cajolery or threats can induce him to resign his claims and pretensions to the crown of Spain, which is his by the real laws of the country.

A tragic event occurred here yesterday in the Bois de Boulogne, about two hundred yards from the house. A young hairdresser from Paris brought down a young woman, to whom he was to be married on the following day. After walking about in the most public part of the promenade, and taking some refreshment together at the ***restaurant,*** they turned up one of the allées, when he drew out a pistol, and shot her dead; he then attempted to commit suicide with another, but only wounded himself slightly, and the police immediately took him into custody. Jealousy was supposed to be the cause of this horrid act.

Saturday, 5*th.*—Don Miguel arrived at Genoa on the 20th ult. Immediately on landing he went to the nearest church, threw himself on his knees, and remained for a long time with his face covered with his pocket-handkerchief.

Sunday, 6*th*—One of the men who has run a long political career, the Duc de Cador [Note *: Champagny.], minister and ambassador under Napoleon, died on Thursday, aged seventy-seven.

Monday, 7*th.*—Mr. Stanley made a violent speech, on Friday, against the Government on the Irish Church Bill. The Queen embarked on the 5th, from Woolwich, in the royal yacht, for Rotterdam, on her journey to visit her relations in Germany.

She was received with great demonstrations of loyalty by the spectators.

Tuesday, 8*th.*—On Sunday last, two young men-one a law student, the other a medical one—repaired to the Bois de Boulogne to settle an affair of honour of so serious a nature (at least in their opinion) that it was resolved that one should die. After a vain attempt at reconciliation, one of the seconds demanded that the delay of one hour should take place before the combat commenced, This being agreed to, he returned with all speed to Paris, and informed a priest, who had been chaplain to the college of the students, of what was about to occur. The worthy ecclesiastic hurried to the spot, and after a vain endeavour to bring one of the adversaries to listen to reason, who insisted on blood being shed, the clergyman said to him, "If you must shed blood, let it be mine: I willingly offer myself as a victim; for I may say, without presumption, that I am better prepared at the present moment to quit this world, than the young man whose life you seek." This touching apostrophe had the desired effect, and a reconciliation took place, all parties doing honour to the venerable peacemaker.

Extract of a letter from Rome, 24th June:—

"On a créé hier quatre cardinaux, savoir Canali, Bottiglia, Polidori et Trigona, le sacré collége est presque au grand complet La papauté est commeces femmes coquettes, qui aiment à être conchées dans le cercueil, ornées de tous leurs joyaux, et dans tout l'éclat de leur parure."

Thursday, 10*th.*—This evening, at La Muette [Note *: In the Bois de Boulogne, then hired by Lord Ranfurly; at one time it belonged to Madame du Barri, afterwards to Marie-Antoinette; and was the scene of many fêtes in the time of the Empire, as mentioned by Madame d'Abrantea.] Lord Leveson brought the account that Lord Grey and Lord Althorpe had resigned. On the 9th inst, Earl Grey in the Lords, and Lord Althorpe in the Commons, announced the complete dissolution of the Whig Ministry. The former rose, under great agitation, to explain the circumstances which led to this event, viz., the impolitic communications of Cabinet intentions by Mr. Littleton to Mr. O'Connell, and the internal dissensions among his colleagues. *This time* the King has accepted the resignations: time only will show the result; but a great change seems inevitable.

Two years ago the Whigs boasted, that, if they were turned out of office by the Tories, they would leave the country in such a state that no other party should be able to govern it: they have outdone their assertions,—they have rendered it ungovernable even by themselves. In the present instance, the Tories have had no hand in their downfal; at no period have they been so inactive, or made so little opposition; upon great questions, indeed, they have more frequently voted with the Government than against them.

Saturday, 12*th.*—There is no ministerial arrangement announced, but the Whigs are struggling to maintain their hold. The Chancellor asserted, in the Lords, that Lord Althorpe had acted under a mistake when he announced the complete dissolution of the Cabinet. *He himself had not resigned* the Woolsack.

Monday, 14*th.*—- The embarrassments in forming a new administration still continue; nothing as yet decided.

Wednesday, 16*th.*—The Cabinet menders are still in difficulty. The Bang has now empowered Lord Melbourne to form an administration, who best consults the indolence of his nature by persuading the lost sheep to return to the fold. Lord Althorpe is yielding to his seductions; but if anything could prove the dearth of public men and public talent in the ranks of the Whigs, it is the fact that William Lamb should become Prime Minister of England.

In the midst of this confusion, to the great surprise of all Europe, Don Carlos has privately made his escape from England, and is gone to join his adherents in the North of Spain, in defiance of the quadrupartite treaty signed by France, England, Portugal, and Spain.

Friday, 18*th.*—As if the march of the two countries was to proceed ***pari passu,*** Marshal Soult has resigned, and is succeeded by Marshal Gérard, as President of the Council and Minister at War. Great opposition has been made to him of late in the cabinet, with reference to the appointment of a civil governor at Algiers, which he would not allow; but the more immediate cause of his secession is the apprehension of meeting the new chamber, which, however it may be of a ministerial colour, is still pledged to economy and the strictest investigation of his military budget. He is said to have realised an immense fortune.

C. Greville writes me from London: "The King wanted to have a coalition, which was out of the question; no party could have agreed to it. He then wished Lord Grey to return; but he was told this could not be. He desired Lord Grey might be consulted, and considered throughout the whole transaction; and it was at his (Lord Grey's) especial Tequest to Althorpe, that the latter consented to stay with Melbourne. Nobody thinks this Cabinet will last long, still less can anybody guess what will come next. Public men seem generally at a discount; and the late proceedings have certainly not exhibited the candidates for political power in a very advantageous light, either as to wisdom or honour. The Coercion Bill will pass the House of Lords, and the Commons will throw out the three clauses: some think that when it is sent back to the Lords, they will refuse it, which I do not; they will prefer taking the bill without the clauses, to having no bill at all. I cannot say that I ever expected to see Melbourne Prime Minister of England, or its destinies committed to such a triumvirate as he, Althorpe, and Brougham. I am not on the whole, however, a great alarmist; and though fully alive to all the difficulty of forming a government, and the obstacles which the Reform Bill has cast in the way of any that can be formed, I am not apprehensive of a revolution, nor of the decadence of our moral, social, or political condition. It would be a tedious dissertation, if I were to attempt to give any reasons for this impression; and I am not sure that I could do so, nor that my convictions are not rather the result of instinct than of an inductive reasoning process; but after hearing the most elaborate arguments to prove that we are on the road to ruin, I feel tempted to answer, 'circumspice;' for I think nobody who does dispassionately, can really believe it."

Sunday, 20*th.*—The patchwork Ministry is settled ***pro tempore:*** Lord Duncannon takes Melbourne's place in the Home Office, and Sir J, C. Hobhouse has the Woods and Forests, with a seat in the Cabinet. Their first act is to expunge from Lord Grey's Irish Coercion Bill the three most efficient clauses, from a fear of the House of Commons.

Michael Angelo Taylor died, on Wednesday last, at his house in Privy Gardens. He was a good-natured, hospitable man, and a great feeder of the Whig members of the House of Commons, who readily obeyed his invitations to turbot and lobster sauce.

Monday, 21*st.*—Lord Duncannon is made a peer.

Friday, 25*th.*—I had a letter from Glengall. He says, "that Lords Brougham and Holland offered Lord Grey the Privy Seal: he almost kicked them down stairs. * * * * Durham is gone northward in disgust. The King would not send to the Duke personally, as he has not forgot old grievances; but he desired Melbourne to form a coalition, which the Tories refused.

Saturday, 26*th.*—I called on Pozzo di Borgo, and sat some time with him. He thinks the present state of England worse than if it was a republic, and the downfal of the House of Lords inevitable. With this exception, the state of Europe generally is improved. The Three Powers have completed their measures, and though they do not wish for war, they are now prepared for it, if necessary. The contentions in the Helvetic cantons are settled to their satisfaction; the word was, faites ça ou la guerre, and the threat succeeded. There are private accounts from Don Carlos's headquarters of a favourable nature; but he was afraid of being too confident. The riots which took place in Madrid last week, when four convents were destroyed and sixty monks massacred, were excited by the Urban guard, who lent arms to the populace, while the government looked on and encouraged the excesses. The English, said he, are now suspected wherever they go. At Paris, perhaps, and at Rome, they are well received; but in every other part of Europe they will be subject to the strictest scrutiny as to passports; and, indeed, without certificates of good conduct and good intentions, they will be vigilantly watched. They are much more to be dreaded now as propagandists than the French, whom Louis-Philippe is bringing into proper subjection and is anxious to go with the good cause; while every day proves the mischievous manœuvres of the English Government. He particularly alluded to the recent election for F——as a proof that they would support any character, however flétri, if it suited their purposes; and said (I fear with great truth) that the moral and honourable feelings which formerly distinguished the English nation from all others, had undergone as great a change as their politics. The power and wealth of the country were still undeniable, even under the present system, though our late colonial measures might eventually undermine that prosperity; but as to the British Constitution of King, Lords, and Commons, which had for ages been the admiration of the world, it had been destroyed by a stroke of the pen. The only government which remained for England was the reformed House of Commons, or, in other words, a democracy.

I asked him if it was true that Louis-Philippe had just given Montrond a pension: he said 20,000 francs a year, to speak well of him at the Clubs and in England.

Tuesday, 29th.—The glorious three days are past, and the farce of commemorating a revolution by which the people have gained no advantages, either moral or political, while the nation has become an object of suspicion to the neighbouring powers, is just finished. The first day (Sunday) was a mourning for the victims who perished in this fruitless cause; the second day was enlivened by the review of the national guards, and all the troops of the line forming the garrison of Paris, an imposing armed force, ready at the shortest notice to exterminate these sons of liberty, if they should dare to attempt any repetition of the scenes which they are called upon to commemorate. This review lasted several hours. All the troops defiled before the king and his staff in the Place Vendôme, who, by his constant bows and cringing manner, displayed rather too openly his main dependence on them to secure his newly acquired throne. The queen, the princesses, &c., were stationed on a balcony behind him. They arrived in a most unassuming motley cortége of carriages, each with a pair of horses, and a single lacquey on the hind seat. The day concluded with a given quantity of puppet-shows, booths, and gingerbread in the Champs Elysées.

The third day was intensely hot. The *spectacles* were open gratis; a balloon was let off; some ridiculous tilting was exhibited on the river; and at night some beautiful fireworks. A sudden storm of heavy rain and lightning concluded the fête, and sent several hundred thousand spectators drenched and dripping to their beds. Heard of the death of Lord James Fitzroy, after an illness of ten days, on the 26th instant: he was only thirty years old, the youngest son of the Duke of Grafton, and nephew to my brother-in-law Lord W. Fitzroy.

Wednesday, 30*th*—Earl Bathurst died on the 27th instant: he was one of the Tellers of the Exchequer, and Colonial Secretary from 1813 till 1824, and had been long in office during all the Tory administrations. A blue riband is vacant by his death.

A duel was fought on the 26th instant between Count Prosper d'Aubri, twenty-seven years old, formerly a *Garde-du-corps,* and Count Gustave de Blücher, grandson of the Prussian field-marshal of that name, in consequence of a dispute on the preceding day at Baden, near Rastadt. They fought in the Isle of the Rhine between Strasbourg and Kehl. The duel took place, with pistols, at fifteen yards' distance. Count d'Aubri was killed by the ball of his adversary passing through his chest.

Sir John Hobhouse has gained his election for Nottingham, amidst great popular clamour against him.

Thursday, 31*st.*—Lord Mulgrave appointed Privy Seal in the room of Lord Carlisle. The King of the French went to the Palais Bourbon to open the Chambers. The speech from the throne, insignificant. The expressions are peaceable; and but little reference is made to the quadrupartite treaty, or the affairs of the Peninsula.

The opening of the Cortes took place at Madrid on the 24th instant. The speech from the throne was delivered by the queen regent. The Spanish funds have again fallen, from some vague expressions supposed to have reference to a reduction of the national debt.

St. Germains.

Monday, 4*th August*—On Wednesday, last, in the House of Commons, an amendment on the Irish Tithe Bill, moved by O'Connell, was carried against Ministers by a majority of 82 against 33. It was in substance a reduction of 40 per cent, on tithe compositions. The value of tithes, by the latest returns, is about 670,000*l.*, and it is reduced to 400,000*l,* the occupiers of the land being exonerated from the payment, which is thrown now on the landlord. There is a strong suspicion that the Government covertly assented to this defeat, wishing the measure to be carried, though afraid openly to sanction it.

Glengall writes on the 2nd instant: "We threw out the bill for admitting Dissenters into the universities with a grand majority in the House of Lords last night. A meeting was held this morning by all the Tory peers at Apsley House, when it was resolved to stay in town to the end of the season."

Wednesday, 6*th.*—A letter is arrived which mentions the death of Mrs. Arbuthnot at Kettering. It is another instance of sudden mortality amongst our acquaintance. She was a very clever, agreeable woman, and, from her great intimacy with the Duke, a prominent feature in the Tory party. Her death was awfully sudden; she left town a fortnight ago in high health and spirits. The melancholy event took place at a farm-house near Woodford, to which she had walked, and was there seized with spasms: an express was sent for Sir H. Halford, but before he arrived she was no more. She was sister to General Sir Henry Fane, and married to Mr. Arbuthnot in 1814.

Admiral Sir Richard King died on the 4th instant of cholera at Sheerness. The disorder seems gaining ground in England.

Friday, 8th.—M. Dupin elected president of the French Chamber of Deputies. The civil war continues in Spain with little success on either side. Zumalacaraguy defends himself in the fastnesses against Rodil, who has moved to Elisondo, and Don Carlos meets with little encouragement.

Thursday, 14th.—The House of Lords has thrown out Mr. O'Connell's Irish Tithe Bill by a majority of 67; to the great mortification of the Government, who did not support it in the Commons. Glengall writes to me, "we have bearded the Dissenters, the Catholics, and the House of Commons to the teeth."

According to M. Torreno's exposé of the finance of Spain to the Cortes, it appears that the revenue of that country amounts at present to the sum of

Reals Velon.	715,319,139.
The charge of collecting which, with other expenses	195,726,065.
	519,593,074.
While the presumed expenses for the year are	599,033,274.
And a known deficit from various causes	336,264,175.

Friday, 15th.—The Duke of Norfolk [Note *: The Duke of Norfolk has since renounced the Roman Catholic faith.] has got the vacant Blue Riband, being the only Catholic of the Order. In the evening we went to Tivoli, with the Ashburnhams, Howard, and Sir Cavendish Rumbold.

Saturday, 16*th.*—On the 15th, Parliament was prorogued by the King in person. East Gloucester has returned a Tory candidate in Mr. Codrington.

Tuesday, 19*th.*—Marshal Maison, the French ambassador at Petersburg, has had a narrow escape for his life; he was present at a review on the 1st instant, when he was unexpectedly overtaken by a charge of cavalry, his horse thrown to the ground, and himself taken up violently bruised and insensible: he is now recovering from the accident.

Sunday, 24*th.*—Talleyrand arrived in Paris on Friday from London; and on Wednesday the Queen returned from the Continent, and landed at Woolwich, amidst great acclamations.

Marriages are soon arranged in this country, Lady Virginia Murray, with her two nieces, young girls of seventeen and eighteen years old, the daughters of Colonel Murray, was invited the other day to dine with the Prince de la Trémouille, who is seventy-six; on the following day he proposed to Lady Virginia to marry one of her nieces, which she was disposed to decline on account of the great disproportion of age: but, when the offer was laid before the young lady, she accepted it without hesitation, and last week she was made Princesse de la Trémouille.

Wednesday, 27*th.*—The opening of the Chambers has taken place in Lisbon, and the ex-Emperor Don Pedro has addressed them in a long and boasting speech; it will be seen hereafter how far his account of his own illustrious deeds will agree with the character given to them by impartial historians.

Thursday, 28*th.*—One of our best modern English poets, Mr. Coleridge, is dead—and there is little prospect of his place being soon supplied in the literary world. His conversational powers were very great. On an occasion when the doctrine of the Sacramentaries and the Roman Catholics, on the subject of the Eucharist, was in question, he solved the difficulty at once, by saying, "They are both equally wrong,—the first have volatilised the Eucharist into a metaphor, the last have condensed it into an idol."

Friday, 29*th.*—Dr. Antomarchi, who attended Napoleon at St. Helena during his last illness, has written the following account of a recent storm, when the lightning entered the house in which he was: "I was at breakfast with my father and family, and a numerous party of friends, at the little village of Santi, when the lightning entered the room where we were sitting. One branch of the electric fluid made its way through the wall immediately above me, at about a foot from my head, without touching me; but it struck Mademoiselle Blassini, a young lady seated on my right hand, and killed her. The right side of her head and her ear were burnt, and her hair was set on fire. The lightning descended by the neck, the breast, the body, and the leg on the same side, leaving traces of its passage by severe excoriation. M. Stella, a young abbé, who sat next to the young lady, was also struck by the same current, which passed from the silk dress and apron of the young lady to his left knee, scorching his leg from top to bottom, leaving a severe bruise on the top of the foot; while his shoe was torn off and rent in pieces. My eldest sister also received the shock, but it only carried away her shoe, and part of the stocking, without touching the skin. All the other persons were more or less affected, but we were all thrown down. The bronze mask of the Emperor, which was suspended between two openings in the wall made by the lightning, was untouched. Plates, glasses, and other things were broken; a dog was killed at my feet; the damage done produced a frightful scene of desolation."

*Saturday 30*th —A serious fall in the Spanish funds on the Paris Exchange. The 5 per cents, which, previous to the death of Ferdinand, were above 80, have been down this week at 28; while the Cortes bonds, which had previously risen during the last six months from 14 to 36, have also declined to 31. The ruin on all hands among the speculators is enormous, and the papers show that many have balanced their accounts by suicide. The mania for gambling in the funds is vastly more extensive here than in London. The women are deeply engaged in it, and had established a parquet for themselves in one of the galleries at the Bourse, from whence they were lately expelled by an order of the Minister of Commerce, but they still continue their ***agiotage*** to the same extent in the outer passages. When Mr. Jauge was lately arrested by the government on the Exchange for supposed communications with Don Carlos, and aiding in his escape from England, which produced a panic among the bondholders, these irritated viragoes would have torn him in pieces, if the arrival of the gendarmes had not saved him from their fury. Mr. Jauge still remains in prison, though it is difficult to say under what pretence a government in a *free country* could have the right to incarcerate him.

Monday, Sept. *1st.*—Standish came to-day to Paris. He married a French woman, ademoiselle Finguerlin, a relation of Madame de Genlis, and established himself for ten years in France.

Wednesday, 3rd.—I called this morning to return the visit of Count Zamoisky, who is staying at Auteuil in the house of the Prince de Beauveau. His uncle, the Prince Czartorisky, is with him, a melancholy victim of the late revolution in Poland, formerly possessor of an immense fortune, and now reduced to a very small pittance. They are both agreeable men, and live chiefly in English society.

Thursday, 4*th.*—This morning, early, a duel was fought in the Bois de Boulogne, close to our house; one of the combatants was killed on the spot. They both came to the grouud with their horses and servants, and were said to be partners in the same business. The cause of the quarrel was not known. The uncle of one of the parties was his second.

We went to see Meudon to-day, which belongs to the crown, and is occasionally inhabited by the Duke of Orleans. It is a good house, but the furniture is modern, put in by Napoleon. The great beauty of the place is the terrace, and the extensive view which it commands for many leagues of the surrounding country—Paris, the Seine, &c. It was built by Louvois, and left by him to his widow, who sold it to Louis XIV. for 400,000fr. and the palace of Choisy. It then became the residence of Monseigneur le Dauphin; was afterwards pillaged in the Revolution, and then restored in the Empire. Meudon is situated on an eminence above Belle Vue, two miles from Sèvres, and at an equal distance between Paris and Versailles.

Sunday, 7*th.*—Fête at St. Cloud. Donna Francesca, wife of Don Carlos, died on the 4th inst. of a bilious attack at Alverstoke Rectory, Gosport. She was a Portuguese princess, sister to Pedro and Miguel, thirty-six years old, and has left three sons.

Wednesday, 10*th.*—Glengall writes from Caher.—"This country is improving much, but O'Connell is stronger than ever, owing to the disgraceful truckling conduct of Government; but the Protestants are roused, and will fight to the last: they have refused to surrender the arms of their Yeomanry Corps.

Friday, 12*th.*—Don Pedro has been created Regent of Portugal. In Lisbon as in London, the cabinet has approved the plan of swamping the Upper House, by thrusting twenty-four new Peers into the Chamber, to liberalise that assembly. A duel took place on Wednesday near Paris, which was attended by singular circumstances. One of the combatants having had the first fire, placed himself in an attitude to receive that of his adversary, who took a long and deliberate aim—the ball passed through his skull, and he died immediately. A few seconds afterwards his adversary also fell and expired, for he had received a ball which traversed his lungs; he had nevertheless retained sufficient strength to execute his deadly purpose. The combatants went into the field to revenge a double and reciprocal adultery.

Monday, 15*th.*—There are no less than five suicides in the paper this morning; and hardly a day passes without an instance of this description, or a murder, though seldom so desperate as that of Mr. Steinberg, of Pentonville, who has killed his wife, four children, and himself. The following disaster is of a different nature. On the 3rd inst., Raymond Coubère, inhabitant of the canton d'Aspes (Haute Garonne), sent his daughter Jeanne to the Mountain Charouente, at six in the evening, to bring home a mare which had been turned out to graze. The girl took the dog with her. At half-past seven, Coubère seeing that his daughter did not return, and hearing the barking of the dog at a distance, hastened with his son, about sixteen years old, and his son-in-law, towards the mountain, where they remained till near ten o'clock, vainly calling for the daughter. About this time their continued cries attracted to the spot a large wolf, which immediately sprang on the son-in-law, and seizing him by the back, wounded him severely. It then attacked the brother of Jeanne, and bit him greviously on the left hip. Impelled by despair they both seized the furious animal, and at last succeeded in despatching him and dragging him down to the village. At daybreak Coubère, assisted by the magistrates and the inhabitants of the commune, renewed their search for his daughter. Arrived at the top of the mountain, they found the body in a dreadful state. A part of the head was devoured, the stomach lacerated, the legs and the arms nearly eaten up. A medical man having examined the body of the dead wolf, found in its stomach a part of the skull, to which some hair was still attached, together with the thumb and other parts of the victim.

Wednesday, 18*th.*—Lord Grey has crossed the border to attend a large political dinner at Edinburgh, got up by the Reform *clique* in that city, to commemorate his services as a Minister; Cobbett has crossed the Irish Channel to be greeted by the Unions and Radical Trades in Dublin, who are to present to him an address approving his political conduct.

Colonel D'Este [Note *: Afterwards Sir Augustus d'Este.], son of the Duke of Sussex, has addressed to the Viceroy of Hanover in Parliament a requisition to obtain his acknowledgment as heir to the throne of that kingdom.

Friday, 20*th.*—The Master of the Rolls, Sir John Leach, died on Saturday last in Edinburgh, to which place he had gone a short time since. His health had been long declining, and he had supported one or more serious surgical operations with great fortitude. He was a kind, hospitable man, fond of society; and though his manner was trifling and perhaps finical, he was esteemed one of the best chancery lawyers in England. No one comprehended more quickly the different bearings of a complicated case. Sir John rose from a very humble station in early life to his late dignified eminence in the law.

Tuesday, 24*th.*—Amongst the political tourists in search of popularity, one of the most conspicuous is Lord Chancellor Brougham, in Scotland. At a late public dinner in Aberdeen, he made a long and flighty speech, the prominent feature of which was an excessive adulation of the King, to whom he informed the meeting he should write by the following post an account of the flattering reception which

he had met with in that city. The following has since appeared in the "Examiner,"
entitled, "Letter from a Gentleman who travels for a large Establishment to One of
his Employers, Mr. William King."

"Dear Sir, the account here forwarded
Of favours since the 4th,
Presents a very handsome stroke
Of business in the North.
Our firm's new style don't take at all,
So thought the prudent thing
Would be to cultivate the old
Establish'd name of King.

"Believe me, Sir, so great a zeal
In this behalf I've shown,
Credit's been turn'd to your account
Which strictly was my own.
Does any one admire my nag,
Or think my gig's the thing,
This horse and shay, I always say.
Belong to Mr. King.

"If any friend attention shows,
And asks me out to dine,
When company my health propose,
In toddy or in wine,
My heart's eternal gratitude
About their ears I ding,
With, 'Be assur'd I'll mention this
Next post to Mr. King!'

"I met with Grey the other day,
Who, since he left the firm,

Has travell'd on his own account,
And done, I fear, some harm;
So thought it right, where'er he went,
To whisper round the ring,
'Perhaps you don't know *how* he lost
The confidence of King.'

"With what I still propose to do,
And what's been done already,
I trust the firm will henceforth go
On prosperous and steady.
Should any chance the senior clerk
Into discredit bring,
I hope, Sir, you'll remember who
Has serv'd the House of King.

It has been remarked that the demeanour of Earl Grey and the Chancellor towards each other, at the late dinner at Edinburgh, was of such a kind as warranted the conclusion that no very cordial feeling existed between them.

Mr. Augustus Craven, son of the Hon. Keppell Craven, who is a great performer in private theatricals, has married the daughter of the Comte de la Ferronaye, having, as a Protestant, first received the consent of the Pope. When the parties were assembled in the chapel, the Bishop of Caserta, Monsignor Giusti, refused to give the nuptial benediction, saying, that he would not bless the union of "Una Christiana con un figlio di Satanasso." The astonishment of the whole assembly may well be imagined, and it was some time before a more tolerant priest could be procured.

Saturday, 29*th.*—A duel has taken place at Madrid, between two Englishmen, correspondents of the *Times* and *Chronicle* papers, which is not otherwise of any importance, than that the latter proves to be Mr. Maberly, the contractor, who, having failed two years ago, has been reduced by misfortune to that means of earning a livelihood.

An ingenious mode of forgery to a large extent has been lately detected at Brest, and has been practised by the same set in other towns in France. One of the party applies to a banker, and purchases his bills on Paris or Bordeaux for the purpose of remittance at sight, taking care to demand a bill for 10,000fr. and one for 100fr. By a chemical process the latter is soon made equal to the former, and despatched first for payment, which meets with no difficulty as corresponding exactly with the letter of advice. That point being accomplished, the real bill is negotiated, for which the drawers must always be liable; in the meantime the parties have had time to escape.

Monday, 29 *th*—The accounts from the West Indian Islands are very alarming. The new law of emancipation came into force on the 1st of August, and great apprehensions were entertained for the result. The slave population in Demerara were in a most alarming state of mutiny and insubordination; that in Grenada had evinced a determined spirit not to work. The accounts from Jamaica were highly unsatisfactory, and the next despatches are awaited with much anxiety.

Don Pedro is at the point of death. The Cortes of Portugal had consequently declared the young Queen of age, and the Duke of Palmella bad been charged by the Queen to form a new administration.

The Chamber of Procuradores in Spain has just acknowledged all the foreign debts contracted at different periods, and particularly the loans as well prior as subsequent to the year 1823. This tardy act of justice, in which much hesitation has been shown, originates in the necessities of government, which is anxious to raise further supplies abroad; but the aggregate of their debt will have become so enormous, and so disproportionate to their means of paying the interest, that it becomes a question whether they would go into the market with better credit than if they had made what Cobbett and Co. call an ***equitable adjustment*** Their resource will now be, and in the present times it will not be difficult, to engage the Rothschilds, Aguado, Ardouin, &c., loan mongers, to come to their assistance with a loan, which the host of speculators will soon take off their hands at a profit, and then woe to the holders of Spanish stock.

The cholera has made great havoc in Sweden. At Stockholm M. D. Tarrach, the Prussian Minister at that court, died in twelve hours. The disease had made its appearance in the palace. The Intendant of the Household, the Marshal of the Court, and a valet of the Crown Prince, were carried off after a few hours' illness. The daily numbers, between the 12th and the 16th, averaged from 295 to 383.

Wednesday, October 1*st*—Accounts are received through Spain by telegraph that Don Pedro died on the 21st. ult. at Lisbon.

A most singular trial is to take place at the Cour d'Assises in the end of this month, of which the following is the outline:—

M. Lethuillier, proprietor of a maison de santé near Paris, had an intimate friend, M. Vadebant. Suspicions of an improper intercourse between the latter and his wife induced M. L. to send him a challenge. Nevertheless, some inexplicable motive urged him to insist that, whichever might fall, the cause of his death should remain unknown; and he therefore proposed that the duel should take place without seconds, and that each adversary should bear about his person a written certificate that, in case of his body being found, be had not died by assassination. The parties being agreed on this point, proceeded to the Bois de Romainville, armed with pistols. It was decided that the antagonists from a given point should walk towards each other, and fire as they pleased.

M. Lethuillier asserts that, his attention being diverted by a woman who was walking on the road at some distance, he stopped short, while M. Vadebant continued to advance, and fired when he came near him. M. L. being wounded fell, and, if he is to be believed, implored the assistance of his adversary without avail.

M. Vadebant, imagining that he had killed him took up both pistols and disappeared.

The wound, however, of the unfortunate Lethuillier was not mortal; having presented his profile to his enemy, the ball had carried away both his eyes, without injuring the skull, and he managed to crawl from the wood to the high road, where he at last met with assistance. Having recovered from his wounds, M. Lethuillier now brings a civil action, and Vadebant has surrendered himself for trial. Plans of the ground are taken, which, it is said, will be of great importance in the decision as to the good faith of the whole proceeding.

Saturday, 4*th.*—The Spanish financial resolutions, which seem to vary and oscillate by every post, and cause the most fatal fluctuations in the prices of their stock, after having acknowledged the whole debt, then made an exception of Gueb-hard's loan. Now again, after having relieved the treasury of the burthen of Gueb-hard's loan, the majority of the Chamber reduced by one-third the loans of which it had acknowledged the totality, by decreeing that the debt shall be divided into two-thirds active and one-third passive. The undue use which has been made here of the telegraph, to procure early information of these sudden and contradictory decrees, for the purposes of speculation in the funds, has excited a general indignation, and has very properly been noticed severely by the public press. The reply to this on the part of the Government has rather confirmed than removed the suspicions of this iniquitous collusion.

The following curious memorandum made at the École Militaire by M. de Ker-alio, the Inspecteur of that establishment in 1784, on the character of the Elève Bonaparte, is taken from the ***Revue Retrospective:***—"M. de Buonaparte (Napoléon) né le 15 Août 1769, taille de quatre pieds, dix pouces, dix lignes, a fait sa quatrième: de bonne constitution, santé excellente, caractère soumis, honnête, reconnoissant, conduite très régulière, s'ést toujours distingué par son application aux mathéma-tiques: il sait très passablement son histoire et sa géographie. Il est assez faible pour les exercises d'agrément, et pour le Latin, où il n'a fait que sa quatrième; ce sera un excellent marin. Il mérite de passer à l'École Militaire de Paris."

The suicides in France become daily more frequent; every journal announces fresh instances of this destructive mania, which seems to rage through all classes of society. According to the records of his time, Bonaparte stigmatized this crime by a public order to the army.

"Ordre du Jour.
"St Cloud, 22 Floréal, An 10 de la République.

"Le grénadier Groblin s'est suicidé pour raisons d'amour; c'étoit d'ailleurs un bon sujet. C'est le second événement de ce genre qui arrive au corps depuis un mois.

"Le Premier Consul ordonne, qu'il soit mis à l'ordre du jour de la Garde— Qu'un soldat doit savoir vaincre la douleur et la mélancolie des passions; qu'il y a autant de vrai courage à souffrir avec constance les peines de l'âme qu'à rester fixé sous la mitraille d'une batterie. S'abandonner au chagrin sans résister, se tuer pour s'y soustraire, c'est abandonner le champ de bataille avant d'avoir vaincu.

"(Signé)   Bonaparte.
"(Contresigné)   BessiÈres."

This document is said to have had great effect at the time. Louis-Philippe, in imitation of his predecessors, has had a voyage to Fontainebleau, with a numerous suite of ministers, courtiers, and ambassadors, to pass a week in a routine of balls, plays, concerts, and festivities. The artistes of the Italian Opera, the actors of the Français, Gymnase, and the Opéra Comique, have been put in requisition to beguile the evenings, while the mornings have been devoted to reviews of National Guards and drives in the various recesses of the forest. The only circumstance which has excited any remark in the society of Paris has been the distribution of the guests belonging to the Corps Diplomatique. The first three days were devoted to the representatives of the Sainte Alliance, the Russian, Austrian, and Prussian ministers; the later period to those of the liberal system, including the English, Spanish, and Belgian diplomatists.

Thursday, 9*th.*—Boieldieu, the celebrated composer, died to-day at Paris, after a long and painful illness—the Opéra Comique is shut for one day as a token of mourning.

Our national anthem of "God save the King," composed in the time of George I., has always been considered of English origin; but on reading the amusing "Memoirs of Madame de Créquy," it appears to have been almost a literal translation of the cantique which was always sung by the demoiselles de St. Cyr when Louis XIV. entered the chapel of that establishment to hear the morning prayer. The words were by M. de Brinon, and the music by the famous Lully:—

"Grand Dieu, sauve le Roi!
Grand Dieu, venge de Roi!
Vive le Roi!
"Que toujours glorieux,
Louis victorieux!
Voye ses ennemis
Toujours soumis!
"Grand Dieu, sauve le Roi!
Grand Dieu, venge le Roi!
Vire le Roi!"

It appears to have been translated and adapted to the House of Hanover by Händel, the German composer.

Friday, 10*th.*—General Sebastiani, French ambassador at Naples, has married Madame Davidoff, a widow, and daughter of the Duc de Gramont, and sister to the Duc de Guiche and Lady Tankerville.

The vintage in France this year has been so productive, that in many of the vine departments the produce has been one-half more than the usual crop; and the scarcity of casks for this excess of produce was so great, that the farmers would fill an empty cask for nothing if another cask was sent with it. The quality of the wine is also very fine, and even superior to that of the famous year of the comet.

Monday, 13th.—The extraordinary composure with which even a painful death may be contemplated is exemplified by a criminal who is under sentence of execution for a murder in one of the prisons of Munich at this present time. He has made with crumbs of bread and a sort of macaroni several figures illustrating the scene in which he will quit the world. He has figured the instant when the executioner, having cut off his head, is holding it up to public view. A Franciscan friar on his knees is at the side of the headless corpse; near the priest is an invalid with a wooden leg, selling a true and full account of his judgment and execution.

A double suicide took place on Friday night, Rue de la Fidélité, No. 24., at Paris. A M. Malglaive, formerly in the army, was deprived of his fortune by unforeseen calamities. He was found with his wife in their apartment suffocated by a pan of charcoal, having previously stopped up every aperture in the room which could admit of air. He had written the following curious letter to a friend by the *petite poste:*—

"Quand vous allez lire cette lettre, ni moi ni ma pauvre Eléonore ne serons plus dans ce monde: ayez done la bonté de faire ouvrir notre porte, et vous nous trouverez les yeux fermés pour toujours. Nous sommes fatigués tous deux des malheurs qui nous poursuivent, et nous ne croyons pouvoir mieux faire, que de mettre un terme à tous nos maux. Connaissant son courage, et tout l'attachement que ma bonne femme a pour moi, j'étais certain qu'elle accepterait la partie, et partagerait entièrement ma manière de voir.

"Adieu, brave ami, en attendant les effete de la métempsycose, je vous souhaite une bonne nuit, et à moi un bon voyage. J'espère que pour minuit nous serons arrivés au but de notre promenade.

"Vendredi, 10 Octobre, 11 heures du soir."

The following is the enumeration of all the English colonies abroad, independent of those under the government of the English East India Company. In the West Indies and South America: 1. Antigua, 2. Barbadoes, 3. British Guiana, 4. Dominica, 5. Grenada, 6. Jamaica, 7. Montserrat, 8. Nevis, 9. St. Christopher, 10. St. Lucia, 11. St. Vincent, 12. Tobago, 13. Trinidad, 14. Virgin Islands. In North America: 1. Bahama Islands, 2. Bermudas, 3. Lower Canada, 4. Upper Canada, 5. Prince Edward's Island, 6. New Brunswick, 7. Newfoundland and Labrador, 8. Nova Scotia. In Africa: 1. Cape of Good Hope, 2. Sierra Leone and Gold Coast. In the Indian Seas: 1. Ceylon, 2. Mauritius. In the South Seas: 1. New South Wales, 2. Van Diemen's Land, 3. West Australia. To which may be added, in Europe, 1. Gibraltar, 2. Heligoland, 3. Malta, 4. The Ionian Islands.

Mr. Charles Grant has been recommended by the Government to the Court of Directors as Governor-General of India, in the room of Lord William Bentinck, which appointment they have refused to ratify.

Wednesday, 15*th.*—The West India packet has brought more favourable intelligence of the proceedings in the islands; it would seem that the slaves are becoming more docile and tractable, though still unable to comprehend the new regulations. The St. Christopher's insurrection was of a very serious nature. Martial law was in force for fourteen days, and the marines from the six ships of war were obliged to be landed. The Marquis de L——, residing near the Opera, after having squandered an immense fortune in dissipation and the pursuit of pleasure, has lately destroyed himself, because he had only 33,000 fr. a year remaining, which he found was not sufficient to satisfy the caprices of his mistress. Previous to his death, wishing to insure the independence of her whom he accused as the author of his ruin, he left by will to Mademoiselle Dérieux all that he possessed, being 600,000 fr. or 700,000 fr. By an extraordinary fatality this will is dated the 1st of October, 1834, and it was on the 25th of September preceding that he had ceased to live. In consequence of this irregularity, the civil tribunal of the Seine has refused to confirm this donation to Mademoiselle Dérieux, in the absence of the heirs presumptive to the estate.

Monday, 20*th.*—On the night of Thursday last both Houses of Parliament, with a portion of the Speaker's private dwelling, were consumed by fire. The origin of this public misfortune is not known; but it appears to have been caused by some negligence in the House of Lords. The reports are very vague and uncertain. There may be something ominous in such a catastrophe at such a moment; the two contending bodies of the State, just arrayed in dire opposition to each other, the one insolent and overbearing in aggression, the other strict and obstinate in defence of its privileges, both buried in one common ruin. It appears that many of the archives of both Houses have been preserved, but not without considerable damage. The tapestry in the House of Lords, representing the defeat of the Spanish Armada, which was generally admired, has been a prey to the flames.

Mr. Hume during the last session had been proposing without success a vote to build a larger House of Commons; a wag in the crowd watching the progress of the conflagration exclaimed, "There is Mr. Hume's motion carried without a division."

The old walls of St. Stephen's have witnessed a long career of British glory and prosperity; may it not have perished with them!!! Time will show that mystery. But if the character, talent, and honour of those public men who in years gone by have distinguished themselves within *those walls* contributed to support that career of glory, then may we own that they have now crumbled over the heads of men who are utterly incompetent and incapable of maintaining it.

Tuesday, 21*st.*—By the accounts from London it appears that the fire originated in the over-heated flues of the House of Lords communicating with the stove in which the clerks of the old Exchequer Office had been burning the accumulation of old tallies which were condemned to destruction.

The Nuremberg Gazette mentions that last year a Polish gentleman caught a stork on his estate at Lemberg, which he released, having previously fixed round its neck an iron collar with the following inscription: Hæc ciconia ex Poloniâ. *This year the bird has returned, and been again entrapped by the same individual, who has found its neck ornamented with a second collar, but made of gold, and thus inscribed:* India cum donis mittit ciconia Polis. The bird has again been set at liberty for further adventures.

Thursday, 23*rd.*—The following extraordinary occurrence has just taken place at a château near Senlis. The Comtesse Pontalba, whose name has been cited before the tribunals in a trial for separation from her husband, at length found means to interest him in her favour and procure her return home, which very much exasperated her father-in-law. Determined to deliver his family from a woman who branded it with ignominy, he the other day entered her apartment armed with two pistols, and discharged the contents of both in her body: he then retired to his own apartment, in a different wing of the château, and shot himself through the heart. His body was found stretched on a sofa, with the countenance calm but still with a threatening expression. The old count, whose life had been as honourable as his sense of honour was rigorous, had just completed his eightieth year, and possessed an immense fortune. The countess did not die on the spot, though pierced by four balls (for the pistols were double-barrelled); her hand by instinct was raised to protect her heart: but she still lies in very great danger.

It would appear that, in the confusion of removing the various objects during the fire in the House of Lords, the curious document of the warrant for the execution of Charles I. is missing. *November.*—It is since found.

Friday, 24*th..*—William Spencer is dead in Paris. He was son of the late Lord Charles Spencer, and nephew of the late Duke of Marlborough. I knew him well in former times, when he was the wit, the poet, and the welcome guest at every table in London. He married, in 1791, the Countess Dowager Jenison Walworth, of the Holy Roman Empire, in Germany. I think I have heard the late Duchess of York say there was some romantic history attached to this marriage: that the countess was first married to an old man, who, perceiving an attachment gradually increasing between her and young Spencer, destroyed himself, that he might not be a bar to their union. This circumstance is said to have suggested to Madame de Souza her well-known novel of "Adèle de Senanges." William Spencer's translations of Bürger's "Leonora" and other poems are well known. He was a constant guest at Oatlands, and a favourite with both the duke and duchess, who took great pleasure in his society. He was an excellent linguist, a profound classical scholar, and gifted with great conversational talents; one of the last specimens of that old school which is now completely extinct. Alas! where are they?

> "And while the lesson strikes my head
> My wearied heart grows cold!!!"

Saturday, 25*th.*—The mania for suicide seems to increase here like an epidemical disorder, though in some instances the cause is so trifling, that it would almost appear to be a caricature on the malady. A young man in the Collège Louis le Grand has destroyed himself because he did not make the desired progress in his studies; and a young maid-servant of seventeen years, of most irreproachable conduct, beloved by her mistress, No. 20. Rue de Richelieu, has suffocated herself with charcoal because she thought that she was not loved by her parents at home.

Sunday, 26*th.*—The dreadful event which took place at the Château de Mont l'Evêque had made such an impression on the public mind, that no one could be found for a long time to bury the marquis. Little hopes are entertained for the life of Madame Pontalba. A curious circumstance was mentioned the other day, which would increase the faith of those who believe in omens. On the day that Charles X. attended the last séance royale ***in 1830 by some accident his foot became entangled in the carpet which covered the steps of the throne, and he was near falling. This false step caused the*** toque, which he wore instead of a crown, to fall at the feet of the Duke of Orleans, who immediately picked it up and returned it to the king.

Monday, 27*th.*—On the 21st instant died, at Knowsley Park, the Earl of Derby. His first marriage was with a daughter of the Duke of Hamilton, and on her death he married Miss Farren the actress. He was eighty-two years old.

The trial of Vadibant and Lethuillier came on before the tribunal yesterday. As there could be no witnesses, the accusation and defence rested chiefly on the assertions of the principals; but it became very evident, upon the whole, that Vadibant had fired on his adversary before he was prepared for it, and the jury brought in their verdict guilty of attempt to murder, with extenuating circumstances. The court sentenced Vadibant to ten years' solitary confinement.

On Saturday at six o'clock in the evening, three young men, fashionably dressed, went to dine at the Restaurant Legrain, Boulevard du Temple, without a sous in their pocket, but determined to kill themselves as soon as their dinner was finished. They asked for a private cabinet, and ordered a most expensive repast. One of them went down stairs, and told the waiter that they expected a lady, who would arrive in a cabriolet with a white horse, and that he might introduce *the horse* as well as *the lady.* After indulging themselves in every luxury that the house could afford, they wrote with pencil the address of their wives, and desired that they might be sent for immediately; but when the ladies arrived, their appearance gave M. Legrain such an unfavourable opinion of their respectability, that he refused to admit them; and they retired without any further comment from the guests. When at length the bill was presented, the surprise of Legrain may be imagined, when one of the party said, "We have not a sous; if you will not allow us to depart, and raise some money, we will kill ourselves before your face." They produced pistols, and were only moved by the screams of Madame Legrain to suspend their project till the next day, on the condition that they might have beds for the night. As soon as they were housed Legrain sent for the guard, and in the scuffle one made his escape; one absolutely shot himself, after his pistol had missed three times; and the third was conveyed to the corps de garde.

Wednesday, 29*th.*—Went to dine with Macdonald [Note 1: Mr. Archibald Macdonald, brother-in-law to Prince Polignac.] at Paris, who leaves for England to-morrow. His visit to the château at Ham was short. He found Prince Polignac well in health, but him and his fellow prisoners as rigorously guarded as ever. During his stay the permission authorised him to have a daily interview from eleven till five o'clock. On his first visit M. Guernon de Ranville, hearing of his arrival, and delighted with the idea of seeing a new face, hurried into the prince's rooms; but the gaoler with much roughness instantly conducted him back to his own, without allowing any communication. As his room was directly under that of the prince, a signal was given by stamping on the floor when Macdonald took leave, and, as he descended the staircase, M. G. de R. appeared at his door, with the intention of taking his daily walk in the court, and had then a hurried opportunity of shaking him by the hand, which still was viewed with a jealous eye by the attendants. At five o'clock the drum beats, and then all communication with the citadel is interdicted till the next day. Each prisoner has a small room to himself; but their visits, **generally** speaking, to each other are not very frequent. The Princess, with the children and establishment, occupy a house in the village, and they have constant access during the day to the prince; but his table is not allowed to be supplied from thence, only occasionally some trifling articles of gateaux, &c, are admitted. A short time for daily exercise in a confined space, guarded by a sentinel, is only allowed to each détenu; and M. Chanteluze always chooses the moment when it rains, which he seems to enjoy, till he is quite wet through, and uses as a bath. He has a suit of clothes entirely for this purpose.

Thursday, 30*th.*—Marshal Gérard has resigned, and the cabinet is again without a president. Differences with his colleagues about the amnesty is the cause assigned for this resignation. The papers are full of the proceedings before the Superior Council of Commerce, as to a revision of prohibitions and duties on imports. The result of these examinations is very contradictory, and shows as much their extraordinary ignorance as their jealousy of everything that may possibly tend to injure their own individual interest.

Friday, 31*st.*—The Royal Court has declared the prosecution against MM. Jauge, Haber, &c., for raising money for Don Carlos, null and void, and ordered the immediate liberation of the prisoners and their papers. This alone proves that the previous act of the government was tyrannical and illegal. J. King tells me all the Spanish loans are to be acknowledged **tant bien que mal.**

Saturday, 1*st November.*—There seems to be as much difficulty to find a prime minister here as in England; no one seems inclined to accept an office beset with so much difficulty, and with so little chance of permanence. The names of Marshal Mortier and Marshal Maison are mentioned, but it is thought they will refuse it.

Monday, 3*rd.*—Marshal Moncey, Due de Cornegliano, governor of the In-
valides, and one of the distinguished followers of Napoleon, is dead.

Tuesday, 4*th.*—The above death, though announced in the papers, has since
been contradicted. The Court of Assizes has been occupied for the last four or five
days with the trial of a Baron de Richemont, calling himself Duc de Normandie, or
the Dauphin son of Louis XVI., who died in the Temple at the commencement of
the Revolution, Many witnesses were examined; but the plot seemed a clumsy con-
trivance, not even founded upon probabilities. The prisoner was found guilty, and
sentenced to twelve years' imprisonment.

Among the numerous suicides which daily occur here there is generally some
reason assigned for the fatal resolution; but to-day the paper mentions the following: "M. Alphin, jeune homme de 18 ans, appartenant à une famille excessivement
riche et heureuse, vient de se tuer par dégoût de la vie."

Wednesday, 5*th.*—At the opening of the Court of Cassation yesterday M.
Dupin, the procureur-general, who has visited England this year, in concluding his
usual speech, alluded to the destruction of the two Houses of Parliament. "There,"
he said, "were collected, by an uninterrupted series of traditions, all the precedents
of power and liberty; there, may be said to have been breathed the history of Old
England, containing sources of inspiration to the orators whose voices resounded
within its walls. Under the same roof, by the side of the parliamentary forum, sometimes so full of storm, were seated, in all the dignity of the most profound calmness,
the antique Courts of Chancery, King's Bench, and Common Pleas; that immortal
jury so severely rigid in protecting liberty, and on the throne of justice those magistrates so great in power, in doctrine, and in consideration, each of whom alone
represents the majesty of a court, delivering their judgments, surrounded by the respect of their citizens, in the presence of a learned and vigilant bar, which gave Lord
Brougham to the ministry, and which still has at its head a Sir James Scarlett."

The other evening, Ischann, the Swiss Minister, said: "Il y a eu un petit Westminster ce soir chez les Berrys [Note *: The Miss Berrys, friends of Horace Walpo-

le.]; la manche de Miss Agnès a pris feu à la bougie." "En a-t-elle reçu quelque mal?" was asked. He replied, "Non; dans les deux cas on a sauvé les parchemins."

Thursday, 6th.—The difficulties in the cabinet increase. MM. Guizot, Thiers, Hermann, Duchatel, and De Rigny have delivered in their resignations to the King, who it is said has sent for Molé. One of my friends has been staying three weeks at Valençay, where Prince Talleyrand and the Duchesse de Dino have been entertaining a party partly English. Talleyrand expressed himself very openly and satirically about the English Government, whom he considered very deficient both in talent and honesty. He said of Lord Holland: "C'est la bienveillance même, mais la bienveillance la plus perturbatrice, qu'on ait jamais vue." Of Lady Holland he observed: "Elleest toute assertion, mais quand on demande la preuve, c'est là son secret." [Note †: M. de Montrond being asked by the Comtesse J. de N——, a Valençay, if there were reason to suppose, as she had heardt that letters were opened at the Château? He answered, with great, composure, "Je crois qu'on ne le fait plus."]

He says the Duke is the only honest public man in the country; that Peel, by his selfish policy in refusing to join him, is the cause of all the mischief present and to come; the latter of which is incalculable. The English consisted of Lady Clanricarde, Colonel and Mrs. Darner, Henry Greville, and Motteux: the last, who is a notorious epicure, and always talking on that subject, was a source of much amusement to the party. One day at dinner he interrupted Talleyrand in the midst of an interesting anecdote by saying: "Mon Prince, avez-vous jamais entendu ce qui m'est arrivé avec les écrevisses?" and every one burst out laughing.

Monday, 10th.—The Chouans still continue their partisan war in La Vendée and Brittany. A waggon loaded with money on account of government was stopped last week by a detachment of forty men, and twelve bags, each containing 10,000 fr., were the prey of the marauders. The escort only consisted of five gendarmes, who were easily mastered.

After several ineffectual attempts to form a new cabinet, the King sent for the Due de Bassano, who without delay made the following list, which is approved:

himself, president; Bresson, foreign affairs; Baron Bernard, war; C. Dupin, marine; Teste, commerce; Passy, finance. It is a government of no colour, no fixed political principle, and no feeling of sympathy among themselves. Bresson is a pupil of Talleyrand, Bernard is aid-de-camp to the King, Dupin brother to the president of the Chamber of Deputies.

The King was very much incensed against the late cabinet, and very high words are said to have passed between him, Broglie, and Guizot.

Tuesday, 11*th.*—The accounts from Spain are of late more favourable to the cause of Don Carlos. Some advantages have been gained by the army of Zumalacarraguay, and General Rodil has been replaced by Mina. There is much warm discussion in the Chamber of Proceres at Madrid, and considerable excitement prevails in that capital.

I dined with King at Paris. The Chambers are to meet early in December. The new cabinet inspires no confidence. It brings at its birth but one advantage, the expulsion of the Doctrinaires and their system. This is the meaning of the new combination; as the Messager says, "We know what it is not, but we cannot tell what it is."

Wednesday, 12*th.*—Talleyrand since his return has professed his intention not to resume his post in England if Lord Palmerston remained as foreign secretary; but the new changes here will probably decide that question at once by another nomination in his place, as the Due de Bassano's [Note *: Maret, formerly Minister of Foreign Affairs to Napoleon.] antipathy to him is well known.

His severe remark on Maret, when he received his title under the empire,— "Je ne connais pas de plus grande bête au monde que M. Maret, excepté le Due de Bassano,"—is not likely to have been forgotten by the new president of the council.

Thursday, 13*th.*—Charles X. has just made a definitive purchase of property in the Austrian states. The Duchess of Sagan has sold him a fine estate in Stiegemark for 2,000,000 of florins.

Friday, 14*th.*—Earl Spencer died at Althorpe Park on the 10th instant, aged seventy-six. By his death Lord Althorpe goes to the Upper House, and vacates his place.

A grand dinner was given by the Tories on the fifth to Captain Gordon, M. P. for Aberdeenshire, at the Town Hall of Aberdeen.

The frost has set in with unusual rigour.

Saturday, 15*th.*—The new cabinet here seems likely not to have even a week's duration. Difficulties have already occurred with the King, who has taken alarm at some allusion to the principles of the Revolution of July, and still adheres to the Doctrinaire system. The result is, that Passy and Teste resigned yesterday, and their example was followed by Bassano in the evening.

A punishment exists in the French navy called "Supplice de la cale," which may serve as a match to flogging in the English army. It consists in plunging the culprit into the sea till life becomes nearly extinct; a letter from Toulon speaks in the following terms of the infliction of this punishment lately. "As at the execution of a felon, a gun was fired to announce that a sailor was about to undergo the *supplice de la cale,* and crowds flocked to the quay. The unfortunate man, round whose body a rope was tied, after having been plunged three times into the sea to a great depth, was drawn up in a senseless state. The ship's surgeon, however, after great efforts, succeeded in restoring respiration."

Sunday, 16*th.*—The King has sent for Marshal Mortier Due de Trevise, to patch up the *doctrinaires* again. The chief stumbling block of the Bassano Cabinet was the American Indemnity Bill, which having opposed as deputies, neither Teste, Passy, or Dupin could advocate as ministers.

Monday, 17th.—The astonishing intelligence is just arrived that the Melbourne administration has ceased to exist. This time it is not a resignation, but a dismissal in form by the King, who intimated to Lord Melbourne at Brighton, when he went to propose a successor to Althorpe, that the death of Earl Spencer would induce him to take the formation of the ministry into his own hands.

The Radical press are raving. The letters say he has sent for the Duke.

Tuesday, 18th.—A courier went through Paris with an express for Sir R. Peel, who is travelling in Italy. He expected to find him at Florence. The despatches were said to urge his return to England.

Wednesday, 19th.—The King's decision took place on the avowal of Lord Melbourne that he despaired of carrying on the government, and that a dissolution of the cabinet was inevitable before the meeting of Parliament. The conference was carried on in the most candid and cordial spirit on both sides, and the King's letter to the Duke was brought to town by Lord M. himself. On Saturday the Duke arrived at Brighton at five o'clock, and staid till ten. On Monday the King arrived in town, and saw the Speaker, Sir H. Hardinge, the Duke, Lords Maryborough, Cowley, Lyndhurst, Jersey, Rosslyn, &c, after which the Ministers arrived to deliver up their seals. The Duke is now authorised to form a new Administration.

Here the changes are a mere farce. Marshal Mortier is President of the Council, and the old *doctrinaires* have resumed their places. Compared to the great change going on in England, which is an European event, this is a mere harlequinade.

Friday, 21st.—The royal family in France are very much displeased with the accession of the Duke to power. The queen is said to have expressed herself very strongly on the subject. Lord Granville has sent home his resignation; and Sir. F. Lamb is just arrived here from Vienna in time to exchange condoléances.

Saturday, 22nd.—The Princesse de Poix, mother of the late Due de Mouchy, died yesterday, aged eighty-four.

Monday, 24*th.*—The Earl of Hardwicke died last Tuesday, and is succeeded by Captain Yorke. Much comment has been made on the testy manner in which Lord Brougham resigned the seals. He came to the King's Court, and would not deliver them himself, but gave them to Sir H. Taylor.

Thursday, 27*th.*—Colonel Caradoc is gone to England for the winter; but previous to his departure the long-debated marriage with Princess Bagration was privately performed before fifteen witnesses. She was a Mademoiselle Jehavronsky, a Russian, with an immense fortune, married early in life, by the emperor's order, to Prince Bagration, as a reward for his military services. He was killed at the battle of Borodino, and his widow has since lived in France and Italy, distinguished by her splendid establishment and her debts.

Friday, 28*th.*—Lady Granville gave her last assembly in Paris, or, as she styled it herself, her funeral; upon which Yarmouth observed, "I believe in a resurrection." Flahault, just returned from England, seemed little pleased with the new changes there. He said, "I should not like to have all my eggs in your basket." The proportion of French was small.

Sunday, 30*th.*—No tidings of Sir R. Peel; and the Duke is left to keep the disjointed offices in order by himself. Notwithstanding the efforts made by the mortified Whigs, and that part of the press which is attached to them, to create agitation in the country, it is astonishing to observe the calmness which generally prevails, and the failure which has attended some partial attempts at public meetings, made by the Radical agents at various places. It may be inferred and hoped, that the nation is decided on giving the Duke a fair trial; while, on the other hand, he seems anxious to show that he is guided at least by no ambitious feelings for himself. The accidental absence of Sir R. Peel at such a crisis is still very unfortunate: so long an interregnum, without any positive government at all, must tend to dispirit and dishearten those waverers, whom a strong and promptly-formed administration would have attached warmly to the cause; independent of which, such an unusual state of things furnishes additional grounds of attack to the opposite side.

Earl Spencer's blue ribbon was given by the Whigs to the Duke of Grafton, who has constantly supported them.

Monday, ***1st December.***—The Chamber of Deputies met this day.

A curious banquet took place yesterday in Paris, being the 122nd anniversary of the birth of the Abbé de l'Epée. Above fifty ***sourds et muets*** met at this dinner, to celebrate the birth of him whom, in their poetic language, they call their père intellectuel. A bystander gives the following interesting description of the meeting:—

"L'intelligence enflammoit leurs yeux, elle étincelait au bout de leurs doigts, avec une rapidité que la parole peut égaler, mais qu'à coup sûr elle ne surpassera jamais. Pendant trois heures j'ai pu me croire dans un de ces mondes, où Swift a jeté son Gulliver; pendant trois heures, les rôles ont été renversés, et je me suis trouvé moi l'homme incomplet, l'infortuné privé de la parole; le paria de la société; obligé de recourir au crayon pour entrer en commerce avec ses frères. Informé que je ne connaissais pas même les premiers élémens de la mimique, l'un de ces heureux du moment a donné à sa physionomie une expression d'ineffable pitié, et puis il a dit: que je plains ce monsieur, il ne pourra pas se faire entendre. Quand Berthier harangua ses frères, comme président du banquet, faisant l'é-loge de l'abbé de l'Epée, devant cinquante hommes, pour lesquels de l'Epée a été un autre créateur; vis-à-vis de lui étaient deux yieillards honorables, anciens élèives de l'abbé, ceux-là n'applaudissaient pas comme les autres, ... ils pleuraient."

Wednesday, ***3rd.***—On the 20th ultimo died at Bagshot, His Royal Highness the Duke of Gloucester, after a painful illness of fifteen days, aged fifty-nine: born January, 1776. He married in 1816, the Princess Mary, his cousin, sister of His Majesty. He was not a man of talent, as may be inferred from his nickname of ***silly Billy,*** but he was a quiet, inoffensive character, rather tenacious of the respect due to his rank, and strongly attached to the ultra-Tory party. His father, the late Duke, married Lady Waldegrave; thus he was uncle to Mrs. Damer.

Thursday, 4th.—M. de Vatry told me at dinner, at the Darners' to-day, that he had seen a manuscript correspondence between Talleyrand and Casimir Perier, so curious that he had obtained permission to copy it, and which proved that the system of policy pursued by that minister during his short political life, and particularly called his system, was in fact dictated and chalked out by M. de Talleyrand entirely.

Friday, 5th.—It is announced that Sir Robert Peel has accepted the Ministry. His brother Colonel Peel stated the fact at M. Dupin's soirée.

Sunday, 7th.—Sir R. Peel arrived at the Hôtel Bristol at eleven o'clock last night. This morning he received the visit of Lord Granville, and at eleven o'clock left Paris for London, big with the fate of Cæsar and of Rome.

Tuesday, 9th.—The following is the account of the suicide of M. Daure, formerly secretary to M. de Talleyrand, from one of the journals:—

"Il y a un mois et demi qu'un étranger portant moustaches, à figure pâle et romantique, à manières distinguées, à élocution facile et élégante, se présenta à M. le Maire de la petite ville de Prune, pour lui dire, que son intention étant de passer une partie des vacances dans ce pays, il avoit cru de son devoir de se faire connoitre à lui. Il exhiba son passe-port, qui le qualifia d'homme de lettres, âgé de trente-sept ans, et ajouta que le motif réel de sa présence étoit de prendre des renseignemens sur la valeur de la fôret de Gresigne, qu'une société de spéculateurs, dont il faisoit partie, se proposoit d'acheter. M. le Maire, séduit par la tenue et le langage de cet étranger, lui offrit une chambre et sa table, ce qui fut accepté, mais sous clause de remunération. M. Daure s'y établit, il avoit apporté beaucoup de livres, beaucoup de linge, et de vêtemens, et tout l'attirail d'une toilette fashionable. Sa lecture constante et favorite étoit la Bible, dont un exemplaire ne le quittoit jamais. Il mettoit toutes les semaines dix francs à la disposition de M. le Curé pour les pauvres, alloit à la messe le dimanche, s'y tenoit décemment, mais il paroissoit absorbé par une lecture, étrangère sans doute au saint sacrifice. Il reçut la visite de sa mère, qui demeure à Montauban; il la reçut bien, et lui donna 40 Napoléons. Son tems s'écouloit ainsi dans les promenades romantiques, dans des conversations instructives, lorsque M. Daure fit trouver M. le Curé de Prune pour lui demander un service funèbre et solennel, pour un de ses amis. Pendant le chant du Dies iræ l'étranger versa d'abondantes larmes, cela fut d'autant plus remarquable, qu'habituellement il paroissoit froid et insensible. Après cette cérémonie funèbre, il paroissoit éprouver beaucoup de sérénité. Le lendemain matin il sortit, sans rien dire, s'achemina vers les mines du château, et un instant après on entend l'explosion d'une arme à feu, et on trouve le cadavre du bienfaisant étranger horriblement mutilé; il avoit appuyé le canon d'un pistolet attaché à son bras par un crêpe, sur l'orbite de l'œil, et s'étoit fait sauter la cervelle; de l'autre main il tenoit un rasoir. En fouillant dans sa chambre, on trouva plusieurs lettres, entre autres une à M. Bonniquet, propriétaire des mines, dans laquelle il lui faisoit ses excuses de s'être tué sur sa propriété.

"Voici ce qu'il prescrivit touchant ses funérailles: le corps couché de l'orient & l'occident, enveloppé de bas de soie blanc, d'un pantalon de bazin, les mains couvertes de gants blancs, la tête serrée d'un Madras, et reposée sur une Bible voilée d'un crêpe. Dans une lettre à son cousin, il lui préscrit un silence éternel sur la véritable cause de sa mort."

Thursday, 11*th.*—Sir Robert Peel reached his house in Privy Gardens on Tuesday morning, at eight o'clock, having travelled day and night. The Duke called on him at eleven o'clock, and they both had a long audience of the King at one o'clock. The arrangements of the ministry are in full train.

Saturday, 13*th.*—Moved to Versailles. On Thursday died, in the Rue de Rivoli, General Sir W. Keppell, aged above eighty. He was merely staying here on his way to England. He was a constant favourite of the late King, and long attached to his household. He was a quiet, good-natured man, and very gentlemanlike in his manners; the long-standing attachment of his fickle master may, perhaps, be attributed to this, that he said little, and was a most attentive listener. Those who have in former times been admitted to the intimate society at Carlton House, may have learnt the value of that qualification, or afterwards lamented the want of it. He was one of the witnesses to the King's marriage with Mrs. Fitzherbert.

Monday, 15*th.*—The invitation which was sent to Lord Stanley to join the new administration, has met with a courteous, but cold refusal; and the Whigs, encouraged by this incident, are making the most triumphant boastings; but every thinking man must feel that an awful crisis is approaching for England.

Wednesday, 17*th.*—The administration is formed without any coalition, and of pure Conservative materials. At the head is Sir R. Peel, First Lord of the Treasury and Chancellor of the Exchequer, and the Duke Secretary for Foreign Affairs; Goulburn, Home Department; Lord Lyndhurst, Chancellor; Lord Jersey, Chamberlain; &c.

Friday, 19*th.*—Talleyrand hesitates whether he shall resume his post in England. The English seem to be going home to prepare for the dissolution of Parliament. Belfast must resign his place; Castlereagh is to succeed him as Vice-Chamberlain. Lord Chandos refuses to join the new Government, being pledged to the repeal of the Malt-tax. During the conversation at dinner, some circumstance was mentioned, on which Burdett observed, "In such a case, il faut faire le philosophe." Montrond, who had joined us remarked, "Il faut être philosophe, on ne peut pas le faire;"—which is very true.

Monday, 22*nd.*—Sir R. Peel's address to the electors of Tamworth, exposing the principles on which his government means to act, is arrived. It is a manly and sensible document, calculated to inspire confidence in the country; expressing readiness to reform real abuses and defects, without seeking for a false popularity by adopting every fleeting popular impression of the day, and promising the instant redress of any thing which any one may call an abuse.

Lord Aberdeen, Colonial Secretary; Earl de Grey, First Lord of the Admiralty; Beckett, Judge-Advocate; Lord Rosslyn, President of the Council.

Tuesday, 23*rd.*—Lord Londonderry goes ambassador to Petersburg; the Duke of Buccleuch receives the Garter, and goes to Ireland; Lord Combermere, it is said, will be Governor-General of India.

The Court of Cassation in Paris has been just occupied with the following case:—After the assassination of the Due de Berri by Louvel, at the door of the old Opera House, in the Rue Richelieu, a royal edict appeared, ordering the demolition of that building, and the erection of a monument to the memory of the murdered prince. This edict was afterwards carried into effect, and on the spot was erected a church, which was nearly completed, but the Revolution of July produced a change of sentiments as well as of government, and a fresh edict of Louis-Philippe has not only commanded the discontinuance of the works, but also the entire removal of the monument, which is now razed to the ground. The legality of the proceeding has been brought before the court, which, after some discussion, has declined to interfere in the matter.

Thursday, 25*th.*—Christmas Day. Called on the Duchesse de Guiche, who is living with her family here, since their removal from Prague and the court of Charles X. She is sister to Alfred D'Orsay. We had much conversation about what is going on here and in England. Talleyrand has had an attack of illness, and does not resume his post as ambassador; but still it is his wish not to die in France, his position as a moine défroqué, ***an ex-bishop, and a*** married priest give reason to suppose that some serious tumults would arise at his funeral, from the animosity and opposition of the clergy, which would not be very creditable to the conclusion of his history. On any other account, I should think, it must be a matter of great indifference to him.

Friday, 26*th.*—It is announced that General Sebastiani, who is now at Naples, will be the new ambassador to England. His first wife was the daughter of Madame de Coigny. He is a man without much talent, but of considerable vanity. Some idea may be formed of his character, by the following speech of his mother-in-law, on the occasion of some defeat which he had sustained in Spain:—

"Mon gendre," said she, "ressemble à un tambour; ne fait du bruit que quand il est battu."

Mons. Buchon, whom I see frequently here, is an *homme de lettres,* very intimate with the most distinguished of the Liberal party here, and a great admirer of Napoleon. He told us several interesting anecdotes of the late revolution, and of Louis-Philippe.

That the latter had any idea of the approaching crisis in July, 1830, was quite impossible. The promulgation of the ordinances was so sudden, that none but the ministers themselves, and the very intimate *coterie* of the royal family, were aware of the fact; and that only so late as the preceding night (Sunday), when the measure was finally decided. He, moreover, partook of the general alarm, and during the struggle of the three days, shrunk in retirement at Neuilly from public observation. Louis-Philippe, though no ways wanting in that physical courage which would confront personal danger, is not endowed with that moral courage which can preserve coolness in difficult moments, and take advantage of events which present a threatening aspect. His course has always been of a more tortuous nature; and to effect his plans, he will always prefer the byways of wily cunning to the straight road of manly resolution. He is notoriously designated as *faux comme un jeton.*

But for a long period back he had foreseen, and prepared to avail himself of, the entanglement into which the prejudices of Charles X., and his infatuated attempts to restore the old monarchical system in France, which existed before the great revolution, infallibly tended to precipitate him and his branch of the family. His object, therefore, was to draw a line, and separate himself as much as possible in the eyes of France, from that infatuated branch. While he on one side paid assiduous court to the king, he on the other privately communicated with the Liberal party; to them he deprecated the insanity of the measures going on, and as if he considered himself as far removed in blood as in principles from the reigning dynasty, he has often been heard to remark, "Mais c'est que les Bourbons ont toujours fait comme ça"

Some years back, Buchon said he had written a book on the American constitution, and knowing the tendency of the Duke of Orleans' politics, he begged permission to dedicate it to his royal highness, which was readily granted. On reflection, however, it occurred to him, that the principles of the publication, as well as the style of the dedication, might perhaps be of a more revolutionary character than the duke would like publicly to avow. He, therefore, thought it right to seek another interview, and express his apprehensions on the subject, offering to modify the same if necessary. Great was his surprise when the duke replied, "Ne changez rien, j'avouerai tout. Allez, je suis bien plus republicain que vous. Oubliez-vous que j'ai vécu en Amérique? J'y ai été laboureur fermier; j'en adore la constitution: avec vous c'est théorie, avec moi c'est pratique."

The revolution came, and Louis-Philippe was placed on the throne of France. In two short years the Liberals were dismissed, proscribed, and massacred; and when the Duke Dalberg consulted the king on the propriety of recognising the order of the St. Esprit, which had been proscribed at the revolution, his answer was, "Attendez, la chose n'est pas encore mûre, mais nous verrons."

So little prepared was the public mind for this revolution of July, that even the chiefs of the republican party were almost all absent from Paris on the Monday, the day of the explosion. Lafitte was on a visit in the country, Lafayette was at Lagrange, and Benj. Constant at Bagneux, where he was confined to his room by a severe illness (an affection of the spine), for which he had lately undergone a severe surgical operation. The first two lost no time in coming to Paris, occupied in taking their measures to resist the ordinances, one of the first of which was to have been a refusal, at all risks, to pay any taxes. But the conflict and confusion had now become general, and the assistance of B. Constant was deemed essentially necessary at such a crisis.

Lafayette then sent for Buchon, and said, "You must get on horseback, and, sick or well, you must induce Constant to come to Paris; the barriers of the city may shortly be closed, and then he will have no chance of joining us." Buchon set off, and on the road met M. B——, Constant's physician, who asked him where he was going. On explaining his mission, M. B——exclaimed, "It is impossible! If Constant moves from his home, he is a dead man; in such a case, I pronounce his death to be inevitable. If, however, you are determined to proceed, I can only insist that in conveying the message of Lafayette, you will also deliver to Constant this, my decided opinion. Adieu." Buchon arrived at Bagneux, and found Constant in a very weak state, who, after learning the state of affairs, consulted him how he should act. The other replied, that he did not feel competent to give him advice; that his health was unquestionably a great obstacle; that a man whose character for fortitude and patriotism was already so strongly established, might without any risk of obloquy be permitted to take a line of conduct, which another man, less supported by public opinion and the convictions of his friends and party, could hardly venture to adopt at such a moment, without giving a handle to censure and imputations, however unmerited, but still liable to misconstructions. He at length determined to go to Paris without delay. It happened, unfortunately, that when the carriage arrived at the Barrière de Sèvres, the barricades were already constructed, and Constant was obliged to proceed from thence on foot, in his then weak state, first to the Hôtel de Ville, and afterwards to his house in the Rue d'Anjou, an exertion which shortly afterwards verified the forebodings of his physician. This, I think, was on the Friday; on the Saturday morning, the Duke of Orleans was induced to come from his retreat to the Palais Royal, where it was deemed necessary that the leaders of the Liberal party should meet, and consult with him without delay. Amongst the rest, the presence of B. Constant was felt to be indispensably necessary, but his strength had begun to fail, and to walk that distance was impossible. He was placed on a mattress, and conveyed on a ***brancard*** by ten men to that assembly, escorted by the armed mob; and what was very curious, Lafitte, who had sprained his ankle, was conveyed thither in nearly a similar manner. The rest is well known; but the health of Constant had received a shock from which he could never recover; he lingered on for a few months, and died just late enough to see, that the cause for which he had risked his life had been strangled in its birth. If he had in that interval refused the donation of 200,000 fr. from the Trésor (not, as was reported, from Louis-Philippe), it would have saved an imputation on his patriotic life.

Sunday, 28*th.*—The selection of Sebastiani for the embassy to England has created some surprise, but it is accounted for in this way;—Louis-Philippe will only select a man with whom he can stipulate that he shall keep up a private correspondence with him, independent of the minister for foreign affairs; the suppleness of Sebastiani's character is a sufficient pledge that he will comply with any terms that may be dictated to him, however degrading to his post and unfair towards the cabinet. Upon the same principle, Louis-Philippe dictates in the council, while his ministers alone are responsible; a fair idea of the ***doctrinaire*** government may thus be formed. No independent man could take office under him, neither does he wish to have any of that description with him, although ***he did live in America, and admired her institutions.***

Monday, 29*th.*—The Duc and Duchesse de Guiche, with whom we passed the evening, were sitting with their three boys and the two tutors: as they were generally allowed when they married to be the handsomest couple in France, it is not surprising that the children should possess the same advantages, and they really are the finest family I ever saw, and brought up with the greatest care and attention. They are living here in great retirement, and not mixing with the society, either here or in Paris; their attachment to the late Royal Family remains unshaken, and no inducement would tempt them to approach the Tuileries under the present government. The Duke said to me, "If France should be engaged in an aggressive war, I would not serve even as a general; if she was invaded, I would serve even in the ranks."

I have already mentioned that at the death of Madame de Vaudemont, much anxiety was felt in certain quarters for the publication of her correspondence. particularly that with Talleyrand; but Louis-Philippe, aware how much he was implicated in all these details, despatched a party of gendarmes to her house, who broke open all the écritoires, and carried off her papers.

Tuesday, the 30*th.*—Some surprise is occasioned in England by the appointment of the Earl of Haddington as Lord Lieutenant of Ireland. Glengall writes to me from Dublin, 24th December, "There certainly is an extraordinary reaction here, but to expect to obtain 170 changes at the elections is far too much. However, it is the last stake, and if Stanley gives a fair support, the thing will do. We have every reason to believe he ***will.*** I saw a letter from the Duke saying it was ***certain.***

O'Connell will be knocked about here very much, and will lose several of his tail. The fault in the new government is, that we have too much of the old leaven."

END OF THE FIRST VOLUME.

The Codes Of Hammurabi And Moses
W. W. Davies

QTY

The discovery of the Hammurabi Code is one of the greatest achievements of archaeology, and is of paramount interest, not only to the student of the Bible, but also to all those interested in ancient history...

Religion   ISBN: *1-59462-338-4*

Pages:132

MSRP $12.95

The Theory of Moral Sentiments
Adam Smith

QTY

This work from 1749. contains original theories of conscience amd moral judgment and it is the foundation for systemof morals.

Philosophy ISBN: *1-59462-777-0*

Pages:536

MSRP $19.95

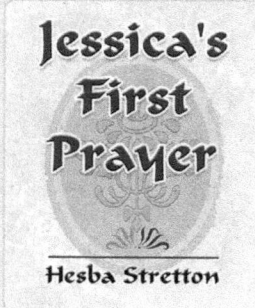

Jessica's First Prayer
Hesba Stretton

QTY

In a screened and secluded corner of one of the many railway-bridges which span the streets of London there could be seen a few years ago, from five o'clock every morning until half past eight, a tidily set-out coffee-stall, consisting of a trestle and board, upon which stood two large tin cans, with a small fire of charcoal burning under each so as to keep the coffee boiling during the early hours of the morning when the work-people were thronging into the city on their way to their daily toil...

Childrens   ISBN: *1-59462-373-2*

Pages:84

MSRP $9.95

My Life and Work
Henry Ford

QTY

Henry Ford revolutionized the world with his implementation of mass production for the Model T automobile. Gain valuable business insight into his life and work with his own auto-biography... "We have only started on our development of our country we have not as yet, with all our talk of wonderful progress, done more than scratch the surface. The progress has been wonderful enough but..."

Pages:300

Biographies/   ISBN: *1-59462-198-5*

MSRP $21.95

The Art of Cross-Examination
Francis Wellman

QTY

I presume it is the experience of every author, after his first book is published upon an important subject, to be almost overwhelmed with a wealth of ideas and illustrations which could readily have been included in his book, and which to his own mind, at least, seem to make a second edition inevitable. Such certainly was the case with me; and when the first edition had reached its sixth impression in five months, I rejoiced to learn that it seemed to my publishers that the book had met with a sufficiently favorable reception to justify a second and considerably enlarged edition. ..

Reference   **ISBN: *1-59462-647-2***

Pages:412

MSRP $19.95

On the Duty of Civil Disobedience
Henry David Thoreau

QTY

Thoreau wrote his famous essay, On the Duty of Civil Disobedience, as a protest against an unjust but popular war and the immoral but popular institution of slave-owning. He did more than write—he declined to pay his taxes, and was hauled off to gaol in consequence. Who can say how much this refusal of his hastened the end of the war and of slavery ?

Law   **ISBN: *1-59462-747-9***

Pages:48

MSRP $7.45

Dream Psychology Psychoanalysis for Beginners
Sigmund Freud

QTY

Sigmund Freud, born Sigismund Schlomo Freud (May 6, 1856 - September 23, 1939), was a Jewish-Austrian neurologist and psychiatrist who co-founded the psychoanalytic school of psychology. Freud is best known for his theories of the unconscious mind, especially involving the mechanism of repression; his redefinition of sexual desire as mobile and directed towards a wide variety of objects; and his therapeutic techniques, especially his understanding of transference in the therapeutic relationship and the presumed value of dreams as sources of insight into unconscious desires.

Psychology   **ISBN: *1-59462-905-6***

Pages:196

MSRP $15.45

The Miracle of Right Thought
Orison Swett Marden

QTY

Believe with all of your heart that you will do what you were made to do. When the mind has once formed the habit of holding cheerful, happy, prosperous pictures, it will not be easy to form the opposite habit. It does not matter how improbable or how far away this realization may see, or how dark the prospects may be, if we visualize them as best we can, as vividly as possible, hold tenaciously to them and vigorously struggle to attain them, they will gradually become actualized, realized in the life. But a desire, a longing without endeavor, a yearning abandoned or held indifferently will vanish without realization.

Self Help   **ISBN: *1-59462-644-8***

Pages:360

MSRP $25.45

QTY

The Rosicrucian Cosmo-Conception Mystic Christianity *by Max Heindel* ISBN: *1-59462-188-8* **$38.95**
The Rosicrucian Cosmo-conception is not dogmatic, neither does it appeal to any other authority than the reason of the student. It is: not controversial, but is: sent forth in the, hope that it may help to clear... *New Age/Religion Pages 646*

Abandonment To Divine Providence *by Jean-Pierre de Caussade* ISBN: *1-59462-228-0* **$25.95**
"The Rev. Jean Pierre de Caussade was one of the most remarkable spiritual writers of the Society of Jesus in France in the 18th Century. His death took place at Toulouse in 1751. His works have gone through many editions and have been republished... *Inspirational/Religion Pages 400*

Mental Chemistry *by Charles Haanel* ISBN: *1-59462-192-6* **$23.95**
Mental Chemistry allows the change of material conditions by combining and appropriately utilizing the power of the mind. Much like applied chemistry creates something new and unique out of careful combinations of chemicals the mastery of mental chemistry... *New Age Pages 354*

The Letters of Robert Browning and Elizabeth Barret Barrett 1845-1846 vol II ISBN: *1-59462-193-4* **$35.95**
by Robert Browning and Elizabeth Barrett *Biographies Pages 596*

Gleanings In Genesis (volume I) *by Arthur W. Pink* ISBN: *1-59462-130-6* **$27.45**
Appropriately has Genesis been termed "the seed plot of the Bible" for in it we have, in germ form, almost all of the great doctrines which are afterwards fully developed in the books of Scripture which follow... *Religion/Inspirational Pages 420*

The Master Key *by L. W. de Laurence* ISBN: *1-59462-001-6* **$30.95**
In no branch of human knowledge has there been a more lively increase of the spirit of research during the past few years than in the study of Psychology, Concentration and Mental Discipline. The requests for authentic lessons in Thought Control, Mental Discipline and... *New Age/Business Pages 422*

The Lesser Key Of Solomon Goetia *by L. W. de Laurence* ISBN: *1-59462-092-X* **$9.95**
This translation of the first book of the "Lernegton" which is now for the first time made accessible to students of Talismanic Magic was done, after careful collation and edition, from numerous Ancient Manuscripts in Hebrew, Latin, and French... *New Age/Occult Pages 92*

Rubaiyat Of Omar Khayyam *by Edward Fitzgerald* ISBN: *1-59462-332-5* **$13.95**
Edward Fitzgerald, whom the world has already learned, in spite of his own efforts to remain within the shadow of anonymity, to look upon as one of the rarest poets of the century, was born at Bredfield, in Suffolk, on the 31st of March, 1809. He was the third son of John Purcell... *Music Pages 172*

Ancient Law *by Henry Maine* ISBN: *1-59462-128-4* **$29.95**
The chief object of the following pages is to indicate some of the earliest ideas of mankind, as they are reflected in Ancient Law, and to point out the relation of those ideas to modern thought. *Religion/History Pages 452*

Far-Away Stories *by William J. Locke* ISBN: *1-59462-129-2* **$19.45**
"Good wine needs no bush, but a collection of mixed vintages does. And this book is just such a collection. Some of the stories I do not want to remain buried for ever in the museum files of dead magazine-numbers an author's not unpardonable vanity..." *Fiction Pages 272*

Life of David Crockett *by David Crockett* ISBN: *1-59462-250-7* **$27.45**
"Colonel David Crockett was one of the most remarkable men of the times in which he lived. Born in humble life, but gifted with a strong will, an indomitable courage, and unremitting perseverance... *Biographies/New Age Pages 424*

Lip-Reading *by Edward Nitchie* ISBN: *1-59462-206-X* **$25.95**
Edward B. Nitchie, founder of the New York School for the Hard of Hearing, now the Nitchie School of Lip-Reading, Inc, wrote "LIP-READING Principles and Practice". The development and perfecting of this meritorious work on lip-reading was an undertaking... *How-to Pages 400*

A Handbook of Suggestive Therapeutics, Applied Hypnotism, Psychic Science ISBN: *1-59462-214-0* **$24.95**
by Henry Munro *Health/New Age/Health/Self-help Pages 376*

A Doll's House: and Two Other Plays *by Henrik Ibsen* ISBN: *1-59462-112-8* **$19.95**
Henrik Ibsen created this classic when in revolutionary 1848 Rome. Introducing some striking concepts in playwriting for the realist genre, this play has been studied the world over. *Fiction/Classics/Plays 308*

The Light of Asia *by sir Edwin Arnold* ISBN: *1-59462-204-3* **$13.95**
In this poetic masterpiece, Edwin Arnold describes the life and teachings of Buddha. The man who was to become known as Buddha to the world was born as Prince Gautama of India but he rejected the worldly riches and abandoned the reigns of power when... *Religion/History/Biographies Pages 170*

The Complete Works of Guy de Maupassant *by Guy de Maupassant* ISBN: *1-59462-157-8* **$16.95**
"For days and days, nights and nights, I had dreamed of that first kiss which was to consecrate our engagement, and I knew not on what spot I should put my lips..." *Fiction/Classics Pages 240*

The Art of Cross-Examination *by Francis L. Wellman* ISBN: *1-59462-309-0* **$26.95**
Written by a renowned trial lawyer, Wellman imparts his experience and uses case studies to explain how to use psychology to extract desired information through questioning. *How-to/Science/Reference Pages 408*

Answered or Unanswered? *by Louisa Vaughan* ISBN: *1-59462-248-5* **$10.95**
Miracles of Faith in China *Religion Pages 112*

The Edinburgh Lectures on Mental Science (1909) *by Thomas* ISBN: *1-59462-008-3* **$11.95**
This book contains the substance of a course of lectures recently given by the writer in the Queen Street Hall, Edinburgh. Its purpose is to indicate the Natural Principles governing the relation between Mental Action and Material Conditions... *New Age/Psychology Pages 148*

Ayesha *by H. Rider Haggard* ISBN: *1-59462-301-5* **$24.95**
Verily and indeed it is the unexpected that happens! Probably if there was one person upon the earth from whom the Editor of this, and of a certain previous history, did not expect to hear again... *Classics Pages 380*

Ayala's Angel *by Anthony Trollope* ISBN: *1-59462-352-X* **$29.95**
The two girls were both pretty, but Lucy who was twenty-one who supposed to be simple and comparatively unattractive, whereas Ayala was credited, as her Bombwhat romantic name might have, with poetic charm and a taste for romance. Ayala when her father died was nineteen... *Fiction Pages 484*

The American Commonwealth *by James Bryce* ISBN: *1-59462-286-8* **$34.45**
An interpretation of American democratic political theory. It examines political mechanics and society from the perspective of Scotsman James Bryce *Politics Pages 572*

Stories of the Pilgrims *by Margaret P. Pumphrey* ISBN: *1-59462-116-0* **$17.95**
This book explores pilgrims religious oppression in England as well as their escape to Holland and eventual crossing to America on the Mayflower, and their early days in New England... *History Pages 268*

QTY

The Fasting Cure *by Sinclair Upton*   ISBN: *1-59462-222-1*   **$13.95**   ☐
*In the Cosmopolitan Magazine for May, 1910, and in the Contemporary Review (London) for April, 1910, I published an article dealing with my experi-
ences in fasting. I have written a great many magazine articles, but never one which attracted so much attention...* New Age/Self Help/Health Pages 164

Hebrew Astrology *by Sepharial*   ISBN: *1-59462-308-2*   **$13.45**   ☐
*In these days of advanced thinking it is a matter of common observation that we have left many of the old landmarks behind and that we are now pressing
forward to greater heights and to a wider horizon than that which represented the mind-content of our progenitors...* Astrology Pages 144

Thought Vibration or The Law of Attraction in the Thought World   ISBN: *1-59462-127-6*   **$12.95**   ☐

by William Walker Atkinson   *Psychology/Religion Pages 144*

Optimism *by Helen Keller*   ISBN: *1-59462-108-X*   **$15.95**   ☐
*Helen Keller was blind, deaf, and mute since 19 months old, yet famously learned how to overcome these handicaps, communicate with the world, and
spread her lectures promoting optimism. An inspiring read for everyone...* Biographies/Inspirational Pages 84

Sara Crewe *by Frances Burnett*   ISBN: *1-59462-360-0*   **$9.45**   ☐
*In the first place, Miss Minchin lived in London. Her home was a large, dull, tall one, in a large, dull square, where all the houses were alike, and all the
sparrows were alike, and where all the door-knockers made the same heavy sound...* Childrens/Classic Pages 88

The Autobiography of Benjamin Franklin *by Benjamin Franklin*   ISBN: *1-59462-135-7*   **$24.95**   ☐
*The Autobiography of Benjamin Franklin has probably been more extensively read than any other American historical work, and no other book of its kind
has had such ups and downs of fortune. Franklin lived for many years in England, where he was agent...* Biographies/History Pages 332

Name	
Email	
Telephone	
Address	
City, State ZIP	

☐ **Credit Card**   ☐ **Check / Money Order**

Credit Card Number	
Expiration Date	
Signature	

Please Mail to: Book Jungle
PO Box 2226
Champaign, IL 61825
or Fax to: 630-214-0564

ORDERING INFORMATION

web*: www.bookjungle.com*
email*: sales@bookjungle.com*
fax*: 630-214-0564*
mail*: Book Jungle PO Box 2226 Champaign, IL 61825*
or PayPal *to sales@bookjungle.com*

Please contact us for bulk discounts

DIRECT-ORDER TERMS

**20% Discount if You Order
Two or More Books**
Free Domestic Shipping!
Accepted: Master Card, Visa,
Discover, American Express

www.ingramcontent.com/pod-product-compliance
Lightning Source LLC
Chambersburg PA
CBHW080900020726
47502CB00008B/2302

* 9 7 8 1 4 3 8 5 3 7 2 0 7 *